Leave Me Breathless

Leave Me Breathless

HelenKay Dimon

BRAVA

KENSINGTON PUBLISHING CORP.
www.kensingtonbooks.com

In memory of Kate Duffy—there aren't adequate words to express my appreciation for your support or my sadness at your passing.

ACKNOWLEDGMENTS

This book is about fictional lawyers and judges in Montgomery County, Maryland. I know a little about the courthouse because I practiced law there for twelve years. As something of an expert on the place, I can honestly say nothing in this book actually happened, and none of the characters are based on real people. It's all a product of my imagination. The lawyers, judges, and clerks I knew and worked with were smart, savvy, and dedicated. My special thanks go out to my former fellow partners—Pat, Cindy, Jeff, Kevin, and Vince—for showing me how to practice with integrity. You are good people doing tough work.

I also want to thank Megan Records for stepping in and helping out on this book. You were patient when I needed more time to revise. For that I am eternally grateful.

As always, I couldn't write a book without the support of my husband, James, who also happens to be a pretty amazing lawyer.

Chapter One

"I don't need a bodyguard." Judge Bennett Walker delivered his observation as he unclipped the top of his black robe and stripped the garment off his shoulders.

Callie Robbins had to fight hard to keep from rolling her eyes. Three denials in two minutes. Yeah, she got it. The big tough guy in the flower-print tie somehow thought he could stop a bullet simply by pretending it didn't exist.

Gavel or not, she was not a fan of pigheaded stupidity, even if it did come in a six-foot-three package of smoldering eye candy. And this guy had the smoking hot thing down. A square jaw and light brown hair that fell in a soft line over his forehead were just the beginning of the impressive package. She'd heard about the broad shoulders he hid under the required work outfit. Watching his white shirt pull across his chest, she now could vouch for his linebacker form. Thirty-eight and sat on his butt all day, but there wasn't an ounce of fat on the guy that she could tell.

Still, all of the idol worship surrounding him in the Circuit Court for Montgomery County, Maryland, struck her as overkill. From what she could tell, Ben Walker was a prosecutor-turned judge-turned-superstar in the uber-wealthy area north of Washington, D.C. He wielded a heap of power and had all the female courthouse clerks scurrying around to catch a peek at him. But, really, he was just a man. And from Callie's 120 seconds of experience, a very stubborn one.

"If there's nothing else . . ." Ben let his voice trail off as he slid into his oversized leather desk chair.

Callie didn't bother to respond to the not-so-subtle dismissal, because he wasn't talking to her. Hell, he hadn't even sent a small glance in her direction since she'd dodged his gaggle of admirers in the outer office to follow him into his private chambers. No, the judge saved all his wrath and attention for the other man in the room, his older brother by one year, Mark Walker.

"This isn't up for discussion, Ben," Mark said in a clear attempt at reason. "You have a target on your back."

"I'm not the one in danger."

Mark shook his head. "Your job is to rule on cases. Leave the law enforcement decisions up to me, will ya?"

Callie knew Mark could handle the worst. He had turned his tenure at the FBI into a position with an undercover division within Homeland Security charged with protecting high-profile targets in the D.C. metro area. Callie wasn't sure what the job entailed, but she knew it was a big one. The kind where her record would likely disqualify her for regular duty, which explained why she was an independent contractor doing Mark a private favor on this job.

Since the judge hadn't acknowledged her presence except for a brief nod after Mark's introduction, she decided to force the issue. She was standing right there next to the judge. Hard to imagine he could miss her, what with his big brain and all.

"Did you forget the part where someone blew up your car?" she asked.

Silence slammed through the large room. For a second, nothing moved. Callie was pretty sure even the wall clock stopped ticking. Then the judge turned in his seat and glanced at her with a blank expression. "Hard to do that since it burst into flames about ten feet away from me."

"A smart guy would take that as a sign," Mark said.

With that, the judge went right back to talking to his brother. "Emma was the target, not me."

The long breath eased from Callie's chest. Something about having the man's sole attention turned on her made her nerve endings jump and twitch. An odd shakiness flooded through her. And she didn't like it one bit.

She watched the brothers argue, marveled at how different two men who were raised in the same household could be. Mark sounded reasonable, smart, focused. The judge came off as a pompous jackass. Attractive in a make-your-eyes-cross kind of way, but still a pompous jackass.

He tried to put her in her place by pretending she barely existed. She had seen the tactic before. A woman didn't rise in the ranks of the FBI without throwing a few elbows. Sure, she'd thrown one too many, which explained why she was here without her badge instead of sitting behind her desk in an office nearby, but she could fight back. If the good judge wanted attitude, she could shovel plenty of it right on top of him.

"Look, *Your Honor*," she said in the least respectful tone she could muster. "Your girlfriend has security protection. You've refused it. From what I can tell, that makes her the smarter of the two of you."

He smiled. "Emma Blanton is not my girlfriend."

Not exactly the response Callie expected, but at least he finally bothered to stare at her for more than two seconds. And without throwing her in jail, that had to be considered a success. "You and your girlfriend would be barbeque right now except that the bomb went off too early."

Ben folded his hands together in front of him on the desktop. "True, but she's still not my girlfriend."

Talk about fixating on the wrong point. "Fine. What do you want me to call her?"

"You could try Judge Blanton." Ben glanced at his brother. "And the bomb was meant for her."

Mark shook his head. "It was your car, genius."

"Emma doesn't drive. The fact we'd been attending the judicial conference together is not exactly a secret. We were on the same panel when she made the inflammatory comments that resulted in all the bad press. Her speech has been all over the news. I'm assuming that's how this lunatic tracked her down. I just got in the way."

Callie thought calling the other woman's talk "inflammatory" was like calling Ben somewhat good looking—a wild understatement. "Judge Blanton told a criminal defendant he was 'filth' as part of her sentencing decision and then reiterated her position in front of a room filled with reporters at your conference," Callie pointed out.

Ben's eyebrow lifted. "I was there for the latter."

"Then you know what I'm talking about."

"Steve Jenner was a pretty bad guy."

Callie knew that. Despite what Ben might think, she read a newspaper now and then. She'd called criminal scum worse names than filth, but she wasn't a judge. The lack of restraint from the top was the problem. Having judges refer to defendants as inhuman, or worse, strained the appearance of impartiality to the breaking point.

Though Callie believed there was a special rathole in hell for violent offenders like Jenner, there was a system in place to take care of them. If she wasn't allowed to ignore the rules, despite how much she might want to, neither could the judges.

She decided to point out the obvious logic to Ben. "Your

friend angered everyone from defendants to the Defense Bar and human rights groups. The press has been all over this story."

"I know. I live here and get the newspaper delivered to my house."

Everything the man said irritated the crap out of Callie. She wondered if he saved up his smartass comments just for her or if all the women in his life got this treatment. Either way, he had one day to knock it the hell off or she'd shoot him in the foot. Wouldn't be the first time, and it wasn't as if she had anything left to lose professionally.

"My point is that it's not hard to compile a list of enemies for Judge Blanton," Callie said.

His smile came back even wider this time. "Which supports what I've been saying. The bomb wasn't meant for me."

He could not be this clueless. "Since you're sleeping with her—"

Ben held up a hand. "Friends."

"—you're in danger."

Mark pushed away from the bookshelves and stood at the front of the big desk, across from his brother. "Enough arguing. You lose. Like it or not, you're getting protection."

"I don't want it."

Mark snorted. "You don't get a choice on this. You either accept what I'm offering or you take a leave of absence."

The judge's jaw tightened in response to the threat. "Since when do you run my schedule?"

"I'll go right over your head to Heath Samson."

"Who?" Callie asked, feeling more than a little ignored.

"The administrative judge. He runs the courthouse and has to think about all the judges and people in it, not just Ben." Mark rapped his knuckles against his brother's desk.

"I'll convince him your presence at work puts everyone in the building in danger."

"Do it and I'll kick your ass."

Callie wondered which one of the two uncompromising alpha males would win that brainless battle of testosterone. Mark dealt in strategies and big guns, but she'd bet Ben knew his brother's weaknesses. Despite his current display of bone-headed tendencies, Ben had earned an impressive list of military honors before his turn on the bench. She'd read his file. She knew all about his sharpshooter days as well as his courthouse days.

What she didn't get was his reluctance to take the much-needed protection his brother offered. Apparently Ben thought the judge's robe worked like a Kevlar shield. Like he was a freaking superhero or something. She would have thought that dodging that fireball the other night would have made him see reason. Just proved her initial reaction to Judge Ben was right: the guy was a bonehead.

"I will pull whatever string I have to, use any threat, to get you a full-time security detail. This is not up for debate." Mark's shoulders stretched even tighter. "You know I'm not fucking around on this."

Something in Mark's dark eyes or stern voice must have gotten through, because Ben exhaled loud enough to be heard in the hallway. "What do you have in mind?"

"Protection. Covert. A person placed in your office and with you at all times."

"So, I was right. A bodyguard."

Callie loved this part. She'd been waiting to drop this verbal bombshell. Thought it might give way to a whole new level of jackassery on Ben's part. "He means me."

Ben's eyes bulged. "Excuse me?"

"I'll be the one assigned to protect you."

"You?"

"That a problem?"

The usually well-spoken judge floundered around, stuttering, before he actually came up with a sentence that made some sense. "You weigh a hundred and twenty pounds."

If he was trying for flattery . . . well, he came close with the wild underestimate. "I'm more than qualified."

Mark eased back on his fighting stance. Actually unlocked his knees and stopped clenching his jaw every two seconds. "She's ex-FBI. She's good."

The judge looked at her then. Really looked. His heated gaze roamed up and down before it settled on her face again. "You're kind of young to be a former anything."

Mark shifted his position until he blocked her from Ben's direct line of sight. She knew the chivalrous move was ingrained, locked somewhere deep in Mark's protective DNA. Still, despite the mistakes she'd made she didn't need a champion. Having Ben see her as weak would only make her job tougher.

Callie stepped out from behind Mark's shadow and took her position beside him, putting her directly in front of Judge Grumpy Pants. "I'll be your new assistant."

"I have a clerk."

"Did I say clerk?"

Ben's lips thinned until they almost disappeared. "So that you know, I don't accept that sarcastic tone from my employees."

Talk about an ego problem. "Do you want me to call you Sir? Maybe I should bow when I see you. Wipe your feet when you come in from the outside."

"The feet part is unnecessary."

Mark slapped his palm against the desk. "Would you two get serious?"

She had a few insults stuck in her throat but decided to save them until later. "Mark's right. You have a stalker. That's what this protection detail is about. We'll figure out the rest as we go."

Mark nodded. "I already cleared the assignment with Judge Samson. Callie will move in here under the guise of a new judges' assistant program. She'll share your office—"

Ben's head snapped back. "What?"

"Where else would I put her?"

Callie really wasn't in the mood to be "put" anywhere. "Could we not refer to me as if I were a plant?"

Ben ignored her. He was too busy grabbing the edge of his desk with enough force to snap off the wood trim. "That is never going to happen."

"I can't really protect you effectively from the hallway," she pointed out.

"No one will buy that you're working for me." Ben held up both hands and shrugged his shoulders in what Callie assumed was some sort of peace offering. "No offense."

"How could I possibly be offended by that," she mumbled.

He shook his head, refusing to give up the fight. "There's security here. We've got a metal detector and there are emergency call buttons hidden everywhere in the office."

"Which will be very helpful if you're shot in the head before you can reach it." Callie knew the guy had to be smarter than this. He passed the Bar and managed to get appointed by the governor. That suggested there was a working brain in that head somewhere.

Ben glared at her before continuing his brother-to-brother negotiations. "There's no need for additional protection."

"Your car blew up in a locked government parking lot."

Mark folded his arms in front of him. "That changes everything."

She glanced at Mark. When he nodded, she took the lead. "It means the person who planted the bomb had access to the facility. Probably has a badge and can come and go in the courthouse without being noticed. He or she is on the inside, which makes you vulnerable even with all the uniforms around you all the time."

"Which is why Callie is your new right arm. Where you goes she goes. Work or work function, she's with you. I'll handle the at home part," Mark said.

Ben closed those chocolate brown eyes of his for a second. When he opened them again, some of the fight had left him. Even his shoulders appeared more relaxed. "We haven't shared a bedroom since we were eight."

"And we're not going to now." Mark glanced at his cell and started talking faster. "Look, I know this is a pain in the ass, but I need you to listen to me."

Ben tipped his head back against the chair. "I get it."

An unspoken emotion passed between the brothers. Callie had no idea why Ben caved, but the verbal and psychological battle had ended. Both men wore grim lines of resignation on their mouths.

She suddenly felt as if she were intruding. "I can wait outside."

Ben shook his head. "No need. We'll set you up here somewhere."

It was Mark's turn to smile. "Nice try. She'll be in here with you. I've taken care of that part and you are not going to overrule me. I get paid to do the tactical stuff, so let me do my job."

Out of nowhere, Ben turned on her and flashed a smile

full of perfect white teeth. "So, you ready to spend ten hours a day with me?"

She shook off the feeling of being in the spotlight. "No."

"If it's any consolation that makes us even."

Funny, but that didn't make her feel one ounce better.

Chapter Two

B en walked into his private chambers the next morning at his usual seven-thirty start time to enjoy a half hour of quiet before the workday madness descended. He had to wait until Mark checked the suite, but Ben wasn't even a little surprised to find Callie there waiting for him. Not in the receptionist's waiting room outside. Not in the front area of his office, where the sofa and chairs were arranged for informal meetings. Not by the bookcases that lined the walls. No, she actually stood behind his desk looking out the window to the concourse seven stories below. He guessed he should be grateful her butt wasn't actually in his chair.

Some guard dog she turned out to be. She hadn't even noticed him or seen Mark do his check. What if someone had come in carrying a gun instead of a paper and a coffee cup, then what—

"Have a good night?" She asked the question without turning around.

Or maybe she was paying attention.

Still, Ben appreciated having an uninterrupted minute to study her. From a pure male appreciation standpoint he had to give her points. She stood about five-eight with a body more curvy than athletic, which was just his preference. He took in her nice round ass and the way her black pants showed it off. A matching short blazer highlighted her trim waist and straight blond hair pulled back in a ponytail at her neck hung partway down her back. Even though those soulful brown eyes weren't glancing at him right now, he'd bet that same mix of pissiness and frustration remained from their meeting yesterday.

Yeah, staring at her every day wouldn't exactly be a hardship.

Dealing with that mouth would be the challenge.

Protecting that fine ass of hers from whomever seemed so determined to chase him down and take him out would be the biggest issue. No way was he letting her step into danger over him. That meant he'd have to watch over both of them, make sure Emma stopped drawing attention to herself, run his office, and hear a case or two. Not exactly what he had in mind when he left the military for the calmer life of a practicing law.

"Uh, hello?" Callie turned around to face him as she talked.

There it was. Flat lips and angry eyes. The look of pure pissiness she did so well. "Sorry. I'm having trouble getting started this morning," he said.

"Why?"

"Let's just say there's a reason I don't live with Mark."

A night of listening to his brother drone on about Callie's shooting abilities without divulging one interesting piece of information about the rest of the woman sure didn't help Ben's sour mood. Neither did the lack of sleep due to Mark's old-man snoring. Ben planned to kick his brother to the downstairs guest bedroom tonight because the one right next door didn't have enough soundproofing to cover the noise.

"Is your brother cramping your style already?" she asked, her smile suggesting that she found the situation funny.

That made one of them. Ben motioned for her to step out from behind his desk. "You seem awfully concerned with my love life."

Callie took her time getting to the front of his desk and dropping into the guest chair there. She started to put her feet up but stopped when he stared her down. "The only way I can protect you is if I know about the people around you. That includes the women you date, sleep with, and know. Also includes your staff here, friends, and—"

"I get it."

She flipped through a small notebook as she clicked her pen. "Then let's start with the women."

"I'd rather start with my impressive *staff*."

Her gaze made the slow trail up until her eyes met his again. "Excuse me?"

"Your word, not mine." Though he did use it as a test. Wanted to see if Ms. All Business All the Time could get thrown off task, and now he knew. "I'm talking about the other people in this office. Since you're going to be here until Mark lets you leave or we kill each other, we may as well get going on the introductions."

"We need to work on our background story first."

Ben waved that suggestion off as he sat down. Today would be filled with enough boredom without adding more. "I got it."

She handed him a file anyway. When he didn't immediately reach for it, she dropped it on his desk, letting it smack against the wood. "I've worked up some information for our cover."

"I said I got it."

"Then you *get* that I'll be with you during every case, and at lunch, and any private discussions you have with lawyers."

As far as he was concerned she took her job a bit too seriously. "Are you going to follow me into the bathroom as well?"

"I might."

He leaned back in the chair and tapped his fingers together in a triangle. "Don't you think people are going to find it a bit strange that you're stapled to my hip?"

"This Samson guy—"

"Administrative Judge Samson."

"He already sent out an e-mail to everyone in the building explaining the new assistant program."

"Leave it to Mark to take care of . . ." Something clicked in Ben's head. "Wait, how do you know about the e-mail?"

She bit her bottom lip but stayed quiet.

That couldn't be a good sign. "You were on my computer?"

He knew the answer but wanted her to own up to the misdemeanor. Maybe apologize.

"I was checking for e-mail threats." She scribbled down something on the lined paper. "Get used to it."

She sure didn't sound sorry to him. "You were violating my privacy."

"We can call it whatever you want."

"How about illegal? I could have you arrested."

Callie snorted. "Oh, please." She made the annoying sound a second time as if trying to prove her point.

It was hard to threaten someone who refused to be afraid. "Which reminds me, how did you get in the office this morning?" he asked.

She reached inside her blazer pocket and flashed a courthouse I.D. badge at him. "I also have a key to the suite and my own desk."

Ben followed her head nod to the small setup perpendicular from his under the window. How in the hell had he missed that? Instead of a two-shelf small bookcase filled with me-

mentos from his pre-lawyer days there was a place for her complete with fake files and a black briefcase he'd bet was empty.

"I don't think so," he said.

"You don't get a vote."

She needed to understand how this arrangement was going to work. Her pushy demanding act was not the right answer. "The governor who appointed me and the electorate that keeps me here would disagree."

She rolled her eyes. Made quite the dramatic scene of it, too. "Must you talk like that?"

"Like what?"

"All hoity and superior."

He tried to remember the last time someone fought him this hard and showed so little respect for his position. He came up with an answer fast: never. "Was it the word 'electorate' that upset you?"

She threw her notebook on his desk. "To be honest, most everything you say annoys me."

He was starting to see why she no longer had a job with the FBI. That mouth could not have been an asset in a rule-oriented, follow-the-chain-of-command government agency. "Right back at you, sweetheart."

"Tell me something. Is your problem with me or with women in general?"

Definitely with her. "I happen to love women."

"So I've heard."

The playboy chatter echoed in his head. Not exactly the reputation he wanted or sought. "If you're getting your information from gossip, then you have the facts wrong."

"Why don't we get started and you tell me what the truth really is?"

"Isn't it your job to know this stuff already?"

She shrugged. "I'd like to hear it from you."

"I'm not playing that game."

"This is serious."

"It's a waste of time, but if we're being forced to do this you first need to meet the rest of the group." He glanced over the daily schedule his secretary Elaine printed out and placed on the corner of his desk each night. "Then you get to sit through my trial calendar."

"Meaning?"

"If you survive the first day, I'll be stunned."

She smiled, but it faded when he didn't reciprocate. "How bad can it be?"

"Spoken like someone who never had the pleasure of listening to lawyers whine about missing documents for hours on end."

"What?"

"Have you ever been shot at?"

Her brown eyes narrowed. "Uh, yeah."

Interesting. "You'll hope for an outbreak of gunfire by the time lunch rolls around."

Callie didn't even make it to eleven o'clock. By ten seventeen, just over an hour into something called the Motions Docket, she almost did a face-plant into the desk in front of her. Sitting at the front of the room and five feet from Ben stopped her, but only barely.

Thanks to the stack of agreements and waivers she signed that morning for Mark, she'd likely be arrested if she even tried to close her eyes. As it was, she only got to keep her weapon strapped to her side after engaging in United Nations–style negotiations with the county sheriff, the man in charge of providing protection for the courthouse. He insisted the gun-carrying activity be limited to his men despite the clearances Mark had secured. She threw around Judge

Samson's name and won the argument. It paid to know people in power, or at least pretend you did.

But there was an even bigger problem with her dozing-off plan. With Ben looming above her on the raised dais he'd probably miss a quick nap, but everyone else could see her just fine.

Lawyers dressed in indistinguishable dark suits lined the pews at the back half of the room facing her. Ben had introduced Callie at the beginning of the docket only as his new assistant. A few of the older gentlemen exchanged questioning looks, but no one said a word. Good thing or she might have been tempted to draw her gun. Would have added some excitement to the otherwise headache-inducing boredom of the rest of the morning.

But nothing so interesting had happened during the last hour. As Ben had called case numbers, groups of attorneys filed up to stand at two long tables in front of Ben to argue about damn near everything. Through it all the blasting air-conditioning helped her stay awake, but the steady hum of the lights and recording equipment kept lulling her back into dreamland. She lost count of the number of missing documents and destroyed documents referenced. The entire process made her rethink the benefits of being employed.

Ben did provide some entertainment. Sure wasn't a hardship to stare at him, either. He asked questions and broke up childish arguments between lawyers who should have known better. And the way he took notes suggested he was engaged in the circus around him. Callie had no idea how he did this part of his job. Being in charge of a big courtroom with its soaring ceilings and historic paintings probably had to appeal to a guy who liked to be in control, but this dry stuff lacked the sexiness of television courtroom scenes.

"We'll take a ten-minute recess." Ben banged the gavel and reached for the top file on his stack.

Then nothing.

The room grew quiet. No one moved, but everyone looked at her. It took her a few seconds to remember her one re-quired line in this whole dreary scene. "All rise."

Ben smiled as he passed by her and whispered low enough not to be picked up by the microphones surrounding them. "Little slow there, Ms. Robbins."

"I think I lapsed into a temporary coma."

"Won't be the last time." Ben opened the door behind the bench and walked down the short hallway connecting the courtroom to his private office.

They made it to the threshold before Ben's law clerk, Rod Banks, appeared out of nowhere. Rod had a clean-cut con-servative look about him with his oxford shirt and pressed dress pants. The kind of kid you'd feel comfortable opening your front door to if he rang the bell. Someone you half ex-pected to be selling Bibles.

Callie didn't like him at all. She was pretty sure the feeling was mutual. Until she showed up, Rod had been Ben's go-to person. The one who got to sit by Ben's side in the court-room, as if that was some freaking prize. But now she held that job. Rod smiled through the change of power, but she saw something stormy in his blue eyes.

"Judge, I was wondering if I could talk to you later," he said.

Rod didn't say "alone," but Callie knew it was implied.

Ben looked up from the file he was reading and circled around Rod to head into his chambers. "Is it an emergency?"

"No."

"Then as soon as I'm finished with this afternoon's docket."

Good Lord, she had a whole second half of the day to

live through. Callie vowed to strangle Mark later for this assignment. First, she had to put the kibosh on the private meeting with Rod.

She closed the door before the clerk could follow them inside Ben's private office. Then she turned to Ben. "You can't meet with him."

Ben glanced up, squinting at her. "What?"

She grabbed his file and dropped it on the coffee table in front of his couch. "No one-on-one meetings."

"I was reading that."

"I'm talking."

Ben sat down and slipped his arm along the back of the sofa. "Rod is my clerk."

"I know the players in this game. So?"

"The worst thing he's ever done is lie about his golf score at the country club."

Ben unclipped the hook at the top of his robe. For a second, she lost her train of thought. Not that she could see anything under the big black garment. No, it was the way his long fingers moved. With precision and a smoothness that had her mind wandering to his activities outside the office. She loved strong hands. Loved it even more when a man knew what to do with them.

"Callie?"

Right. "Rich people can blow things up, too, you know."

"You think Rod is the stalker?" The joking tone of Ben's voice told her what he thought of the theory.

"I have no idea, but I don't plan to give Rod a chance to be alone with you." She sat down next to Ben. Close enough to let him see how serious she was but far enough so that they didn't touch. "He could have a knife, a gun—"

"You watch too much television."

"And you don't understand just how dangerous this situation is."

"Really? Let's see." He sat up straighter and started ticking off a list on his fingers. "I have my brother up my ass, Emma's calling every two seconds, journalists want quotes for the newspaper, the administrative judge is insisting I take a vacation, and you're falling asleep in my courtroom."

Ouch. "You saw that, huh?"

"It was tough to miss." Ben's mouth broke into a sexy little smile. "I heard you snore."

"That's not true." At least she hoped it wasn't.

"And why do you think I stayed awake? One of us had to know what was going on in there."

She cleared her throat. "Either way, no meeting with Rod."

"I'm willing to placate Mark, but I need to be able to run my office."

"Let me shortcut the meeting for you. Rod is going to complain about my presence here. He feels threatened and pushed out. He wants to be the one sitting in that courtroom with you, although I have no idea why, because it sucks."

"Thank you. I aim to please."

She ignored the sarcasm. "Rod definitely doesn't like the fact that my desk is in here with you."

Ben exhaled loud enough to be heard on the next floor down. "You've been here less than a half day and already you're making trouble."

"Imagine what will happen if I have to put a bullet in the kid."

"He's twenty-four. You can't be that much older."

"Thirty, and there is a world of difference between a kid like that who has had everything handed to him and me." Rod had every opportunity open to him. She tripped through the past two years and was only now getting back up off her ass again.

"Feeling judgmental today, are we?"

"I've done some background research on you and everyone who works for you."

"Interesting." Ben smacked his lips together as if he had gone into deep contemplation. "When did you find time for that?"

"Last night."

"Very enterprising of you." He shifted his weight, edged a little closer.

She could smell the citrusy scent of the soap on his skin. "I have my talents."

"I'll bet you do."

The room shrank. Callie knew that the laws of physics made that impossible, but the air grew thin and his hand now rested just inches from her knee. "Uh . . . ?"

His eyebrow kicked up. "Yes?"

"Are you flirting with me, Your Honor?"

"Of course not." The hitch to his voice said differently.

That would be a disaster. Fun but dangerous. She knew how this scenario played out. She went through these cycles of attraction. Someone would appeal to her, they'd connect, the sex would consume her, and then she'd lose.

One of them had to exercise some common sense. From the way her palms started sweating and the rush of excitement that just shot through her stomach, it better be her before she lost all control. "In addition to the fact I don't like you all that much and have been tempted to shoot you several times since meeting you—"

"Thanks again, this time for refraining from homicide."

"—it would be a conflict for you to be involved with anyone who works for you."

"Well argued. You could be a lawyer with that reasoning. Except that you've forgotten one very important fact."

That was quite possible, since she couldn't remember anything at the moment. "Which is?"

"You work for my brother, not me."

Chapter Three

"Tell me Callie's story." Ben took the cap off the bottle and slid the beer across his kitchen counter to his brother. With dinner over, Mark fired up the laptop. That meant Ben had a short window to grab his brother's attention before he drifted off into law enforcement worker mode.

"What do you want to know?" Mark shuffled his papers, scanning them for something, but didn't bother to look up.

"Why isn't she with the FBI now?"

"You'll have to ask her."

"I'm asking you."

Mark glanced up then. He leaned his elbows on the counter and passed the bottle back and forth between his palms. "She chose to move on."

"That's not a real answer. Hell, I could get that information without much digging." Ben wanted something more. Something personal that would give him a little insight into Callie.

"Need-to-know only."

"Don't give me that. Was it an assignment gone bad? She swore at the director? She shot a witness who pissed her off, which I could absolutely see her doing, by the way. Or was it something worse?"

"You might want to be careful. She's considered excellent with that weapon."

"So noted."

"And she's very private. She took on this job as a favor to me. I wanted someone smart and tough to watch over you. Someone from the outside who you couldn't boss around or intimidate."

"You make me sound difficult," Ben joked.

"You're a complete pain in the ass about all of this."

"Apparently you're not alone in thinking that. She's already threatened to put a bullet in me."

"No surprise there."

Ben looked down at the bottle in his hand. He picked at the edge of the label, trying to get lost in the mundane activity rather than let his mind wander to memories of how tight Callie's ass looked in those pants today. "But her accuracy on the gun range doesn't really answer my question."

Mark didn't say anything. He just let the quiet fill the room, as if silence somehow answered his brother's question. Finally he spoke up. "Let me ask you something."

Ben swallowed a groan. "Can I stop you?"

"Why the intense interest in her personal life?"

"She's in my office."

"You know everything about Elaine or that Rod kid?" Mark punctuated the remark with a knowing smile. "Don't remember you insisting on a background check when those two came to work for you."

Ben thought about throwing his brother's laptop out the window. "This is different. I couldn't move two inches today without tripping over Callie."

And then there was the part where he wanted her until his mind blanked on everything else around him. The woman had a smart mouth and sweet curvy body. He'd never had a preference for blondes versus brunettes. Now he did.

She pretended to despise him, said all sorts of shit he'd never let anyone else say to him at the office. More than once he caught her staring up at him from her seat in the courtroom. Sometimes he saw a soft awareness in her eyes. Other times she threw him a want-to-squash-you glare.

The reality was her feigned disinterest drove him to his knees. There was something pretty damn hot about a woman who acted as if she could live without him, who didn't care about the rumors of his bedroom skills or how fast he could get tickets to whatever event she wanted to see in the area. Independent and feisty. Yeah, Callie appealed to him on a fundamental level. Rubbed him raw and had him thinking up new uses for his desk.

And despite the not-interested act, there was a "got the green light" vibe zapping off her that had made it tough to concentrate on the middle-aged men parading through his courtroom all afternoon. He called two extra breaks during the afternoon session just to have a few seconds alone to think. Of course, she followed him everywhere, so he had to go to his only private space anywhere at the moment—the bathroom. The second time he stood in there with one hand against the wall mirror and mentally listed out all the reasons making a move on a prickly woman who carried a gun was a dumb idea.

Mark clicked his tongue against the roof of his mouth. "You can't sleep with her."

"Whoa." Ben held up his hands and tried to deliver his best shocked look. "Where did that come from?"

"Thirty-eight years of seeing that stupid smile on your face and the past twenty plus watching how you operate with women."

Ben balanced his hips against the counter and swished his drink around in the bottle. "Despite what everyone in the courthouse thinks, I've never had a relationship with some-one who works for me."

"So?"

"What, you don't believe me?" That possibility hit Ben like a sucker punch. Through everything that happened in the past, they believed in and supported each other. They owed the lives they had now to that fact.

"I mean 'so' as in Callie works for me. Your impressive statistic isn't relevant."

Ben relaxed, but not fully. He had hoped Mark would miss that distinction. "What's your point?"

"She's there to protect you."

She excelled at distracting him. Ben didn't buy into the rest. He could watch out for himself. Had been doing it for years no matter the cost. "So you keep saying."

"I am not paying her to slide all over you."

"I'm not sure which one of us is the whore in that scenario you're describing, but for the record, I'm outraged on Callie's behalf," Ben said in his most sarcastic voice.

"She's off limits."

"Come on. She's a grown woman and can make her own decisions."

All the humor faded from Mark's face. "Not her, Ben."

Ah, shit. All the oxygen sucked right out of the room. Ben could handle Mark's interference at work. Ben understood where the concern came from and forced back his refusals to let Mark win that one. But Ben refused to fight his brother over a woman. They'd never done that before, despite what Mark might think, and were too old to do it now.

"You want her," Ben said.

"What? No." Mark's eyes grew wide enough to take over his face. "I mean, she's *fine*. Don't get me wrong. I have a pair of fucking eyes, so I can see how good she looks."

Mark could get off that subject damn quick, as far as Ben was concerned. "So?"

Mark squirmed in his seat as he picked up his bottle and

set it back down again. And then repeated the exercise four more times.

The fog cleared from Ben's brain. He got it. "This isn't about Callie."

"It's just that—"

Ben forced his hands to unclench from the counter behind him. "You're stuck on someone else."

Mark's anger came fast. "That's over."

"It doesn't have to be."

"We're not talking about my love life. We're on yours." Mark shoved the laptop and everything in front of him off to the side and then started to pace. "Look, there are about a hundred women who would love to say they got nailed by the popular young judge. You've got power, and that stupid robe seems to drive the courthouse ladies wild. You need a good time? Pick one of them."

Ben tried to think of something less appealing. "I can't date anyone who works for me or in the same building."

Mark stopped. Even gave a forced smile. "Then you have your answer."

"To what?"

"Callie works there. Right in your office, in fact. By your logic, she's in restricted territory."

"She doesn't really."

Mark shrugged. "Besides, she probably isn't interested."

"What about my aphrodisiac robe?"

"You're not her type."

Ben refused to ask. This amounted to brotherly warfare. He set his empty bottle in the sink and thought about . . . *Hell*. He turned back around. "What's her type?"

"A guy who's smart enough to take a bodyguard without whining when one's offered," Mark said as if he'd been waiting to fire off that response.

"You're wrong."

"About?"

"Almost everything, but mostly about Callie's feelings. She wants me back." Ben was counting on being right about that important fact.

"She better not."

Ben was thinking the exact opposite.

Chapter Four

The next day, Callie stepped off the elevator and rushed down the hallway leading to the private judges' chambers. That was her deal with Mark. They would exchange the responsibility for Ben no later than seven thirty each work morning. The fact the plan worked a bit like a kid's day care drop-off made her smile. She bet Ben loved that.

But funny or not, she vowed to arrive even earlier each day and get settled in. Since she didn't have any real paperwork to do, getting ready for work consisted of walking through the office's four rooms and reception area to make sure no one else was there. The only barrier between the elevator and the office was a sign at the top of the hallway that read "RESTRICTED AREA" and warned of electronic monitoring. Yeah, that would stop the bad guys. Stern written warnings *always* scared men who liked to blow things up.

Idiots.

She made a mental note to go a second round with Sheriff Danbury over the need for a guard station on each of the floors where the judges had offices. She knew the man would ignore her, but there was an "I told you so" moment coming and she planned to be ready for it. The truth of looming disaster gnawed at her gut.

Her shoes tapped against the marble floors as she walked past the stupid sign. There was something unsettling about knowing security guards sat in a room somewhere in the building watching her walk. Kind of made her want to do something inappropriate, but since the gossip about her new position with Ben had already started rumbling in the women's restrooms and at the tables in the cafeteria she skipped the offensive gestures. It had been hard enough to make a salad under all those watchful eyes at lunch yesterday. No need to make people think she had an insanity issue on top of having a mysterious job.

She stopped at the far end of the hall near the emergency door to the stairwell. The locked door on the right side led to Ben's offices. The one directly across on the left led to Emma Blanton's space. A very convenient arrangement for their so-called friendship and for anyone who might want to take the judges out together.

Callie swept her key card through the reader and heard the door click open. On her second step, her heel hit on something that made her leg slide a few inches. She noticed the envelope with Ben's name on it. Reaching out, she closed the door behind her.

The air in her lungs started to whirl, but she refused to panic. The man was a judge. He probably got messages under his door all the time. It could be work or personal. It didn't mean anything. Because her stomach kept jumping around, however, she decided to ignore the rational theory and explore.

She slipped her gun out from under her arm and swept through the office, stalking around the reception area, then down to Rod's tiny room and across the hall to Ben's airy office. She led with her weapon, waiting for someone to jump out and attack. With her back to the wall she checked under desks and behind curtains, even pushed open the suite's closet with the tip of her foot before peeking inside the courtroom from Ben's private entrance. No one else was in there.

Her head said everything was fine. The dropping sensation inside her convinced her to remain wary. She returned to the reception area and grabbed a tissue off Elaine's desk. With the mysterious envelope pinched between her fingers, she walked back to Ben's office. Careful not to drop it or smudge any prints, she carried the paper and placed it on his desk. Studied it for anything unusual.

She grabbed for her cell phone to call Mark.

"What are you doing?" Ben's amused voice rang through the room.

And scared the hell out of her. She almost wasted all her careful efforts by putting her hands on the envelope when she jumped. "Where's Mark?"

"Good morning to you."

"I'm not kidding. We need Mark."

"I saw you in here and told him to go. He's over in Emma's office." Ben dropped his briefcase on the couch and walked over to stand beside her. "Why?"

"We may have a problem."

"And you plan to resolve it with a tissue?"

She glanced up at him. His black suit and bright blue tie highlighted his dark good looks. The joking smile on his lips gave him a younger and softer look than the one he wore while sitting on the bench listening to cases. On the job he wore his stern judge face, never unfair but not one to take any crap, either. In this office he seemed more . . . human. Right now he was a stalked human.

"You got a letter," she said.

"I get mail all the time."

"Who opens it?"

"Elaine."

"Well, this is different."

Ben stared at the envelope and then back at Callie. "Because?"

"It was on the floor by the door when I came in."

"And?"

"That's a problem."

His eyes narrowed. "Is it possible you're overreacting?"

No way was she agreeing to that. "It's just as possible I'm not."

"Hard to argue with that logic. Let me open it." He reached for the envelope, but she pulled it out of reach by body-blocking him with her hip.

"No."

The touch of her thigh against his stopped them both, but she shook off the shiver and focused on the problems in front of her—the paper and the knucklehead standing next to her. For some reason Ben refused to see the danger around him. She didn't understand his blockage. Nothing in his file explained how a man who once thrived on the adrenaline rush of carrying a gun and fighting for his country could be so cavalier about his own safety. She would figure it out eventually, but not today. The job right now was to keep him alive long enough to smack some sense into him.

Callie tried reason first. "We need to have a forensics team come in here and—"

"We need to open it to make sure it's not a regular letter from a lawyer. An admirer."

"You get a lot of fan mail, do you?"

He shrugged. "Other people like me."

It was the one guy who wanted Ben dead she worried about. "I find that really hard to believe."

He exhaled. "I'm opening it."

"We need Mark."

Ben's stance changed. The lazy smile disappeared and his shoulders tensed. "I'm a grown man. I can open my own mail."

So this was a guy thing. The big bad judge didn't want the little woman saving his ass or calling in reinforcements. Yeah, well. Tough. "This isn't a test of your virility. Something could be in there. You could destroy evidence."

"Then we'll do it another way," he said.

"What do you—" Words caught in her throat when he slid his arm between her stomach and the slim top drawer of his desk. The sleeve of his jacket brushed against her and his scent filled her senses as he leaned with his mouth so close to her breast.

Visions of being with him in a different time and place danced in her head. What he was doing was mundane. What his presence did to her deep inside could only be described as violent. She wanted to feel the hot rush of his breath against her. Shook with the need to run her fingers through his hair and watch as his head turned from the desk to her body.

She inhaled through her nose, trying to calm her breathing and pull her mind back to the job. She had to at least pretend to be professional, but her heartbeat had taken off at a full gallop. In her head, she struggled to like Ben. To ignore his stubbornness and obvious need to control everything and everyone around him.

Her body arrived at a very different conclusion about the man. He got close and she turned to pudding. Her muscles strained and her mind spun with ways to get him out of his suit.

"What was your assignment before this?" he asked in a husky tone that broke her out of the sexual fantasy spinning in her head.

"Why?"

"It made you paranoid." He stood back up holding a letter opener. "I'll slice the top. You can hold the paper the entire time."

"I don't—"

"So that you're clear for the future, that was a statement and not a request." He held the very edge of the envelope and cut it open. "See? No need for a recon team."

"Uh-huh."

His smile fell. "What's wrong with you now?"

Other than the fact seeing the guy with a letter opener got her all hot and bothered? Nothing. "What does it say?"

She read over his shoulder. Heard a gruff rumble hit his chest right before he swore. Tensed when he tensed. The big bold letters written in blue ink didn't say much, but they said enough: *It's Your Turn.*

He slapped the desk before he backed up and paced to the window. "Son of a bitch."

"We have to get Mark." She started to dial but Ben folded his fingers over hers.

"No."

"Ben, this is a direct threat against you. Maybe the bomb had Judge Blanton's name all over it, but this person, whoever it is, is dropping a not-so-subtle warning about the next time. It could happen in a minute or next week. We don't know, but we have to be ready."

The idea of Ben being in that much danger sent a shot of anger spinning through her. She vowed to keep him safe. No one was going to kill him but her.

"Callie." He stepped in close, blocking out her view of the rest of the room. His palms brushed her upper arms in a gesture so intimate she froze.

He leaned in until his body overwhelmed hers. This close

she could see the mix of anger and sadness in his brown eyes. Could smell the shampoo in his still damp hair. She should have stepped back and insisted on a separation between work and play. Instead, her fingers fondled his tie.

"Don't ask me to ignore this, Ben. I can't do it."

"I'm asking you to wait." It was a whispered desperate plea.

"Trust me on this."

This time she found the will to push away. Two more seconds with him right there and he'd be able to talk her into handing over her gun. "I'm calling Mark."

A half hour later Callie sat next to Emma Blanton on the sofa in Ben's office. Rod and Elaine buzzed around on the other side of the door. Both judges had canceled their morning dockets after complaining for what felt to Callie like a month. Apparently their concession meant shifting cases and otherwise screwing up the entire courthouse calendar. For some reason, both judges viewed a schedule snafu as more important than a threatening note. Or they did until Mark overruled them.

The scheduling clerks had demanded an explanation. Ben refused to offer one and hung up the phone without delivering his usual dose of charm. Callie could just imagine the e-mails shooting around the building as the courthouse's female employees tried to figure out what was happening with Judge Cutie Pie behind closed doors.

Callie didn't know if that's what had Ben sitting in a chair with his arms crossed and jaw slammed shut, but something sure had ticked him off. Rather than dwell on Ben's reaction, Callie studied Emma. The other woman looked normal enough. Not like the fire-breathing defendant hater Callie expected. Emma's shoulder-length brown hair and bright blue eyes gave her round face a soft glow. At forty she had reached the age where people threw around words like "handsome" instead of pretty, but Judge Blanton definitely qualified as pretty. No wrinkles, and with an open warmness that only added to her attractiveness.

Callie tried very hard not to hate her.

If Ben had shown any heated interest in Emma, Callie knew she would have wrestled the other woman to the ground. Felony charges be damned. But nothing in their body language or conversation explained what the two of them meant to each other. Ben sat across from his supposed girlfriend and hadn't said a word in more than ten minutes. Neither did Emma's bodyguard, Keith, who stood with his back to the door and his hands folded in front of him. From the way he frowned at Emma, Callie assumed the guy didn't like his assignment all that much.

Mark ran the meeting. Sitting in the open chair next to Ben and across from the couch, Mark went over a new set of courthouse security procedures. "Sheriff Danbury is up to speed on the threats. He's personally checking the security tapes to see who slid the envelope under the door. He's also running through the morning's recordings to see if anything unusual happened at the metal detectors downstairs."

"He's not going to find anything." Callie knew that as sure as she knew the size of her pants. The real size, not the one she told people.

"Probably, but it's worth a try. In the meantime, we need to deal with something else." Then Mark dropped the biggest bombshell. "Judge Samson wants you both to take a vacation."

"I'm not going anywhere," Ben said, finally speaking up but not sounding one ounce happier at being there.

"I agree." Emma ran her fingers through her short hair. "We have work to do. Sitting at home worrying isn't going to help you catch the person any faster."

"But it could keep you alive," Mark said.

Emma kept her focus on the bookshelves lining the wall perpendicular to her instead of looking at either of the Walker men. "I refuse to let this piece of garbage run my life."

Ben stood up. "Are we done here?"

Again with the stubborn act. Callie had just about had enough. "What the hell is wrong with you?"

Ben turned to face her. The slow-motion move carried a menacing quality. "When did I give you permission to talk to me like that?"

The fury in his voice hit her like a slap. She expected frustration about the situation, but this was different. The stupid man was actually angry with her. That realization fueled all the anxiety brewing in her gut. "Probably about the same time I agreed that I needed your okay to do anything."

"Stop." Mark stood up and held his hands out as if he were refereeing a fight. "Let's all calm down."

"Just find the guy." Ben walked over to his desk. "In the meantime, I'm going back to work."

Callie wanted to kick him, but she stuck with the facts instead. "Your morning caseload was canceled."

"I've still got plenty of paperwork to do."

"Right." Mark pointed to the door. "Callie, Keith, let me see you two outside."

Ben waited until they hit the door to fire off one last verbal attack. "Aren't you afraid someone will attack me while you're gone for three seconds?"

Mark pursed his lips together as if he were considering the possibility. "Unless Emma plans on stabbing you, I'm thinking you'll be fine."

"I'm betting she'll be tempted," Callie said, making sure Ben could hear her on the other side of the room.

Emma smiled. "I promise Ben will be alive when you come back."

Callie didn't doubt that. It was the leaving them alone part that had her back teeth snapping together.

As soon as the door closed behind Mark, Ben tried to concentrate on the blank piece of paper in front of him. For the first time in forty-eight hours he could move around his chambers without tripping over Callie. He didn't have to worry about her snide comments or her tendency to put her feet up on his desk.

The moment of quiet should have felt great, but nothing fit together right. He had wanted her to side with him about the note. When she put the job in front of him, his stomach burned. He knew his anger didn't make any sense. She didn't owe him anything. Still, he had counted on her loyalty, and when she failed to give it the need to lash out at her flashed through his mind.

But now he had a different female problem on his hands. One a bit more refined but equally formidable. "What?" he asked Emma.

"They're trying to help, you know."

He could feel his friend's gaze boring into his forehead. After a silent minute of her staring and him ignoring, he looked up. "The situation is suffocating."

"You'd do the same thing for Mark if the roles were reversed."

The calm comment tamped down the fire racing through Ben. He threw down his pen and leaned back in his chair. "If you're going to be logical, it's going to be hard for me to be an irrational ass."

Emma finally got up and walked over. With her hip resting on the corner of the desk and her hands planted on her lap, she gazed down at him with the wise-beyond-her-years look she had perfected in the tenth grade. "You sure your problem is really with the note?"

"Meaning?"

"We've known each other forever, Ben. I can see it. The way you grumble. The short temper. The longer than usual hours in the office."

"You do think I'm being an ass."

Emma smiled. "I think you're attracted to her."

"Who?" Oh, he knew, but stalling for time seemed like the best plan of action at the moment.

"Don't play dumb. I'm talking about the bodyguard you stare at every second you think she's not looking."

Hell, a guy couldn't even plan a move without having an audience. "Exaggerating a bit, aren't you?"

"Not by much."

"Yeah, well, you've read this all wrong. Callie is a menace. She swears like a drunken defendant and insists she runs the place. She's been here for two days and the entire office is upside down. I haven't had a second alone except to take a piss—" He held up his hand. "Sorry."

"I've heard worse."

"Probably from me."

"And others, but none of that changes the facts. She pushes you."

"Exactly." He snapped his fingers. "That's what I'm saying."

"And you like it. You like her, even though you're too thick to admit it." Emma played with a pen on the edge of his desk. "Callie is different from your usual dates. She gets you riled, challenges you."

"You somehow get attraction from that? I get frustration, anger. The desire to fire her ass."

"You love the hunt. That's always been a huge turn-on for you, which is why you seem so uninterested in the women in your life lately."

Where had that come from? "Jesus, you make me sound like a predator."

"More like a single guy who thinks he needs one type of woman but really wants another." Emma continued to spin the pen. "You get bombarded with offers from women who are more interested in your position than about who you are. You go out and get bored and move on."

"You've clearly spent some time thinking about this subject."

"I've watched this dance for years. The more they fight it, the more effort you put in. It's part of why you hate the whole playboy talk. It suggests you'll drag anyone home. You and I both know you're more discriminating than that." She lined the pens back up in straight lines again. "I know the man behind the superstar judge persona."

He pounded his fist against his chest in false bravado. "There's just more superstar underneath."

She reached over and took his hand. "No, there's a sensitive guy who long ago lost the desire to chase an easy score."

"Emma—"

"When people said things about us, you didn't lose your temper or rush to deny. You kept your control and ignored the lies."

"That's different."

Emma squeezed his hand. "Of course it is. Because there's nothing between us." She pressed even tighter when he tried to talk. "But there *is* something between you and Callie. She digs and you take the bait. It's interesting to watch, actually."

Ben folded his free hand over their joined ones. "Happy I could entertain you."

After a barely audible knock, the door to his office flew open. Callie stepped in, ready to say something he was sure would annoy him. But her mouth froze in the open position. She stared at their hands on the desk before looking up at him again with red-stained cheeks.

He couldn't believe she managed to stay quiet for a full ten seconds. "Yes?"

"Sorry. I'll wait outside." Callie slammed the door shut again before he could yell at her for interrupting.

"That was interesting." Emma eased her hand out from under his and stood up. She brushed the wrinkles out of her skirt. Made quite a show of the process, as if she were trying not to look at him. Or laugh.

"You mean the part where Callie is a grown person but for some reason doesn't know when to knock on a closed door?"

"I was too busy noticing the stunned look on her face."

He refused to read anything into Callie's shocked flush. She was rushing around and feeling left out. Nothing else. "She's probably upset that I had five minutes of freedom."

Emma cocked her head to the side. "Come on."

"I'm serious."

"You know women better than that."

"She's not a typical woman."

"Sure seems like one."

Subjects like Callie's looks and exactly how he planned on undressing her once he got her alone were off limits. He shared a lot with Emma but drew the line at locker-room talk. "I admit Callie is attractive in a could-kick-my-ass sort of way."

Emma laughed. "See, many men would not find that aspect of her too compelling. You do."

Which only proved men were idiots. "I was kidding."

"Sure you were." Emma's voice dripped with sarcasm. "You still trying to tell me there's nothing between the two of you?"

Something pulsed there with Callie. It breathed and kicked, begging to get free, and he had no idea what the hell it was. "She's ticked off."

"And the funniest part is that you don't even know why." Emma winked at him. "But you will, and I can't wait to be there to see you figure it out."

Chapter Five

Seven hours later, they left the courtroom with Callie convinced the mind-numbing afternoon killed off a few thousand brain cells. She thought about telling Ben that little fact, but he practically ran back to his office, ignoring her every step of the way.

Then he tried to close the office door on her face. Apparently he thought she could watch over him from the crack under the door.

Jackass.

"What's wrong with you now?" Callie pushed the door open and then banged it shut as hard as she could behind her.

Ben slowly turned around. Something rumbled around inside him and it wasn't happiness. Tension radiated off him, pulling every part of his body tight. For the first time all afternoon he glanced at her.

An apology for his grumpiness was in order. He should have been embarrassed for flirting with her while his true love Emma sat only an office away. Instead, his brown eyes smoldered with . . . was that fury?

"Don't do that again," he said through a clenched jaw.

"What?" she asked, mystified about the cause of his sour mood.

"Slam my door." He threw his files against his desk with enough force to send a few flying to the carpet.

She sure as hell hoped he didn't think it was her job to race around and pick those up. Just to be clear on that point she didn't move. "But I like the sound."

"Well, I don't, and since I run this office I decide what happens here. It's about time you realized that."

Looked like they were back to the me-boss-you-stupid-girl routine. "Care to tell me what crawled up your ass?"

"Excuse me?"

"Up. Your. Ass."

"I'm not in the mood for your attitude or a shadow."

"You don't get that choice."

"Yes, I actually do."

To be fair, the day had been an absolute pisser. When a threatening note turned out to be the highlight, a shit storm of bad news was inevitable. Mark wanted to beef up security. The courtrooms had to be locked down during business hours. And there was that whole hand-holding thing she witnessed.

But Callie still had a job to do. If that got in the way of his office loving with Emma, then tough shit. "After this morning, I'm not going anywhere."

"Don't remind me." Ben stripped off his robe. The jacket came next, leaving him in a white dress shirt and tie.

"What is that supposed to mean?"

His hands dropped to his sides. "Did it ever dawn on you that I didn't want to share the note with Mark?"

Callie realized they were talking about two very different things. She worried about Ben's safety and assumed he was tired of having someone with him at all times. He got stuck on the chain of command. Looked like a case of Ben being knocked flat by his oversized ego.

"Mark is trying to protect you," she pointed out for what felt like the three hundredth time.

"I don't need my big brother to rescue me."

"Is that what this is about? You're having a crisis of male self-worth? If so, snap the hell out of it." She grabbed Ben's arm and forced him to look at her. "For God's sake, you're smarter than this."

"I told you once that I don't accept a belligerent tone from employees."

"And I ignored you."

"I've earned the right to expect more respect than you show me." His voice stayed sharp, but he didn't pull away from her touch.

"First, as you pointed out, I don't work for you." She eased up on her grip because he didn't seem to be running away. Well, not physically. Mentally he had left the building. "Second, you have to earn respect, and stomping around and acting stupid is not the way to do that."

"Did you talk to your supervisors at the FBI like this?"

"No."

That was the truth. Even though it killed her inside, she had shown deference and played by the rules. She took crap from her boss and refrained from pushing him out a window, because that's what she had to do to keep the job she worked so hard to get. When all of that reluctant patience backfired, she learned a hard lesson. Now she refused to hide and stay quiet. No longer would she wallow in false obedience. If someone needed to be called a jackass, she would do it.

Which probably explained why she had been unemployed for almost two months before Mark came knocking and offering odd jobs. Then came the Ben gig. Callie said yes but attached some strings. She didn't have to toe the line or cut through bureaucratic bullshit. She could say what she needed to say as long as Ben stayed safe, and it was up to Ben to figure out how to deal with her truthfulness.

"Why did you get fired?" Ben asked.

He was fishing. If he had the facts he would have chosen his words more carefully. "I didn't, and my life is not your business."

"That goes both ways."

"No. I need you to listen and follow my lead."

His teeth slammed together hard enough for her to hear the click. "This is my fucking office."

He delivered his observation in a resounding yell. The grating sound brought Rod running. He knocked once, not waiting for permission to come in before opening the door. "Is everything okay?"

"We're fine," she said as she dropped her hand from Ben's arm.

But not before Rod's gaze went right there. "Sir?"

Ben shook his head. "You can leave."

Rod's face fell at his boss's abrupt tone. Callie almost felt bad for the poor little sycophant.

"I'm just outside if you need me," Rod said.

Callie waited until the clerk left again to say anything. "You didn't have to scare the hell out of the poor kid."

"Since when do you care about Rod?"

The man made a good point, but the nastiness was way out of proportion for the situation. Callie knew she should drop it and let Ben fester in his male stupidity, but a voice inside her head told her to keep digging.

"What's really going on here?" she asked, fully expecting another screaming match.

"I just told you."

They stood a few feet apart. If she reached out she could

touch him again, which was exactly why she kept her arms strapped to her sides with invisible tape. "You had to know what would happen with the note."

"Excuse me if I'm ticked off that my work life has turned into this load of crap."

She guessed she was the "crap" in that description. The guy could be a little more appreciative that her sole purpose in life at the moment was to keep him alive. Some hours, like now when he spent most of the time snapping at her, she debated taking him out herself.

But she did understand the panic that rolled over you when you lost control of everything around you. She spent her entire life chasing the dream of joining the FBI. She read books, worked on her shooting, and built her endurance. With the tests and training behind her, she hit the streets. She never imagined the most dangerous part of the work would come in the office, at her desk and at the hands of a supervisor with a God complex.

"Is this about Emma?" Callie forced the other woman's name out over a lump of envy.

"No."

Ah, hell. Even though her mind played an endless loop of getting Ben naked while she crawled all over him, Callie knew she didn't actually have any rights to the man. Her debilitating case of lust didn't have anything to do with his very real relationship with Emma. Time to step back and be professional.

"Look, I'm sorry I came in during your . . . well, your thing." She didn't know what to call that spectacle, so she didn't try to define it. Talking about it would only put the image of Emma and Ben together back in her head, and Callie had spent all day trying to stamp it out.

"Thing?"

Callie heard a tinge of amusement in his voice. "I don't know what the correct name is."

His shook his head. "I said no. That's not it."

"I can talk to Emma if that will help." Callie had no idea how to start that conversation or what to say, but she made the offer anyway. This being the bigger person stuff just sucked.

"I got it, but not necessary."

He liked using that phrase even when it didn't make any sense or have an understandable context. "Got what?" she asked.

Ben exhaled as the rigid anger left his body. "Stop talking about Emma."

Seemed Ben turned a bit touchy when the topic of his girlfriend popped up. Probably a guilt thing. That's what happened when a guy tried to dip his pen in too many wells.

"I'm trying to ignore your jackassery here and apologize."

Instead of revving up again, Ben smiled. "My what?"

"I was going to call you a douche and the bag it came in, but I thought you'd have me arrested."

"And here I thought you didn't know where to draw the line." He leaned back against his desk with his feet out in front of him at an angle. The move put his thigh right next to hers. "So tell me why you keep apologizing about Emma."

Callie only remembered one time, but arguing about that struck her as lame. Now that Ben's temper had returned to human levels, she didn't want to send him racing back to crazy town again. "You two were in a clinch when I came in."

"You call that a clinch?"

Whatever it was it made Callie's head explode. "Sure."

"Tell me something."

No way was she agreeing to that without more information. Hand this man an opening and he'd steer a submarine through it.

He kept talking anyway. Looked pretty relaxed in his slouch as his smile inched up on his lips. "Do you have a boyfriend?"

If he wanted to shock her . . . well, he did. "How is that relevant?"

"Call me curious."

"Are you allowed to ask me about that?"

"You think there's a law against it?"

"There should be."

"So, you're not going to answer?"

Not until she knew where this was going. "What does the state of my love life have to do with anything?"

"You know all about me. Only seems fair I get some background on you."

"I need to know about your life in order to do my job." At least that was the excuse she used when she ventured outside the file Mark gave her. She'd lost her clearance when she walked away from her job at the FBI, but she still had friends of the computer-hacker variety. In just a few hours she had all the paperwork that existed on Ben.

She had to admit her little search mission turned out to be a huge disappointment. His background was so clean it squeaked. If he hadn't passed through screening committees and all sorts of interviews to get his current judicial position she would have thought someone manufactured his past. No arrests. No trouble. Great grades. Always within the law. For some reason she expected to find a smart guy with a bad-boy past. That sounded good in the fantasy she created in her head but looked as if it wasn't true.

"So, you're not poking around in my life just because you're nosy?" he asked.

No way could he know about her travels through his personal history. She'd been careful and cleaned up behind her. "I don't poke."

"Tell me what you want to know."

She smelled a con. "Anything?"

"You get one question."

She thought about his decision to leave the military and about the scarce information on his parents. She skipped all that and went with the issue at the front of her mind. "What's going on between you and Emma?"

"I've already answered that. We're friends."

Callie snorted just to let him know what she thought of his fake deals. "I don't climb all over my friends when the door shuts."

"Really? When do you climb on them then?"

"Huh?"

He closed in. One minute he shot her a lazy smile. The next he stood up straight and hovered over her with his cheek right next to hers. "What do you do with your friends?"

Heat thrummed off him, surrounding her and filling her with a tingly sensation from shoulders to toes. "I don't—"

"Do you touch them?" Ben trailed the back of his hand down her cheek. Dragged his thumb across her lips.

"I . . ."

"Smell them?" He leaned down and nuzzled her ear. "Do they smell as good as you?"

His mouth traveled down her neck, nipping and kissing. Hot breath tickled her skin as his fingers caressed her waist. The double whammy of touching slammed her breath to a halt in her chest. Her body strained to get closer to him as her palms skimmed up his back.

Holy crap. "This isn't a good idea," she said.

"Probably not, but I've been wanting to do it all day."

"I thought you were mad at me."

"Be quiet for a second," he said.

Then his mouth covered hers. His lips pressed deep and strong and his tongue brushed against hers. There was nothing teasing about this kiss. It shot through her hot and wet, electrifying every cell inside her. She fell into the sensation of being overpowered and claimed. Her stomach tumbled and her knees dipped. Muscles relaxed as her brain shifted into neutral.

"God, yes," he mumbled when their mouths lifted on gasps of harsh breaths.

He dove back in. His lips met hers over and over again in a kiss that had her winding her arms around his neck and pulling him close.

Him. Her. Touching. Nothing else mattered. Pleasure crashed over her, drowning out everything around them. Fingers searched and sculpted. Her hands swept into his hair while his pushed against her lower back, easing her closer to the juncture between his thighs. She heard the grumbling moan in his chest and the deep breaths from her own.

She lifted her head in an attempt to get some air. "Ben . . . that . . ."

"You taste so good."

His mouth found that sensitive spot right at the slope of her chin. Her kryptonite. A few nibbling kisses and she wanted to strip that conservative shirt and tie right off him.

She dropped her head back to give him greater access. "Right there."

When his mouth found hers again, lights exploded in her brain. He kissed like he worked, with an intensity that sent her common sense screaming in wild defeat. The touch of his lips was all she dreamed about and everything she feared.

But her mind shouted out a red-light warning through the sensual haze. She had a job and he had a girlfriend.

Callie pulled her mouth away, letting her forehead rest against his cheek as she struggled to breathe without wheezing. "We have to stop."

"God, why?" He mumbled the question into her hair.

"Emma." Callie now hated that name.

With the gentle touch of his palms, he lifted her head and stared down at her. The gaze from deep brown eyes searched her face. The rapid beating in his chest thumped against her as his eyes grew soft.

"I don't cheat," he said in a husky whisper. "If I were with Emma I wouldn't be kissing you."

Callie knew she should pull back, but she rubbed her hands up his back instead. "But, I saw—"

"Evidence of a lifelong friendship." He traced her cheekbones with his thumbs. "That's it."

"You're not—"

"No."

"Does Emma know that?"

His chuckle vibrated against her from everywhere their bodies touched. "Definitely."

Relief washed through Callie. She balanced her head on his chin as she tried to figure out what it all meant. "Now what?"

"You invite me to your house."

"That crosses a line." She could recognize that over her misfiring brain waves and damp panties.

"I'd carry you to mine right this second, but Mark will be there eventually to screw everything up." Ben dropped a quick kiss on her mouth.

"Oh, yeah. Your brother." And her boss.

"And we're going to need hours of privacy."

She debated the pros and cons for all of two seconds. The temptation proved too great. "Well, as you keep telling me, you're the one in charge."

Ben's smile lit up his face. "About time you admitted that."

Chapter Six

Emma finished her afternoon docket and left the bench in time to see Mark storm into the back room of her suite and grab her clerk by the arm. He dragged Scott MacAllister behind him down the hall to her private office, and was not too subtle about it. Scott's high-octave screaming didn't help, either.

Everyone came running. Emma waved off her bodyguard and reassured her assistant as she followed in Mark's footsteps. "What the hell are you doing?" she asked in a harsh whisper as she shut her door.

Mark barely spared her a glance. "Get out of here, Emma."

"Absolutely not." She used her best judge tone to convey her anger over his disrespect.

If Mark picked up on her mood he didn't let on.

"This is between me and young Scott here." Mark's face flushed with fury as he dropped Scott into the nearest chair and held him there.

She feared he'd kill Scott if she moved away. "This is my office," she said, trying to break through the irrational mood that gripped Mark.

"This is my case."

Dread settled in her stomach. "What has happened?"

"Your clerk has the starring role on the security tapes of Ben's office."

"No, Judge Blanton. I didn't. I wouldn't." Scott shook with fear as he tried to get up.

Mark grabbed Scott by the collar and shoved him down again. "Shut up."

"But you've got this all wrong." Scott's voice grew louder as he tried to reassure Mark of his innocence.

"I have eyes, Scott."

And the strength of the devil. Emma stepped up, hoping to calm both men with her presence. "Tell me what's going on," she said as she unwrapped Mark's fingers from Scott's shirt.

Scott rubbed his arm from the spot of Mark's earlier vise-like hold. "Someone gave me the note."

Mark scoffed. "Nice story."

Mark's anger and Scott's fear still didn't rise to the level of an explanation for her. "I don't understand why you're all over my clerk."

"He's there on the security tapes. I watched it myself. He came down the hall and slid the threatening letter under Ben's door." Mark turned his wrath back on Scott. "I want to know why."

"I just delivered a message. I do that all the time."

"It's true, he does," she said.

Mark wasn't ready to calm down. "If that's true, why didn't you tell me that earlier?"

Emma shifted through the information in her mind. "He was probably afraid you'd kill him."

"I might yet."

They barely made it inside the front door of her apartment before Ben pinned Callie against the wall. In their rush of entwined legs and arms, they knocked over a small table in the entry, sending something glass crashing to the floor. He heard the shattering fall as he shoved the front door shut with his foot.

He hoped whatever had broken didn't matter much to her, because he couldn't stop to investigate even if he wanted to. And he didn't. The sole purpose of his wanting stood locked in his arms with her hand on his ass.

Everything moved in a haze of color and light. He remembered making a somewhat clumsy pass at her in his office and then struggling to drive his car while she shouted out directions and slid her hand along his inner thigh. The only thing that saved them from an accident where he wrapped his car around a tree was the desire to get her home and naked. No way was he checking out of this world before he got that opportunity. He stayed focused for that reason alone.

But they were home now. In her domain, where she would be comfortable and in charge. Where he could learn every inch of her skin without worrying about Mark busting in or anything stopping them. Where he could run the live version of the movie that had been playing in his head, the one where she could give free rein to the energy burning through her and use that hot mouth of hers for something other than giving him shit.

The threats and frustration faded into the far distance. Whatever or whoever plagued him and wanted him dead could wait. He concentrated solely on Callie—the eager touch of her hands and fierce heat of her kiss. Nothing else mattered but that.

Their bodies rolled against the wall until he moved them out of the way of the broken glass. Sharp breaths mixed with searching hands as their mouths slanted over each other again and again. Need flushed through Ben until all he could think about was getting her onto any flat surface and peeling that navy suit right off her.

Blond hair spread over white sheets as he pushed deep inside her. Yeah, he had been dreaming about that one since he met her.

"Lock the door," she whispered against his lips.

This was one order he didn't mind her giving. "At your service."

He left her for the second it took to throw the bolt, then he came back even more eager to pull her close. Fingers dove through her hair and knocked the barrette loose. Silky strands fell over his hands and across her shoulders. Long and smooth. Just as he imagined.

And he wasn't alone in searching. Her hands moved to his belt, shifting and tugging until he felt the tightness around his waist loosen. The belt hit the floor. When his fingers returned to the button at the top of his pants, his stomach dipped, giving her easier access to ripping the clothes right off him. The kiss in her hair, the brushing of his palms over her collarbone, all of it allowed her to take the lead. To be ready on her terms.

The clicking of his zipper got him moving again. He chanted her name as he stripped off his jacket and dropped it to the floor. Without breaking a kiss he reached for her blouse. One, two, three. The pearl buttons slipped from their holes, revealing miles of creamy skin and a pink lace bra that begged for sex.

But he didn't need an invitation. He rubbed his palms over her breasts, learning every curve and caressing until her back arched and her nipples puckered. A finger eased under the material's thin edge, giving him access to her bare skin. When he folded the silk back and slid a thumb across the plump top of her breast, she broke off the kiss and stared down at her chest.

Every time his thumb passed over her nipple, her body jumped in response. Her high, round breasts lifted and fell on harsh breaths.

"Bedroom," she said in a breathy voice.

He wanted to do the romantic thing and carry her to the bed, but his erection pounded too hard to let him do it. "Can't make it."

She glanced over his shoulder, her eyes wild with need. "Sofa."

"Yes." Hell, the wall worked for him. He still couldn't believe they made it out of the car and up a flight of stairs to the front door without peeling their clothes off.

She grabbed his hand and dragged him into her small living room. A couch and a chair and . . . some other piece of furniture. He didn't really give a shit what. All he wanted was her. He could do an inventory later. Maybe after they had sex six or seven times and his dick no longer threatened to burst.

But all of his good intentions fled when she dropped down on the cushions in front of him. The sexy move put her eye level with the part of him that was most desperate for her. She didn't play games or hesitate. No, she knew exactly what they both wanted. She slid her hand inside his pants, under the elastic of his briefs and straight to his cock. Her fingers squeezed, caressing his tip before sliding down the length of him.

His knees buckled.

Seeing her hair fall over his lower body made him rock hard. He wondered how he would survive the delicate torture of her exploration. When she took him between her lips and down her throat, he knew he wouldn't. His body bucked and trembled. Every time she eased him back out of her mouth, his hips tensed and pushed forward as if his lower body could not tolerate the separation from her.

The gentle assault of hands and tongue continued until his

mind crashed. All the fantasies about taking her long and slow vanished. Something primal and raw replaced them. He wanted her naked and panting, spread out on the floor before him while he pushed deep inside her.

"Protection." Ben forced the word with a groan.

She glanced up, her mouth wet and her eyes glazed with longing. "What?"

"We need a condom." If she didn't have one, he would go door to fucking door of the condo complex until he tracked one down.

"Right." She placed a kiss on the tip of his cock and stood up.

He immediately regretted speaking up. A flaming heat gripped him. With her gone, his muscles refused to relax. Rather than waste time standing there with his erection pressing against his pants, he started to strip. Off came the tie and shirt. He shoved his pants and briefs down and stepped out of them. There he waited, naked and still in the center of her living room.

Callie reappeared in the doorway with a box in hand and wearing nothing but her shirt. Slim feet with bright red painted toenails showed off the bit of sexy whimsy she hid under her sensible bodyguard shoes. Her lean legs went on for miles, disappearing right at the dark edge of her crisp dress cotton. If she had panties on under there, they sure were tiny.

And he damn well planned to solve that little mystery in the next few minutes.

"You should wear skirts to the office," he said, thinking they'd never get any work done if she did.

"I can move better in pants."

"I can get to you faster in a skirt."

She shot him the sort of knowing smile women had used throughout the ages to signal a flashing "yes" sign to their lovers. "Why don't you concentrate on getting to me now?"

That was the type of invitation she only had to issue once. "Come here."

She threw a box on the couch next to him and walked over to stand in front of him. Her arms curled around his neck as her body slid next to his. Skin met skin. Sweet curves touched tense muscles. Everywhere he was hard, she was soft. Firm and athletic, but very womanly.

His hands settled on her ass. It took only a shocked second to flip up her shirt and find skin. "You're not wearing underwear. Not that I'm complaining, because I'm not."

"Seemed unnecessary," she said as she kissed her way along his jaw.

"Smart woman."

Trying to imagine her panties had been bad enough. Now he'd have to deal with the idea of her going without. He felt a sudden surge of gratefulness that he sat behind a big desk in his courtroom. Seeing every inch of her body and thinking of her bare under her conservative suits would make the barrier to wandering eyes a necessity.

"Please tell me you weren't like this today at work," he said, half hoping she was.

"Would that upset you?"

"I may die from it."

"Poor baby."

"If I start thinking about this—" He squeezed her ass in his palm. "We're never going to get through a court docket without at least two breaks to go back to my office so you can show me."

"The naked part?" Her lips moved against his throat. "That's all for you."

"Sweet Jesus."

"So is this."

She tried to step back, but he held her close. With his hands on the small area of warm flesh between the tops of her thighs and bottom of her ass, he kept the connection. His head fell forward, his gaze glued to her fingers as she slid the shirt off her shoulders and let it fall to the floor behind her.

She wasn't wearing a damn thing underneath there, either.

Ben's gaze wandered over the tops of her breast to her tight rosy nipples. Down her flat stomach to the soft flare of her hips. Ending at the thin strip of hair covering her very core. She didn't try to hide or talk, but her skin flushed pink under his inspection. Soft breaths skimmed his cheek as he trailed his fingers past her waist and kept going.

When his thumb slipped into her heat, her legs opened in silent invitation. He pressed and brushed until her wetness bathed his skin. With each pass her inner muscles clenched, as if trying to drag his fingers deeper inside. The more he touched, the more he wanted to taste. To accomplish that, he slid to his knees. Her salty scent filled him as he widened her legs to fit between.

Her nails scraped down his back as he found her clit. Licking and sucking, he whipped her into a frenzy. Her thighs tightened against his shoulders as her lower body swayed in time with the rhythm of his mouth.

She begged. She pounded on his shoulders. Still he held her steady and swept his tongue over her clit while he stretched her open with two fingers. A husky moan rumbled up her chest and echoed in his ear.

Her pleasure only made him work harder. The taste of her on his lips and feel of her against his hand fueled his needs. His body ached and strained. Pleasure mixed with pain as he held back and concentrated on her pleasure. Faster and harder he caressed and inflamed until her lower body pulled into a tight spring. With one last pass of pressure on her clit, she exploded, arching in open-mouthed ecstasy.

Callie shouted his name as the muscles in her legs gave way. Her body collapsed. Damp skin and soft hair fell against his back. Heavy breaths forced her body up and down as she fought to regain her breathing.

The romantic thing would be to let her mind calm and her body cool, but his cock twitched with the need to get inside her. As gently as possible, he put his hand on the small of her back and eased her to the tan carpet. At this angle he hovered over her, able to see every delicious inch of her heated skin.

The back of her hand rested against her open mouth as her legs fell open in welcome.

"Callie . . ."

"Now, Ben."

As far as he was concerned they were fifteen minutes past the point of comfort. His lower body had pulled tight enough to make the blood pound inside him. She was ready for him and he couldn't get enough of her. With his hands on her knees, he moved between her thighs. He didn't even remember ripping open the box and fishing out a condom, but he wore it, which meant nothing could stop him from fulfilling the fantasy now.

The tip of his cock entered her tight passage, pushing and stretching as he slipped deep inside. Her body clamped down on his as he pulled out and then thrust back in again. He tried to set an even pace to let her body adjust, but she wouldn't let him go slow. Her palms grabbed his ass and brought him in even tighter against her. The shocking sensation sent his stomach tumbling as if he just raced the highest point of a roller coaster.

It had to be now.

He pinned her hands to the floor and threaded his fingers through hers. Closeness, not control, was the issue. He wanted to feel every part of her as his body ratcheted up even further. When she dug her heels into the back of his thighs, the last of his control snapped. Speed and intensity overtook finesse. From her knees to her breasts, every part of her touched a part of him as their bodies bucked and their moans filled the quiet room.

Her head fell back and an orgasm ripped through her. He followed right after. Flexing his hips, he lodged his cock deep inside her one last time. Jerking and pressing, his body clamped down hard. Everything inside him stiffened as his breath caught on a gasp. A second later, the vise-grip hold on his lower body loosened and he emptied into her.

It took another ten minutes for his breathing to return to normal.

Five minutes after that, she led him to her bedroom to start again.

Chapter Seven

By eight that evening, the courthouse had quieted down. Except for a few law enforcement officials stationed at the entrance to the building and others signing off shifts down in the sheriff's area, no one was around. Emma welcomed the calm. Knowing Keith sat just outside her office helped soothe the queasy unease that had filled her ever since the bomb went off.

Her anxiety had only heightened earlier when Mark dragged Scott to the hidden elevator at the side of her courtroom. The same elevator that led straight to the sheriff's office holding cells downstairs. As Mark led him out, Scott lost his control and promised to sue, a threat that just damned him further in Mark's eyes. It all happened hours ago, but no matter how many times she shut her eyes, Emma couldn't block that image from her mind.

She heard shuffling and glanced up to see Mark filling her doorway. Dark with shocking green eyes and a brooding air, he commanded every room he entered. The lines of his face were sharper than Ben's. Where Ben smiled and his face lit up, Mark usually wore a stern frown. They were both handsome, Ben more classically so, and athletic in a could-lift-a-car kind of way.

A whiff of danger followed Mark. He worked in secret and thrived on the adrenaline of walking on the edge. Compared to her and Ben, who lived in the open, constantly subject to public scrutiny, Mark moved only in shadows and refused to let anyone share that gloomy space with him.

The women in the courthouse and managers of the newspaper's society section developed a crush on Ben the minute he stepped on the scene. He put on that robe and otherwise sensible females went wild. Emma loved Ben, but like a brother.

There was nothing brotherly about her feelings for Mark. Never had been.

"Hey." Mark stood with his hands resting on either side of the threshold. He called to Keith in the outer office. "Go ahead and take a break. Get some fresh air. I'll watch over Judge Blanton for the next half hour. Check back at exactly eight thirty."

A shiver ran through her at Mark's remark. She held a position of power, made decisions about freedom and forgiveness every day, and still this man could shake her to the core.

"How's Scott?" she asked, trying to keep their communication as routine as Mark did.

"He finally stopped whining. I had one of my men take him home."

Leave it to Mark to find a young man's protests of innocence to be nothing more than a nuisance. "I guess that means his story checked out?"

"A delivery kid met Scott by the elevator, and then Scott walked the envelope back and slid it under Ben's door. Tracked down the delivery service and it was a cash job. Kid has no connection with Scott. Insists Scott just happened to be there and wouldn't let the kid go back to the restricted chambers area."

Emma exhaled for the first time in hours. "So, Scott was telling the truth."

"About this, but I'm still checking on his background."

"It's clean. Just be relieved Scott isn't the problem." She knew she was.

"It would have been easier if Scott was behind all of this."

"Why?"

"It'd be over."

The edge to Mark's voice worried her. "But you let him go, right?"

"Scared the hell out of him first."

She'd be lucky if Scott even showed up for work tomorrow. As if the office wasn't enough of a mess without losing her clerk. "Was that really necessary?"

"Thought so at the time." Mark pushed off from the door and walked toward her. More like stalked. His sleek body moved with a rhythm that mesmerized her.

"Either way, thank you for assigning Keith to me."

"He's good at his job."

As usual, Mark jumped right to work and avoided anything personal. Their relationship had moved in and out of the bedroom for years, yet he still talked to her like they just met. Except for a short period of time in her life, Mark came to her after every difficult job. Didn't talk. Just used his key to get in her house, climbed onto the mattress, and released his frustration and anxiety through rounds of high-energy sex.

"How did you know I'd be here tonight?" she asked.

"You're a workaholic. Ever since . . ." Mark coughed. "You're here a lot now."

"You mean since I left Jeff." It had happened a year ago. The rumor mill buzzed about the circumstances surrounding her breakup with her former fiancé. Her ex fed the frenzy by suggesting Ben had played a role. The headlines painted her as a woman out of control in her private life, sleeping with both a prominent partner in a prestigious law firm and the handsome judge across the hall.

The real reason for leaving before walking down the aisle turned out to be much more mundane. She backed out because she refused to settle. She loved Mark. Ben helped her to see that truth, and then he got dragged into her nasty all-too-public breakup as a thank-you.

"You've been busy pissing off the public, making speeches," Mark said, broaching a subject she knew picked at him but which he hadn't mentioned. Until now.

"Someone is always going to be upset with my decisions. That's the nature of the job."

Mark slid into the seat across from her and balanced an ankle over his other knee.

"I heard someone filed a complaint against you challenging your fitness as a judge."

That part ate away at her. She gave up so much for the job and in return had grievances filed against her. There was a public movement to remove her from the bench, a plan that left her empty and restless.

"The new theory is that I skew the cases against defendants and bias juries. Funny how no one ever questioned my professional integrity until a year ago, and now everyone watches every move I make," she said.

"A bomb did go off in front of you. Some folks are watching and talking because of that and not because of anything else."

"Admittedly, the timing was not great."

"Is there ever a good time for attempted murder?"

"Not that I can see."

Mark tapped on the bottom of his shoe. "What did you

think would happen when you said those things to Steve Jenner at his sentencing hearing? Reporters were in the court-room. His attorneys were looking for grounds for appeal."

"I am aware of that."

"Hell, his wife continues to deny the reality of being mar-ried to a rapist and murderer. She wants someone to blame for the crapper of a life she's been handed, and you gave her a prime target. All but painted a bull's-eye on your back."

"You think she's behind the threats?"

"If so, not on her own, and I doubt she's paying anyone. She ran through almost every dime on her husband's legal fees. There's just nothing left. Besides, I've had someone on her ever since she started screaming at you in the courtroom. There's no evidence she's physically gunning for you. She's spending too much time going on talk shows and complain-ing about renegade judges. It looks as if she's found her call-ing."

The realization of just how much Mark knew about this other woman and her whereabouts stunned Emma. "Is dig-ging into her life part of your official job?"

"It's one that helps me sleep at night."

Emma knew that was as close as he would ever get to ad-mitting he cared about her. She knew how he operated. They had grown up together. Slept together as recently as a week ago when he showed up on her doorstep and without a word led her upstairs. Otherwise, he stayed disconnected, passing messages through Ben and keeping a safe distance.

But they shared a violent past. Because of that he should understand how hearing the parade of lies about victims would chip away at her reserve. "You don't know what it's like."

"Enlighten me."

"I sit up there day after day and listen to victims get bashed and maligned. I hear fantastical stories about how rape victims asked to be hurt. How being out at night means a woman deserves to be tortured and killed. About how husbands snap and kill the ones they supposedly love and should be forgiven because it was a one-time thing, as if that even makes sense."

"You've been on the bench for seven years. None of this was new."

"But it builds up. You watch the juries and see the defense attorney connect with someone. Feel that one person start to believe that a respectable businessman like Steve Jenner couldn't possibly beat and rape women in the basement of his house. That his wife would know, because any reasonable human would, even though the evidence of his guilt is clear."

"You're too close to this situation."

Emma relived every minute of the damning trial information every time she closed her eyes. "You can't hear that kind of testimony and not feel something."

Mark's eyes clouded with an emotion she couldn't name. "You know what I mean."

"I don't."

"You have to separate Jenner from your mom."

Emma knew the suggestion was coming. Still, Mark's words jabbed at her midsection. "This isn't about her."

"Of course it is." His voice grew softer the longer he talked.

If he had yelled or ordered, she would have had a defense. But he sat there, listening and the words spilled out of her. "I just want to feel clean again."

"Emma—"

"Ben enjoys the job, gets a rush out of the vibe in his courtroom. Not me. Not anymore. I get swamped with a coldness I can't shake."

"Take a leave of absence."

Quit and run. Mark had been pushing that agenda for years. She used to think his words were about protecting her. Now she knew it was another means of pushing her away.

Resolve built back up inside her. "No. Absolutely not."

"You need a break."

"If I walk away, then guys like Jenner win."

Mark let out an exhale full of frustration. "Use your head. Someone is trying to do more than scare you here."

She waved her hand in dismissal. "I'll be fine."

Mark leaned in with a voice rubbed harsh from need. "I don't want anything to happen to you."

A short shocked silence filled the room.

"Ever," he added in a whisper.

She wanted to go to him, to curl up on his lap and let him wash away all the confusion and fear with a rain of kisses. But he'd bolt. He was in superagent mode, all serious and bossy. He could handle being shot at and testifying before Congress. Female weakness, now that scared the hell out of him.

What she needed and what he could give had never matched. Time hadn't changed that obvious fact. So, she settled for letting him know she felt secure. "I have Keith. Nothing is going to happen with him here, or you stopping by, or Ben across the hall."

Mark glanced at his watch. "Where is Keith?"

"Probably walking around the floor." She smiled at the thought of her oversized, no-neck bodyguard pacing the hallway. "I'm sure he just lost track of time."

Mark was already up and out of his chair. "Keith doesn't make mistakes."

Chapter Eight

The call came around midnight. Callie fought through a fog of sexual satisfaction and rabid hunger to concentrate on the rumbling sound. Being pinned to the mattress with an arm wrapped around her waist and Ben's firm thigh pressed against hers, she couldn't move. Wasn't even sure she wanted to.

"What the hell is that?" Ben grumbled against her bare shoulder without opening his eyes.

"Phone." That was the only explanation she could muster in her wiped-out state.

"We're busy."

The noise stopped. She had just closed her eyes when it began again. She glanced over and watched her cell phone vibrate against the nightstand. The blue light flashed, but still she didn't reach for it. Not after the past few hours with Ben. The man sucked the energy right out of her.

But he still had some. Lips brushed against her skin as his fingers traveled to the bottom curve of her breast.

Then the vibrating started for a third round.

Ben's forehead fell against her cheek. "Please tell me you don't have a boyfriend."

"Little late for that talk, isn't it?"

His head shot up and his eyes glowed with an angry intensity. "I'm serious."

"I can see that." With the lights on she could see everything. Him naked . . . furious. That last part caught her by surprise. "Care to tell me what's behind the change in mood?"

"Poaching another man's woman is not an option. Not ever."

She remembered he had started his tenure as a judge by hearing family law cases. Callie figured those early years of contested custody cases and people fighting over forks had taken a toll. "I wouldn't be with you in the middle of my bed if I'd been keeping someone else here."

"So, that's a no?"

Clearly the man's big brain misfired when his dick saw some action, because he sure wasn't catching on very quick. "It's a no. You're not the only one who draws that line." She rubbed her thumb over his frowning eyebrows.

"Okay." He nodded. "Good."

She didn't have a law degree or wear a big black nightgown to work every day, but she knew anxiety when she saw it. Knew when she felt it shoot through the guy laying all over her. "Is there anything you want to tell me?"

The words barely left her lips when her home phone rang. Ben leaned up on an elbow and glared at the thing as if it were a foreign invader. "Who is this jackass?"

Unease washed through her. Someone this insistent planned on delivering bad news. "Maybe something's wrong."

He leaned across her and grabbed the receiver.

Mark. With sudden clarity, she knew who sat at the other end of the line dialing like a madman. Which meant she was in a shitload of trouble.

"Ben, wait—"

"What?" Ben asked the question into the phone, not to her.

When his eyebrows snapped together, she knew the flipping around in her stomach was there for a reason. "Give it to me."

Ben shifted away from her, blocking her hand with his shoulder before she could reach the receiver. "When?"

When what? Yeah, this was bad. "Let me—" She tried another grab, but he used his body as a shield.

"How is he?" Ben asked.

So, not Emma. Callie wondered what "he" other than the "he" next to her was in trouble now. "He who?"

Ben shushed her. Actually sat naked on her bed and made an annoying hissing sound to get her to be quiet. She had no intention of obeying his command. It was her damn house, after all. "Who is it?"

"We'll be right there," Ben said to the person on the other end of the line.

When he handed the phone to her a second later, all she got was a dial tone. "Unless you plan on paying the mortgage, I answer the phone from now on."

"Is this really the time to argue about something so dumb?"

"Would you prefer we make time later?" Instead of answering, Ben flipped back the covers and crawled out of bed. Not being a fan of the sex-and-run type, she grabbed his arm. "Where are you going off to without your pants, Your Honor?"

"There's been an accident."

His serious tone wiped the snootiness right out of her. "What?"

"We have to go."

An hour later, Callie stood in an elevator and adjusted her gun for the third time. During the ride to the fourth floor of the hospital, Ben stood next to her with his fingers wrapped around the handrail behind him. They wore the same clothes from the day before and waited for the bell to ding and doors to open. Neither of them talked. But there wasn't all that much to say. Not until they knew the particulars of what happened.

One thing was clear, someone had attacked Keith. Since the man weighed two-forty, and that was only when he forgot to eat, the danger level for all of them shot up. Even Ben had stopped whining about his protection detail. She would have celebrated his newfound brilliance, but she was too busy trying to figure out how hard Mark would kick her ass when he saw her.

She had spent hours on her back instead of on the job, or at least that's the way Mark would see it. Not answering her phone had been a mistake. Making Mark track her down could spell the end of her freelance career.

"Ignore whatever my brother says when he sees you," Ben said without bothering to look at her. He was too busy staring at the floor buttons as if they held the secret to life's most intriguing questions.

"I can handle Mark." And by that she meant she would stand there quietly while Mark yelled his head off.

"He's not stupid."

"I never said he was."

"He's going to know we slept together. He'll have an opinion, and it won't be good." Ben exhaled loud enough to drown out the soft rock version of some dance song playing in the background. "So, like I said, let me deal with him."

She carried a gun and proved her stamina during the naked slap-and-tickle games of the past few hours, yet Ben refused to concede that she could take care of herself. His Captain Save a 'Ho complex just never stopped. If a female walked in front of him, he felt the need to rescue her.

Fuck that.

"I've been shot at and lived through three days of your bossiness. Mark's yelling doesn't scare me." It did a little, but admitting that would only give Ben an "in" and then she'd never get him out again.

"You're not as smart as I thought."

But she was. She knew Mark would crawl right up her ass about this. When he hired her, he had made a point of mentioning her past. Seemed Mark admired her for turning down her old boss's advances and sticking up for other women who had dealt with the same by reporting him rather than ignoring it like so many other FBI females had been forced to do. Mark understood the chain of command and supervisors with friends in high places. He knew she had been set up and decided to walk away rather than get buried in paperwork at a desk job in Des Moines or someplace cold enough to freeze her fingers together.

Basically, Mark knew she didn't sleep around on the job. Until now.

"If this is your idea of charming post-sex chatter, your bedroom skills need some work. Here's a piece of advice: women don't like being called names as soon as they get their underwear back on." She tightened her ponytail. It was either that or strangle Ben. "Actually, name-calling is always bad, in case you weren't clear."

Ben's mouth fell into a huge smile.

She saw it in the reflection on the back of the doors. "What's so funny?"

"It's about time."

"For?"

He faced her as his hand slid across the railing to touch hers. "You ignored me during the drive over here. I thought that meant you planned to pretend nothing happened tonight. Since you're all feisty, I'm thinking we're back on track."

As if she could push Ben from her mind. Despite the lapse of judgment and the huge mistake of going "no contact" when Mark needed to talk with her, she didn't regret the sex. Her body craved Ben as much as she craved air. She didn't know how the hell she'd break that addiction, but she would. Probably not on Mark's timetable, but eventually.

"Would you like a grade for your performance?" she asked, hoping to get him all flustered and sputtering.

Ben threw her off. If anything, he grew even calmer. With his head balanced against the back wall of the elevator he shot her a sexy smile. "Only if it's a high one."

The highest, actually. Callie might need a new scale to measure his ability, and that was after only a few hours with him. She wondered how much greater he would be with prolonged contact. "Are you always this needy after sex?"

"Are you always this bitchy?"

She couldn't help but chuckle at that. "Touché."

A chime sounded and then the doors opened, and she was saved from hearing whatever gem he might have come up with next. In a way she almost regretted that because the sparring functioned as a form of foreplay with them. Not that now was the time for that, because it sure as hell wasn't. A good man had been injured. That fact trumped sexy talk no matter how much she enjoyed it.

They took a few steps down the hallway. Despite the early hour, nurses rushed around and several people stood by the station in the middle of the open area. Callie guessed this was calm compared to what the place looked like during peak hours.

The harsh smell of antiseptic filled her nose the second they turned the corner and started toward Keith's room. Her lips scrunched up in a frown as she fought off the smell from invading her senses . . . and then she saw Mark. Tall, dark, and furious. He paced around a small waiting room with hunched shoulders, wearing a suit as black as his mood. He hadn't noticed her yet, but she knew she was on his mind. That would explain the tic in his cheek.

The only other person in the area other than the security guard standing next to Keith's room was Emma. Of course. Heaven forbid a Walker brother be somewhere and her not be there, too. For a woman who played the role of non-girlfriend, she sure did show up at girlfriend-like times.

Not that Emma looked any better than the rest of them. Her serene demeanor had vanished. That angelic round face had paled to ghostly proportions. Her mouth pulled tight in a frown as she wrung her hands on her lap.

Emma's gaze followed Mark's long gait, sweeping over him and holding briefly on his face. Until she saw Ben coming toward her. Then she switched focus. She stood up, causing Mark to hit hyper-lawman mode and spin around to see what was coming.

His glare hit Callie with the force of a gunshot. Combined with Emma's stiffness, that was one impressive wall of human anger. Callie wondered if the two practiced that joint disappointed look or if it just came naturally.

Ben spoke first. "How's Keith?"

"In the hospital," Mark said in a voice as rough as the scar that marred the side of his cheek.

Talk about a "no kidding" moment. "Do we know what happened?" Callie asked, hoping to keep the conversation as professional as possible.

Mark shrugged. "As far as we can tell, he was outside the courthouse and got hit in the head. Lost a lot of blood. The doctors stitched him up and gave him something for pain, so I can't talk to him yet, but I'm thinking from the angle of the wound he didn't see his attacker."

"So, he's fine?" she asked, since Mark hadn't volunteered the ending to the story.

Mark just nodded. No words. Just a swift sure movement of his head. Callie knew that couldn't be good for her.

Ben shifted his weight from side to side, as if he were the

one on the firing line. Callie didn't know if the situation caused the anxiety or if standing in their small group where everyone knew he just had sex was a bit "too much information" for his taste. If it was the latter, he could get over it. They were adults. Adults had sex. Maybe not on the job and when danger lurked, but still.

"The police?" Callie asked.

Mark smacked his lips together. "Called. They're investigating. I've worked with the chief before. He understands what's happening and is talking about a joint operation."

She doubted that was the case. "Is it?"

"No, but I let him think that to make things easier."

A question finally popped out of Ben's mouth over all of his uncharacteristic squirming. "Any chance we caught the incident on one of the security cameras?"

Emma shook her head as she tucked in closer to Mark's side. "No. This guy's good."

"I'm not convinced that's true. More likely he has inside information and knows enough to stay out of the way of video," Mark added.

"Damn it." Ben switched to pacing. "Why didn't Keith know about the camera locations and stay within them?"

"Because no one thought Keith was in danger. The tactical plans involved you and Emma." Mark didn't say "dumbass," but Callie was pretty sure she heard it in his tone.

Ben came to a sudden stop. "And where were you during all of this?"

Callie bit her tongue because she had been about to ask that very same question. Since Ben did it for her, Mark could rage at Ben instead of her. She refused to think of that as letting Ben rescue her. It was more like smart strategic thinking.

"Talking security with Emma." Mark's voice grew even chillier as he glanced at the security guard as if to make sure the other man wasn't listening in, though how that was possible when he stood only a few feet away wasn't all that clear.

Emma must have noticed, because she glanced between the brothers and then rushed to fill the conversational void caused by Mark's shot of anger. "Keith was only away from me for about a half hour. Mark stayed with me the whole time. About business, of course." The woman got more flustered and a bit breathless as she spoke.

Now there was an interesting extra sentence. All business? Mark and Emma together at night in a dark courthouse? Callie knew what would happen if she were in that situation with Ben. On her back, legs in the air, and lots of moaning. Hell, it did happen. Three times.

There was some weird non-sibling energy zapping around Mark and Emma. Callie could feel it, thought about ducking to keep from getting hit by it as it bounced around the room. The way they tried not to look at or touch each other was a dead giveaway as well. It was a sign of pent-up sexual frustration if ever Callie saw one. Showed that, maybe, Mark was human after all, though she doubted that could be proven with any sort of scientific certainty.

"We didn't even realize there was a problem until Mark tried to reach Keith on the cell," Emma said, continuing to talk faster than the human ear could hear.

Mark held up the object in question. "Yeah, I had a lot of trouble with phones tonight."

Uh-oh. Time to beg for mercy. Callie decided to launch an offensive strike. "About that."

Mark didn't give her a chance to explain or grovel. "Can I see you for a moment?"

She wanted to say no, even toyed with the idea, but didn't. She deserved this. She had no one to blame but herself. And Ben, but mostly her. "Sure."

"Alone." Mark made the word sound like an opening to a death march.

Apparently he didn't want any witnesses. Callie feared that this request had more to do with his plans for her than with the sensitive topic.

Ben picked that moment to stop pacing and pay attention to the world around him. He crowded next to his brother in what Callie took to be a somewhat macho show of dominance. Brave move, since Mark carried a gun and didn't think twice about using it.

"Mark, now is not the time," Ben said, chest puffing out and eyes daring Mark to test him.

"Callie works for me." Mark matched Ben's puff with one of his own.

The good judge didn't back down. "I'm the only one she's tailing."

Time to step in or risk having the Walker boys roll around the floor punching each other. As awesome a sight as that might be, this wasn't the place. "How about I make my own decision about what I do?" Callie asked.

Her preference was to leave the hospital and never come back, but she knew that couldn't happen. She owed Mark an explanation and an apology. And she was far from being done with Ben. The man knew his way around a bedroom . . . and a foyer. She planned to see what he could do with a kitchen table and a shower, and not necessarily in that order.

"Whatever Mark has to say can wait." Ben stood up straighter, if that was even possible. "In fact, it could probably go without being said at all."

Okay, enough of that. Testosterone all but dripped off Ben to puddle on the floor. He treated her like a breakable doll. On some level Callie found the scene unbelievably flattering. It showed she meant something. But on most every other level it was a demonstration of male chest-beating jackassery that she did not want at the moment. When she told Ben he needed to amp down the rescue dial—and she had—then he needed to listen. This was about being taken seriously and handling her punishment. Ben couldn't do those things for her.

"I doubt Mark plans to shoot me right here in the hospital," she said, hoping to hell that was true.

"I don't think you're his target," Emma said under her breath.

"This isn't up for debate." Mark stared down Callie and then pointed at some distant point down the hallway. "Discussion. Now. Over there."

Callie didn't wait for a second command. She got her butt moving. "Look," she said, thinking to get a jump on the conversation as they reached ground zero. "I messed up."

"That's an understatement."

She didn't exactly agree with that. Seemed to her Mark was blowing this out of proportion a bit, but he was in charge and she would respect that. "Okay."

"I hired you to do a job."

"I know."

"I'm not paying you for sex."

A passing nurse did a double take at that comment. Callie cleared her throat to keep from screaming. "To be clear, no one is paying me for sex."

"With your history—"

Oh, hell no. "That's low."

"But accurate."

It actually wasn't, but she refused to make this conversation about her past. "Don't go there, Mark."

"There is no way you can watch Ben if you're naked with him and nowhere near your phone. Where was your cell while the two of you were . . ." Mark stuttered before letting the subject drop.

"Fucking?"

Her boldness enraged him all over again. His head flushed red from his neck to his hairline. "Being provocative isn't going to work. This is a serious breach of protocol, not to mention an ethical gray area."

"I didn't see it that way."

"That's what has me concerned about your fitness for the job."

Callie sensed disaster looming. She knew there was only one way to handle this. Take more than her fair share of the blame and then try to get the discussion moving in another direction. "I screwed up."

"Damn right."

Apparently he wanted more blood, so she decided to unload another quart. "I'm sorry."

"You should be. You know what I'm talking about. This kind of shit can't happen."

"It won't. Not again." She had no idea how she was going to keep that promise, but she vowed to find a way. Maybe she could throw a bag over Ben's head or order him not to smile, or smell so good, or flirt. It was going to be a long "do not" list.

"I know my brother, Callie. It will keep happening unless you stop it."

It? And since when did big strong federal agents blush at the idea of sex? "Ben is a grown man. While we're on this subject, I'm an adult as well."

"He's got you in his blood and he isn't going to let go until you force him to."

The strength of Mark's assurance swept through her, making her a little breathless. The idea that she had some control over the superstar hottie judge was so ridiculous that it should have slid off her without sticking for even a second.

Instead, she took Mark's words and turned them over in her head. Two days from now she'd be doing the same thing no matter how hard she tried to forget his comment.

"You're giving me too much credit," she said when she finally found the voice to talk again.

"I've been around Ben long enough to predict the ending to this train wreck." Mark closed in and started whispering when a group of nurses passed by. Well, his version of whispering, which sounded more like a thunderous rasp. "And that's how this will end, with an explosion that ruins everything."

"That seems a bit extreme."

"I know what I'm talking about here."

Mark's insistence on images of crashing and big booms made her wonder just how many times Ben had pulled the judge's chambers pick-up scene. Yeah, she'd interrogate the scammer in question on that one later. Right now, she had to deal with Mark and his two-hundred-pound fury.

"Ben's right, you know," she said, thinking a walk down this lane could lead straight to danger alley.

"About what?"

"You're overly invested in saving him."

Mark's fury rolled over him. If possible, his frame snapped even tighter as his voice lowered to gravel levels. "What the hell is that supposed to mean?"

The thought had wormed its way into her brain and stayed there, taking root until she couldn't come up with another explanation for the way Ben shoved back so hard on the issue of protection. She thought it was a pretty dumb position for a very smart man to take. But now she saw it. Mark tried to control everything about Ben, including his choice of bed partners.

"As an outside observer, you treat him more like your

son rather than your baby brother." Callie swallowed hard to keep from outlining the rest of her theory. "That's all I'm saying."

And, yeah, she had said about two sentences too many.

Mark's head snapped back as if she had slapped him. It took a few uncomfortable seconds for him to regain his clenched-jaw stance and respond. "As you both keep telling me, Ben is an adult."

"Yeah, *we* know that."

"Let me worry about my relationship with Ben. Your job is to keep your panties on and your gun loaded." He pointed to the items in question as he seethed. "Got it?"

"Sure."

"You get one more shot."

"At?"

"Getting your job right."

Well, that was going to be a problem since she planned to go right on sleeping with Ben. Rather than point out that little flaw in Mark's plan, she stayed quiet.

Chapter Nine

Ben couldn't take his gaze off Callie. She stood a good five inches shorter than Mark but still managed to hold her ground. When Mark threw out his chest and moved in close to hover over her, when his harsh voice rose until it carried across the floor and grabbed the attention of the entire nurses' station, her gaze didn't change. She listened. She argued. She didn't back down.

Ben couldn't imagine anything hotter in a woman.

"Are you ready to admit that I was right?" Emma asked as she stepped up beside him and out of hearing range of the security guard stationed by Keith's door.

"About?"

Emma folded her arms over her stomach. Even treated Ben to the condescending eye roll she'd been perfecting for decades. "Oh, come on."

"She is my bodyguard." And his one-time bedmate, and if things went as planned and his brother learned when to shut up and back off, the more-than-one-time lover.

"Which explains why you were together at her house at midnight." Emma pretended to think about her comment. "Oh, that's right. It doesn't."

This is what happened when a man spent all of his

nonwork time with smart women. Screwed up his private life. "It's Callie's job to be with me."

"An interesting way of putting it."

He had been a lawyer long enough to know when to stop justifying. Trying to end the conversation seemed like the better plan. "Do you have a point?"

"I'm betting you weren't playing cards."

"I don't like cards."

"From the way Mark tried to hunt you two down and the rise in his voice when you answered your *bodyguard's* phone in the middle of the night, I'm thinking—"

"Midnight is hardly the middle of the night." As far as dodges went, Ben thought that one worked well enough. Not that he was concentrating all that much on the conversation. Hard to do that when he had the full view of Callie's fine ass. And the hard lines of his brother's face. Those were two things that just didn't go together.

"Are you saying the two of you were working at her condo? Looking over briefs and such."

Ben was trying very hard not to tell Emma anything. "What about you?"

Emma's smile fell. "What?"

"Your activities this evening."

"We're not talking about me."

Ah, there it was. His angle to end the conversation and then head over to Callie without looking too obvious. "Maybe we should be."

"I'm not the one who went incommunicado."

Ben kept digging. "You and Mark, alone in the office. That doesn't exactly sound case related to me."

"Your brother is all work."

"No, he's not. You and I both know that's not true."

Not when it came to Emma. Mark didn't talk about his feelings, refused to deal with whatever kept happening with her, but there was nothing neutral about the way he looked at Emma.

There was a time when the brothers ceased speaking because of Emma. Mark's hidden attraction blossomed into rage when he bought into the rumors circulating about Ben and Emma. By the time the last bombshell fell, Ben had been named as the reason for Emma's change of mind about her marriage, which was fair, but not in the way everyone thought. He had never slept with Emma, but convincing the world and Mark of that fact proved difficult. Ben only cared about Mark, so he focused his efforts there. Promised and apologized, explained and begged, until Mark finally relented. Whether he truly believed or not was still a question.

Mark wasn't an easy man, but he was Ben's only family, and Ben refused to lose that along with everything else he had lost from his childhood. His reputation suffered because of the Emma situation, but he plugged along, doing everything he had always done and ignoring the pointing fingers and talk of him being the other man in a love triangle. The accusation touched on the very heart of him. He had learned early that the tentacles of pain from infidelity had a very long reach.

Ben loved Emma, had for years. Not in any romantic way, but as a deep friendship forged by tragedy. They bonded over blood and horror, fought through whispers and family anger. Somehow, their relationship survived. Thrived, even. But never moved past that to anything sexual.

Emma chewed on her fingernail as she stared at the hospital room door. "I still can't believe this happened to Keith."

"Any idea who's doing this or why they're jumping back and forth between us?"

"None." Emma shook her head as sadness moved into her eyes. "Well, that's not true. There's my infamous speech."

"Don't do that. We don't know that all of this is related."

"Mark thinks so. I'm sure Callie does, too."

"That threatening note came to me, not you," Ben said.

If Emma heard him, she didn't show it. Her eyes grew glassy, as if she was lost in the unknown emotions swirling around inside her. "I sat there in the courtroom and saw Steve Jenner's smug face, listened to the litany of horror he inflicted on those poor women—"

"Don't." Ben stopped glancing at Callie and focused on the woman falling apart in front of him.

The last two years had taken a toll. Gone was Emma's wicked sense of humor. She had always possessed an outward calm, but with people she trusted she could be bawdy and fun. Something about her life of late sucked all of the lighter parts out of her.

"He tortured them and took sick pleasure in doing it. After so much pain and so many lies in case after case, I lost it. I said . . ." Her voice broke off. "What I felt. That people like Jenner aren't human. They don't deserve mercy or our concern. Lock him away and forget about him. Preferably execute him. That's the real answer. Why should the taxpayers keep that monster alive?"

"On principle, I don't disagree."

"But you're smart enough not to say it out loud and risk your career."

Ben didn't know what to say to that, so he didn't address it. He wouldn't have brought the integrity of the bench into question. He worked too hard to get his position and make this life to throw it away in a rush of anger. Separating his personal view from the work was a constant battle, but it was one all judges had to fight.

"Mark thinks I got all wrapped up in my feelings about my mother and let that seep into the sentencing," Emma said.

"Did you? I mean, it's not as if we don't all live with what

happened. It touches everything." How any of them separated out the events of all those years ago was a mystery. In
the span of a few minutes and a culmination of months of
sneaking around, his father and Emma's mother were dead.
That sort of thing didn't just go away. Not when you're ten
and the world switches from making sense to total disarray
without warning.

Emma blew out a long breath. "I don't want to do this
anymore."

"What?"

"Be a judge. Pursuing a legal career made sense at one
point. Fighting for the broader principles of justice and right.
But not now."

Here he was thinking about the best way to talk Callie
back into bed, and Emma was toying with the idea of walking away from everything she'd accomplished. "Don't rush
to any decisions."

"I might not have a choice. I'm being investigated. But
you know what? I don't really care anymore. That's what
scares the hell out of me."

"What does?" Mark walked over with his scowl in place
and body in full clench.

Emma waved him off. "Doesn't matter."

The comment started a nerve twitching in Mark's cheek.
He got it under control long enough to bark out another
sentence. "We have a new problem."

"Only one?" Callie mumbled the question as she scooted
around Mark's large frame to join the group.

Ben thought she looked relatively unscathed from the
verbal attack she just lived through. Some of the sass had
left her walk and her cheeks seemed a bit pale, but there was
nothing deferential about her. No feet shuffling or bowed
head. If anything, she held her chin even higher. Stole a peek
or two at him and gave Emma one long stare. Ben had no

idea what the latter was about, but this was hardly the first time a woman confused the hell out of him. Callie excelled at the task. The only place he truly understood her was in bed. Now that he knew that fact, he hoped to keep her there as long as possible each day.

"Keith can't watch over Emma, and I've got my only other available man on Keith's door just to be sure he's not an ongoing target. That means I need you to work around the clock. Problem?" Mark stared at Callie as if daring her to say no. "And I'll stay on duty."

"You always take the night shift," Ben said.

"I'll be with Emma this time."

Emma's mouth fell open almost as wide as Callie's did.

Callie clicked her teeth shut as she bit her lip. Ben assumed she was trying to swallow a smile. "Then I'll take Ben," she said.

"One night only." Mark held up a finger as if to prove his point. "I'll have a replacement for you by tomorrow night."

Ben saw his opening. "No need."

"Don't push me." Mark nodded in the direction of the far elevator bank, then started walking. "Let's go." He took off, leaving Emma to run after him.

Emma sighed. "I guess he was talking to me."

"He sure as hell better not be talking to me with that attitude," Callie said loud enough for the words to bounce down the hallway and reach Mark. Must have worked, because he stopped. Didn't turn around, but didn't go forward either.

"I'll take care of him." Emma smiled. "You two have a good night."

Ben waited until Emma and Mark got on the elevator before turning back to Callie. "You okay?"

"You mean the yelling? Yeah, your brother is kind of an expert at that sort of thing."

Ben's shoulders relaxed for the first time since they got the call. He had worried about Callie's reaction once her clothes were on and Mark laid into her. Women could be funny creatures when the lights came on. But he underestimated Callie. He kept doing that, but he thought he'd learned his lesson this time around.

"You should try being related to him," Ben said.

"I'm an only child and thinking that's a good thing at the moment."

A piece of personal information. She didn't let many of those slip. Since he had more secrets than the average person, he didn't hold her need for privacy against her. "Did Mark warn you away from me?"

"Yes."

"Forbid you from sleeping with me?"

Callie smiled but quickly hid it again. "He had some trouble spitting the actual words out, but yes."

Not a surprise there, since Mark never talked about emotions or women. They each handled their history their own way. For Mark, being painfully private was the answer. "Did he insinuate that your job depended on you keeping your pants on?"

"Were you eavesdropping or something?" She dropped her head to the side in that sexy way that put his mind on hold and gave the green light to every other part of his body.

"Just know the beast."

"Mark threaten your women often?"

Now she was fishing for information. "No. Believe it or not, before the explosion I handled my private life without his help."

"Does he know that?"

"He's lost his mind and his boundaries." Ben made a mental note to talk with Mark and get their relationship back on track. Ben didn't work for him. Didn't like having Mark step in and mess around with his nighttime plans, either.

"So I guess I'm the lucky one." She smacked her lips together. "That's fantastic."

Fantastic was the body she hid under that conservative suit. "I have one crucial question for you."

The corner of her mouth kicked up in a smile. "Hit me."

"You gonna listen to Mark's advice?"

"Advice?"

"Orders. About staying away from me. Staying out of my bed."

Callie shook her head. "Of course not."

His fingers found her waist. "Then I think we should go home and take our clothes off."

"I'm impressed with the way you think."

"I have other skills."

She wrapped her arms around his neck as her lips hovered right over his. "Show me."

Chapter Ten

An hour later, Emma's Georgetown town house stood dark on the first floor. Mark had checked every room, every closet, and underneath every piece of furniture. He locked the doors, did a perimeter check, and looked over everything a second time. Emma knew because she heard every one of his steps echo through her three-story house.

Now she sat on the edge of her bed wearing nothing but a sheer white nightgown and waited for him to come upstairs. He would. That was their pattern. She would turn off the lights and he would show up, strip down, and climb into bed with her. He was strong on the outside and broken deep within.

And she loved him with every breath she took. Something scarred and lonely inside him spoke to her. Ben brought sunshine and Mark wallowed in blackness.

The door opened a few seconds later. The light from the hallway put him in shadow. Seemed fitting somehow.

He stripped as he walked. His tie flew to the right. The buttons of his shirt came open as he practically ripped the thing down the front. His belt clanged as he slid it open and then let it drop to the floor. By the time his knees touched hers, he wore only his pants and shoes.

This wasn't about talking and soothing. It was about deep,

hot sex. A release that would last them until the next time, and there would be a next time until she stopped him. She had tried that before and spent every day in aching pain and every night racked with guilt as she slept with her then fiancé instead of the man she truly loved. She had learned. Mark couldn't give her everything, but he could give her this time.

"Is this okay?" he asked into the quiet of her bedroom.

"Are you?"

"What do you mean?"

She heard his zipper slide down. Couldn't see his face clearly but knew he wore a frown because a certain harshness flowed through his voice. "You were angry at the hospital."

"At Ben. At Callie. Even at myself, but not at you." With material sliding against skin, he let his pants fall to the carpet.

"Why the attitude with Ben?" She gave into the need then and brushed her hand over his cheek.

Mark sighed as he placed a kiss in her palm. "Does it matter?"

On some level it did. "I think it does to you."

"He's being cavalier with his life."

"You don't trust Callie to keep him safe?"

"Can she do that when she's under him?"

Emma had to smile at that. Mark didn't think like other people. Didn't seem to recognize that his self-appointed job was to help her, and yet he was two seconds from making love to her. It was the very same thing he faulted Callie for doing.

But he saw everything in terms of black and white, safe and unsafe. Life was about rules that applied to other people. He was immune. It wasn't a matter of ego. No, it was more a sense that he viewed himself as being different from the people he protected. As if he were disposable and unimportant. He pushed emotions out of his mind and ruled with a fierce determination that demanded everyone else obey.

Nevertheless, Mark was keen enough to understand Ben was falling hard for his supposed bodyguard. Mark's sudden emotional clarity impressed Emma. She was afraid to hope that meant he could learn, but the idea did pass through her mind.

"I don't want to talk about him now." Mark dropped to his knees and put his head in her lap.

She took the opportunity to thread her fingers through his soft hair and place a kiss against his ear. She loved him in private the way she longed to love him when the lights were on and other people were around.

"What do you want to do?" She whispered the question against his closed eyelids.

His hand slid up her bare inner thigh. "You."

Callie grabbed the headboard behind Ben's shoulders with enough force to make her knuckles ache. Her heart thundered as her chest shuddered on hard breaths. From this position, above him, riding him, straddling his lap, she could watch his muscles strain and his eyes light with pleasure every time she eased her body down on his.

It was two in the morning and they had not lost one ounce of energy. The hospital trip prolonged their time between sex sessions but did not stop them. Even now they sat entangled, naked, and damp from a half hour of foreplay. Their clothes littered the floor and the sheets rumpled beneath them.

The soft creak of the bed grew louder the faster they moved over each other. She wanted to slow down and savor. Enjoy the feel of skin on skin. Revel in the sound of his harsh groans as she took charge of their lovemaking and refused to let him find release. But her body betrayed her. The tightening deep in her stomach begged for release. With every move, the tension increased until her head spun with dizziness.

Her bare thighs pressed against the outside of his legs as his fingernails dug into her hips. Using her knees, she lifted her body up, sliding against his erection as the air pounded in and out of her lungs. The friction of his cock pressing up inside her caused everything inside her to clamp down hard against him.

"God, Callie. Now." Ben whispered his plea as he rubbed the stubble on his chin against her breast. Warm breath blew across her skin, making her nipples pucker.

She lifted and then sat back down. A riot of sensations made her tremble at the intimate contact. Her thighs shook as her back arched against him. With every plunge, he pulled deeper into her. His lips sucked and tongue licked. Hands, leg, mouth. She didn't stand a chance of maintaining control.

When she kept the speed steady, he took over. With a firm grasp on her hips, he lifted and pulled her up before guiding her back down again. The bucking motion touched off the spinning inside her. Her stomach fell and a lightness moved through her chest. It was as if she were careening dangerously toward something and not being able to stop. No seat belt and no safety net. Her body separated from her mind as every part of her surrendered to him.

When the first wave of pleasure washed over her, what began as a low mumbling of his name turned into a scream. Blood coursed through her. Her lower half constricted, every inner muscle clenching against him. The pulsing. The burning fever. The pressure built until she couldn't contain it.

Every time his hips moved, hers did, too. The rhythm increased until his final thrust shattered her. An orgasm ripped through her veins, stealing her air and pulverizing her bones into mush. His head fell back against the wall at the same time she collapsed against his chest in a boneless heap.

She inhaled the musky dampness of his skin as she fought to restore her ragged breathing. She knew she should sit up and guide Ben through his orgasm, but she didn't have the strength. And he didn't need any help to come. Even as she wrestled with the lethargy that took her over, muscle by tired muscle, Ben's neck stretched and his jaw locked. The deep whooshing sound in his lungs echoed under her ear.

"Holy . . ." His voice cut off as his lower body pushed up one last time.

She brushed her palm over his shoulder in an effort to soothe his stiff body as he shuddered beneath her. "This time was just as good."

After a few seconds, his hips returned to the mattress. "Better." The word came out in forced pants.

She thought about getting up and sliding off him, but that struck her as too much work in her current drained state. The fact his now limp penis was still lodged inside her also made crawling off him tough. Not that she really wanted to go anywhere anyway. There was something oddly comforting about hearing his heartbeat against her ear with his arms wrapped around her.

He gave her a little squeeze. "It's possible I've had a heart attack."

Since she could hear his breathing return to normal, she kind of doubted that. "Think of the news headlines for that story. Hottie judge succumbs after sex."

"The photos that would accompany the article would be even more interesting."

She lifted her head and stared down their joined bodies.

Legs and arms everywhere. "I'm not sure this kind of scene is appropriate for a family paper."

He glanced over her head. "I sure as hell plan to think about it quite often."

She snuggled back against his shoulder and let her hair fall over his chest. The mellow mood on the heels of such breathless passion made her smile.

"What's so funny?" he asked.

"How did you know I was about to laugh?"

"I can feel your mouth curl up against my skin."

Probably the same way she could hear the smile in his voice without seeing his face. There was definitely something sexy about that. "Can I ask you something?"

He folded one arm behind his head. "Shoot."

"Since I actually do carry a gun you might want to rephrase that."

"Good point." His free hand traveled down her back and skipped under the sheet to land on her ass. "Ask away."

"Not if you're going to do that thing with your hand."

"This?" His finger dipped lower. "Couldn't resist."

She slid his hand higher to keep her concentration. No way was she going to let him sidetrack her with a few caresses. Well, she would, just not right now.

"How long have Mark and Emma been doing the deed?"

Ben sputtered as he sat up straighter, taking Callie with him. "What?"

She fully straddled him now with a leg draped over each of his thighs. The shock of having him push deeper inside her made her gasp. "Whoa."

"Forget where you were?"

"Something like that." She adjusted her position but stopped wiggling around when he grabbed her waist and held her still. "But don't change the subject."

"Did I?" he asked.

"Please tell me this information about your brother's love life is not a news flash for you."

Ben's thumb traveled up to tease her nipple. "I know all about them. I just didn't think anyone else picked up on it." The finger dipped down, circling her full breast and bringing a rush of blood under her skin.

She fought to keep her mind on the question and off his expert hands. "So, what's the answer?"

"They have a thing."

"A thing?"

"You used the phrase, or is the phrase politically incorrect when a man says it?" His head dipped as his mouth settled over her.

Ten more seconds and she'd be flat on her back . . . and totally happy to be there. "Sort of. So?"

His shoulders fell as his lips stopped moving. "You really want to talk about this now?" He mumbled the question against her swollen flesh. When she nodded, he treated her to an exaggerated exhale and then continued. "Suffice to say it's complicated."

"Is that all you've got? Legal speak? Because, honestly, you managed to say quite a few words right there and not make a lick of sense. You learn that in law school?"

"Yes."

"I hate lawyers."

"Thank you." Ben dropped a quick kiss on her nose.

"Tell me something non-legal."

"You want the quick and dirty? It goes like this: Emma and Mark have been dancing around each other for years."

The information managed to be obvious and shocking at the same time. Callie wouldn't have pinpointed Emma as the wild woman in the bedroom type. And the idea of Mark being bound that strongly to anyone was nothing short of a revelation.

"You mean sleeping together," Callie said.

"That and more. They drift apart and then go right back. It's annoying, actually."

"Why?"

"Because it's obvious they're meant for each other and could work if Mark would—what is your phrase?"

"Ah." She trailed her fingers over his biceps, enjoying the firm curve of his muscles. "So all of the men in your family suffer from head-in-ass syndrome. Interesting."

But the pieces started to fall into place. All that pent-up jealousy about Emma vanished in a flash. Callie had seen the other woman's face when she watched Mark. She didn't have that look when she glanced at Ben. Seemed pretty telling to Callie.

"So, whatever they have goes beyond just sex?" she asked.

"Yes, but whether Mark has realized that is the question." Ben's other hand joined the first. He massaged her breasts, pushing them together and switching his tongue between her nipples, licking one after the other, until that squirming need started building inside Callie again.

"Mark doesn't mind your relationship with Emma?" Callie asked as she slid her fingers along the back of Ben's neck.

But the touching stopped. Ben's head came up nice and slow. The haze had cleared from his eyes and the wariness there didn't look all that inviting. "What exactly are you asking me?"

"A simple question."

"One with a load of context behind it."

Callie refused to back down. Probably would have if Ben had just coughed up an answer. It was the bobbing and weaving that got Callie's attention. He was sensitive over this topic and she wanted to know why. "I notice you're still not responding."

"Because we've been over this. I'm trying to figure out

what part of 'Emma is not my girlfriend' you keep missing. I've been saying it since we first met."

Callie no longer doubted that part. From another man a denial or two might have sounded false. From Ben, the words functioned as an unbreakable promise. One she could count on despite everything else she might see, including that disturbing hand-holding incident in Ben's office the day before.

"My only point is that you're close to Emma. If Mark wants to be the man she turns to when things get spooky, then I could see where that might strain your relationship with your brother. A 'too many alpha males in the kitchen' sort of thing."

Tension left the area around Ben's eyes. "Ah. The kitchen. Got it now."

Callie wasn't convinced he did. She wasn't poking around for more Emma information, though another denial about Ben's feelings for the other woman would be welcome. Callie really wanted to understand the brotherly dynamics and what it all meant in the context of who Ben was outside judge mode.

"Our relationship's a bit different now than when you gave those earlier assurances about Emma, don't you think? A little more personal." And if he said anything but "yes," Callie would reach for her gun. She swore she would.

"Clearly, you're right, as evidenced by the fact I'm still inside you while we're talking about people other than us having sex."

Callie pressed her thighs tighter against his hips and watched his eyes roll back. "What, you can't talk when we're like this?" She seriously thought about dropping her hand between them but knew that would end the discussion a beat too soon.

"I'd get to your point fast, if I were you." He half spoke and half groaned. "Like ten seconds ago."

"I was just trying to understand the Mark–Ben–Emma dynamic.

"Didn't I just explain?"

Not in any way where she understood it. "You have an annoying habit of talking in semicircles. Remember how I told you about your tendency for jackassery? Yeah, this is it."

"Are we fighting? Because, if so, I'll have to concede. No way can I follow along when you're pulsing around my dick like that."

"You poor thing." She clamped down even harder on the tiny muscles wrapped around his erection.

His breath rushed in on a rough intake. "Damn, woman."

"Just trying to get your attention."

"You have it." Ben exhaled a few times. "Okay, let's just clarify this so that we never have to talk about this subject again."

Ben slid his hands up and pressed his palms against her cheeks. Bringing her close, he kissed her. It was hot and long and made her heart double thump with each beat. When he finally lifted his head her vision blurred.

"Even though you claim to be asking another question, I do want you to know that I've never," he said as his second kiss followed the first. "And I mean ever, made a move on Emma. We're friends. No sex. No dating. I'm not playing games when I say that. We didn't even toy with the idea."

Callie sensed that was the case, but having it confirmed in the strongest terms possible made her heart do a little dance. "Because of Mark?"

"Because the feelings just weren't there. Not on my side, anyway," Ben said.

Callie tried to remember the last time she heard such a terrific sentence. "Emma is pretty."

"Shhh." Ben slipped a finger over Callie's lips. "For Emma it was a matter of her wanting Mark. I was never even a contender, not that I wanted to be. She turns to me as a friend. She turns to Mark for everything else."

"Interesting." Callie wondered if Mark understood that distinction.

"And that's enough talk about Emma and Mark and every other person we know. It's time for us to concentrate on just us." Ben wrapped his arm around her waist and dragged them both down on the mattress.

On their sides, with their noses touching and their bodies joined, his mouth covered hers. The kiss rumbled through her from head to foot, cascading and swirling until she forgot everything and everyone.

"You make a good argument for changing the conversation," Callie mumbled against his lips as she fought for a quick breath.

She wasn't one step closer to understanding the relationship between Mark and Ben, and there was something funky there that she wanted to analyze, but there would be time for that later. Now was the time for Ben to impress her with his sexual expertise.

"Let me show you what happens when a woman isn't just a friend." His hands moved to her stomach, then lower.

When his fingers found the place where their bodies met and started rubbing her, Callie actually felt sorry for Emma.

Chapter Eleven

The next afternoon, Ben sat in his office and stared across his desk at his brother. Mark's mood was even less pleasant than usual. He had been serious and talking in short sentences ever since he arrived with take-out Chinese food for their informal lunch meeting ten minutes earlier. If Mark was getting regular sex from Emma it was not helping his sour disposition one bit.

"How's Keith?" Ben asked, aiming for a somewhat neutral topic.

Mark pushed the noodles around in his Styrofoam container with his fork. "He gets out of the hospital today."

"Oh, that's good. Yeah." Well, it was for Keith. For Ben, not so much.

Keith checking out meant returning to work, which meant Callie going back to signing off before the sun went down. Sure, they could still be together, but Keith would have to know and all of the details would become part of Keith's nightly report to Mark.

"You're pathetic." Mark shook his head but didn't look up.

Ben realized only Mark could get away with talking to him like that. Well, Mark and Callie. "Excuse me?"

"You heard me."

"Doesn't anyone around here care that I'm a judge and can throw people in jail?"

Mark lifted his head. Instead of frowning, a small smile crossed his lips. "Don't worry. I'm putting Keith on another job. Your arrangement with Callie remains secure."

And here Ben was ready to jump all over Mark. Set him straight and call him off Callie. That one comment saved all of that fight. "I don't know what you're talking about."

"While it's tempting to play musical bodyguards just to piss you off, that sort of thing will only draw more attention to you and cause me paperwork."

Ben hid his smile rather than risk pissing Mark off even more. "I can't figure out if you're a hopeless romantic or just hopeless."

"The latter, but the point is that you get to keep Callie. For now."

Ben doubted Callie would appreciate the way Mark phrased that, but *hot damn*.

"She's competent." Ben decided Mark had spent too much time with Emma when he did a deadpan impression of her eye roll. "Yes? Something you want to say?"

"And people say I lack a romantic side," Mark said.

"I sure as hell say that about you."

Mark used his fork as a pointer. "You're sleeping with her."

"Who?"

Mark's mouth twisted into a not-so-welcoming face. "Don't."

"Callie." Ben figured now was as good a time as any to broach this subject. "About that. Are you going to yell at me like you did her? Or are you smart enough to know that will land you on your ass?"

"Lot of good it did me to try to talk some sense into her.

She crawled right back into bed with you. It's part of why I'm conceding now. It's a lost cause to keep you away from her." Mark held up his hand. "And before you ask, I can tell from the stupid grin on your face, so don't bother denying it."

Ben had no intention of doing that. Not when being with Callie suited him just fine. "Then you can also ease up. Callie knows what she's doing."

"She had a job and failed."

"She was doing everything I wanted her to do."

Mark dropped his fork, letting it thump against the wood desk. "I meant protecting you. Not sleeping with you, you jackass."

"I was fine with her right where she was. Trust me." Yeah, Callie would hate him throwing that out there, but he did it anyway.

"What if—"

Rage banged against the inside of Ben's head. "Mark, knock it off. You have a problem with me, you talk to me. No more beating her up or trying to break her down. The threats stop, as does the meddling."

"Wrong. She works for me. I expect professionalism and a daily report. Instead, she . . . she does whatever she wants. Ignores authority."

"Is that really a surprise from someone who's former FBI and can out-swear a sailor?" Ben waited to see if Mark would take the bait. Ben had tried to get a copy of Callie's employment file. To figure out what happened to her career in the Bureau. No luck.

"I thought she could learn from past mistakes."

Ben had no idea why anyone would think that. There was nothing in Callie's personality that suggested she would bend. She'd been swearing and disrespecting him from the second she met him. He had wanted her in his bed a second after that.

"She's off limits to you from now on." Ben was prepared to back up that statement however he had to. It wouldn't be the first time they raised fists to solve a brotherly argument. "She's strong. I'm trained. I have security all over this building. We got it covered."

"You're talking about the same security that was in place where Keith got attacked?" Mark snorted. "Not your strongest argument."

But Ben had a better one. An obvious one that Mark refused to see.

"I'm not a scared kid anymore." Ben needed his brother to get it.

"I know that."

"Do you?"

"That's not what this is about."

"What the hell is it then? I went off to Operation Desert Storm before I was out of my teens. Got shot at. Killed for my country. Came back and struggled through law school because I didn't want to aim a weapon at anyone ever again. But I can if I have to. I can also fight with my hands and feet, dirty or clean, whatever it takes to win. You made sure of that."

Mark gave a smile tinged with pride. "You were a good student."

"Then tell me why you're so fucking sure I can't handle myself."

"I'll remind you again that someone tried to blow you up. You think your hands will help you in that kind of situation? You gonna pound a bomb with your fists?"

Ben closed his eyes to try to stop the banging in his head. "Mark, come on."

"You know why." Mark delivered the reason on a harsh whisper.

The memories came rushing back. The hounding of the press. The brutal bullying at school. Being shuffled off to live with their grandparents in the short punishing days following their parents' funerals. Those images sat in Ben's mind, fading only slightly with the passing of the years. A name change. A school change. A deafening silence whenever he searched for answers as to what went so wrong that afternoon.

But those days were long gone. Ben sighed, letting his building frustration escape. "I don't need you leading the way or making the bad news better. Not now. Not for years."

"Yeah, well, it's a hard habit to break," Mark said as he shoved the carton of food away from him. "Seeing you in the hospital after the explosion brought it all back."

"When we lost Dad—"

Mark held up a firm hand. "I don't want to talk about this."

"But it impacts everything. You, me . . . Emma."

"She's fine."

Mark could not be that clueless. Hell, Callie knew them all for a few days and already she picked up the vibe. "Emma is not fine, and you know it. Her career is imploding and she's lost her will to hear the cases."

"She's scared, but she'll get through."

Not like this. Not when she put the rest of her life on hold waiting for Mark to get his act together. "You going to stay as her bodyguard?"

"Yes."

"How are you going to explain that?"

"With the bomb, there's nothing unusual about Emma having protection. No need for any special cover for me."

"And what are you going to do about the part where you walk in and out of her life all the time? It destroys her."

Mark went from carving lines in his food container to high alert. "How do you get to that?"

"I have eyes."

The skin pulled tight around Mark's mouth. "*I'm* not the reason she dumped that jackass of a fiancé."

This again. "Yes, you are. It's never been about me. Not for Emma."

Mark held his brother's gaze for an extra beat before talking again. "The report came in on the bomb."

Typical Mark. When emotions hit the table, he hit the streets.

"Are we done talking about you and Emma?" Ben asked.

"Yes." Mark sat back in a leather chair that barely held him. "No fingerprints or fibers. The materials were store bought and nothing special. The squad is sifting through everything looking for a signature because the working theory is that someone paid for a professional to make and plant the bomb."

"You're thinking this was Jenner or his wife?"

"Both are under surveillance, but I don't think so. There's no consistency to the signature. A bomb, a threatening note. This feels messier. Not the style of someone as anal retentive and plan oriented as Jenner."

"You get anything from the note to me?"

"Another dead end."

Silence followed Mark's statement. Ben guessed his brother was winding down, ready to leave. The conversation circled and wandered, but Ben tried one more time. "You'll have to deal with it one day, you know," he said into the quiet.

"What, Jenner?"

"Emma."

Mark's frown deepened. "We understand each other just fine."

"Which is good for me."

"Why?"

"I figure if you're sleeping with Emma, you can't very well turn around and piss all over me for sleeping with Callie." Made sense to Ben. Kept them from throwing off the suit jackets and going into battle.

Mark's scowl suggested he wasn't buying it. "Don't agree with that assessment at all."

Nothing new there. "You better get used to it, Mark."

"I just want to catch the bastard who's after you and Emma, and then let our lives get back to normal."

Ben wasn't sure he even knew what that was anymore. "Agreed."

Chapter Twelve

Callie sat in the small library directly across from Ben's private office and stared at the closed door for the fortieth time. Mark had walked in there fifteen minutes ago. He didn't tell her to keep out. Didn't have to. His lack of communication and stiff body language said it all.

She wasn't really up for another round with Mark. Sleeping two hours at night did that to a woman. Rounds of lovemaking pulled her off her game. She could describe every inch of Ben's naked body without even closing her eyes to call up the memory, but listening to Mark drone on about principles and ethics and whatever other boring topic he had in mind was not on her daily agenda.

She rubbed her eyes. When she dropped her hand again, she saw Rod standing in the doorway. And here she didn't think her day could get worse.

"Hello." She made sure her tone was as unwelcoming as possible.

"You're here."

The kid was a genius. A snarky, ass-kissing genius. "Where else would I be?"

"Good question."

The way he smiled ticked her off. Hell, everything about

him rubbed her wrong. The moneyed affect in his expensive boarding-school voice. The ever-present striped tie. The way he did everything but lick Ben's shoes to get his attention. Rod was everything she hated in a male. But she figured the sooner she let him say whatever it was he wanted to say, the faster she could go back to figuring out a way to infiltrate Ben's office without being seen.

"You want something?" she asked.

Rod continued to lounge in the doorway with an annoying smirk on his face. "He did just fine without an assistant."

Callie wondered how long it would be before Rod would open that door. Four days. Not bad for an annoying shit of a parasite. "I assume you're talking about me."

"Everyone is."

"Oh, really?"

"The news is all over the courthouse."

She had no idea what that meant. "Didn't they teach you to be specific in law school?"

"You slept at his house."

Wow, that was sure some strong courthouse grapevine. The bottom line was right, but the specifics got all tangled up somehow. Made Callie wonder who had been spying and how he or she missed which house she dragged Ben to yesterday. "No, I didn't."

"Don't lie about it." Rod all but spit the words at her.

The little creep was working on her nerves. "I'm not."

"Did you even go to law school?"

She barely made it through community college. Couldn't imagine willingly going through more years of classes and paying an ass-load of money to do it. "Nope, but I never claimed to be a lawyer."

"In his position and with his professional reputation, the judge could have his pick of lawyers to work for him."

"Maybe the judge is sick of snotty-ass lawyers."

"Why you?" The nasty sneer reflected Rod's anger. "I don't get it."

As far as Callie could tell, there was a lot young Rod didn't understand. Knowing when a woman who could kick his scrawny ass stood right in front of him was one of those things. "Why don't you say what you want to say?"

"Not my place."

She threw her arms wide. "Oh, you're all about boundaries all of a sudden?"

Rod snorted. "You should talk."

Yeah, one more sarcastic comment and she was pulling the gun. "Say it, Rod. Whatever it is you are dying to tell me, just say it."

"I don't—"

"Stop being a pansy and say it."

Rod shook his head. "There is nothing special about you. What does he see in you?"

If she were honest, she'd been wondering about that as well. She didn't have Ben's education or reputation. She'd messed up her career by opening her big mouth when everyone else had been smart enough to stay quiet. No one looked at her and saw a superstar. Yet, somehow, she held Ben's interest. The question was how long that would last.

"Most people like me," she said.

"Not around here."

"I'm sure you've been telling nice stories to anyone who would listen." She knew that was the case. Hell, he wasn't the only one who heard things around the courthouse. This kid had been yapping his mouth about her and not saying anything good.

"You're sleeping with the judge. That's your position in the courthouse."

"Be careful with that." She pointed at Rod to emphasize her point.

"It's disgusting. Your whole job is to shut the door and get the judge off."

She had to give the kid some credit for driving right to the basket. Not much, but some. "Nice language."

"So you admit it then."

"No, I was commenting on how you finally stopped sulking around and confronted me. I'm impressed. Reluctantly, but at least you stopped hiding behind the judge's pants leg."

"I don't know who you think you are."

"The person who, as you point out, spends every hour with Judge Walker. Morning, noon, and night." She made sure to emphasize all three. Let the little twerp take that to mean whatever he wanted it to mean. "I have Ben's ear, and you don't."

Rod's mouth dropped open. "You call him Ben?"

She called Ben Studmuffin when he stood in her kitchen wearing only a towel and making her coffee earlier that morning, but that struck her as one of those private bits that better remain quiet. "That's really what's killing you here, Rod. People's titles?"

"You're just a stupid slut. You know it and I know it."

Right over the line. Time for her to smack the little shit back down. "Watch it, kid."

"Why should I?"

She stood up. Tugged on the bottom of her jacket to straighten it. Also had the added advantage of covering her gun, though letting this weasel see it had some merits. "You have two seconds to turn around and leave. Strike that, to *shut up*, turn around, and leave. We'll pretend this never happened. We'll both know you're an ass wipe, but it can be our little secret."

"I'm not afraid of you."

"Because your daddy is some bigwig and you think he'll save your wimpy butt?" She asked the question in a falsely sweet voice before returning to her normal one. "Give me a break."

The fidgeting stopped as a suspicious calm washed over Rod. "Everyone around here will know all about you soon enough."

"You're playing an awful grown-up game. You sure you have the big boy panties to do it?"

"I have all the information I need."

He had passed from annoying to unbearable. She knew it would only get worse unless she ended it. "And just what do you plan to do with whatever it is you think you have, Rod?"

"You'll see."

"You sound like you're five."

"You're winning now because the judge likes sex, that's not a secret, but that's all about to change."

Ben's sexual appetite was part of the courthouse gossip? Yeah, he was going to love knowing that.

"Just wait." Rod ruined a perfect turn and dramatic exit by shifting and running smack into Scott. Rod fumbled, trying to say something. Finally he gave up and stormed down the hall.

"Problem?" Scott asked as he watched Rod flee.

"Other than the fact Rod's an ass?"

"Yeah, no kidding." Scott slipped inside the room and glanced behind him at the closed door to the judge's private chambers.

"So, it's not just me?"

"Nah. Rod dislikes anyone he sees as a threat."

"That's a charming personality trait." Callie didn't realize how tense she'd become until she saw the bent pen in her hands. She eased up on her grip to keep from breaking it in half and getting blue ink all over the place. "What about you? You don't seem to have the 'me, me, me' complex like some of the other judges' clerks."

With his hands balanced on the back of the chair across from her, Scott leaned down. "I don't come from the same entitled background as Rod."

"You're not a millionaire rich kid who got into law school on Daddy's name?"

"Hardly. More like a kid of divorce who had to work his way through college and take tens of thousands of dollars in loans and aid to get there." Scott's mouth twisted as he spoke.

Callie couldn't blame him for being bitter. It was hard to work around a bunch of entitled people and not get a bit testy. "Parts of that story sound familiar."

The sharp look on Scott's face softened. "Look, I heard what Rod said to you—"

She waved him off. Certainly didn't need some twenty-something trying to soothe her. "It's okay."

"I just want you to know that most of us think it's pretty cool."

Her back went rigid without receiving any message from her brain. Just pure instinct. "What is?"

"You with Judge Walker. Most of us are happy that he's found someone else after . . ." Scott shrugged. "Well, you know."

She didn't have a freaking clue. "You lost me, Scott."

"Judge Walker's been hung up on Judge Blanton for so long that we all started to wonder if he'd ever date again."

Callie felt a small tug of doubt over Ben's story. "How long?"

"Some people think their relationship started when he first took the bench and was hearing divorce cases. Judge Blanton was his mentor. A lot of long nights and meals together and then they were dating. Apparently it was a big shock when Judge Blanton picked someone else."

Callie knew she should stop the gossip, but her nosiness took over. For some reason, no one seemed to know that Ben and Emma grew up together less than two hours outside D.C. That missing piece struck Callie as odd, especially since everyone seemed so invested in spewing romantic nonsense about Ben.

"Other people think it happened after Judge Walker had to be moved out of the divorce rotation," Rod said. "But I guess the timing doesn't really matter so much as how it all played out."

Had to be moved? She decided to check on that later. "I'm not sure any of your information is correct."

"Of course it is." Scott's face went blank. "Wait, you don't know."

"About?"

"Judge Blanton's engagement. She and Judge Walker started fooling around and the fiancé walked. That's why the judges are both still single. We kept waiting for them to go public with their relationship, but now . . ." Scott opened his mouth a few times before spitting the words out. "You're in the picture."

He framed it nicer than that piece of crud Rod, but Scott's version ended up at the same conclusion—she spent a lot of horizontal time with Ben. "So, you think it's my turn to step in and sleep with the judge."

Scott waved his hands. "Wait. I didn't mean—"

"That's not what's happening here." Okay, it was *exactly* what was happening, but the scenario got all screwed up in the telling. Made her look easy and opportunistic. When it came to her relationship with Ben, she'd admit to one of those. She wasn't there as some rebound for Ben. Hell, he wasn't even rebounding.

"I didn't mean to offend you," Scott said.

"You didn't." Confused the hell out of her, but that was about it.

"Please don't tell Judge Walker that I'm the one who told you."

Oh, she intended to discuss this with Ben. Absolutely. He deserved to know the misunderstanding swirling around about him. Maybe he could explain why everyone wanted to give him a big high five for nailing the office staff while she got tagged with the whore label. The double standard ticked her off.

Yeah, they'd talk about it, but she'd keep the kid's name out of it. "It's okay. Really."

"Right." Scott nodded but still looked uncomfortable. "Have you seen Judge Blanton?"

"She's being interviewed by the administrative judge about the complaint filed against her." Callie knew that was the only reason Mark would accept for not being plastered to Emma's side.

"I'll leave you alone then." Scott got up. "And ignore whatever Rod says."

She planned to do the exact opposite. A kid with that much anger was just asking to be investigated.

Callie enjoyed her ten seconds of privacy. She wanted more, but the office atmosphere seemed to be sending restless waves her way.

"You're popular today." Elaine, Ben's true assistant, stuck her head in the door. Fifty, smart, capable, and a hard worker.

Callie understood why Ben depended on the other woman so much. Elaine answered phones and kept the true crazies away from Ben. Lawyers and case parties yelled at her all day long on the phone, and Elaine stayed calm. She also had the unenviable job of handling the tons of paperwork that shuffled through the office every hour.

And Elaine managed to listen to Rod without punching him. Callie thought that was pretty damn impressive.

"Apparently Rod thinks I'm a slut," Callie said, expecting a shocked reaction. She got a knowing nod instead.

"Yeah, I could hear him. I just hope the judge didn't."

Callie kind of hoped he did. Someone needed to tear Rod apart, and Mark would be pissed off if she tried. There's nothing covert about stuffing a snotty law clerk's head in a toilet. "For reasons I can't understand, Ben actually likes Rod."

Elaine smiled. "If you say so."

"Since you probably didn't come in here to talk about a bunch of twenty-something boys, what can I help you with?"

Elaine's smile vanished as fast as it came. "This is for you."

Callie eyed the plain envelope in the older woman's hand. Other than her name scrawled across the front, it was blank. "Thanks."

Then the silence stretched. Callie sat there staring. Elaine stood staring back.

Callie finally blinked. "So, if there's nothing else—"

"One of my jobs here is to open the mail." Elaine pursed her lips together. "All of it."

"Uh, okay."

"Unless it says 'private' on it, it's my responsibility."

Callie knew Elaine was trying to tell her something. Not sure what, but something. "Is this another threat?"

"Not exactly."

Callie dragged her finger along the jagged edge where Elaine had ripped the envelope open.

She barely got the papers out of the package when she saw the subject line.

Busted. "I can explain."

Elaine's mood didn't change. "You don't have to. I can read. It's obvious you're investigating the judge."

Callie felt a splash of guilt for her snooping. She had justified her covert actions saying it was all part of the job. Deep down she knew that was total bullshit. Ben intrigued her. They were sleeping together, for God's sake. That had to give her some rights. And, yes, she experienced a kick of something everytime she saw him. She didn't like feeling vulnerable and unsure about where she stood in her life. She liked it even less that she wanted to hold some sort of position with him. In his life.

Emotions were a bitch.

"It's not what you think," Callie said.

"I think it's your job to watch over him." Elaine tapped her fingers together. "The assistant title is clearly a cover. I'm assuming you work with the man who was watching over Judge Blanton and got injured."

Callie tried to force her eyes back to normal size level. "I can't really—"

"I know all about the judge's brother Mark. That one might have an important secret job, but I've been with the judge from the beginning, which means seeing Mark often. What I've figured out is he's an agent of some type."

Callie just knew Mark would blame her for this. "That's not my business."

"I also think that whatever it is you're doing with that quiet investigation of yours has nothing to do with Judge Walker's safety. This is personal for you." Elaine didn't raise her voice. Still, her comments came out like a lecture from a disappointed mother.

Callie had a bigger problem. With the stalker still out there, no one should know about her true position. Elaine might not look like an assassin, but who could tell? Besides that, Callie knew blowing her cover would be the last straw with Mark.

"Do you plan to talk with Ben about the paperwork?" Callie asked.

"I think you should do that, don't you?"

"Of course." In time but not now.

"I trust you'll do the right thing and not sneak around."

Callie hated it when people said stuff like that. It was a ticket to disappointment and guilt. Almost made her wish she hadn't asked her hacker friend to track down Ben's past and dig around, including into the boring stuff that looked too good to be real.

Elaine's gaze never wavered. "I've worked with the judge a long time. He deserves honesty."

Callie vowed to give that to him . . . eventually.

Chapter Thirteen

"You sure know how to show a girl a good time." Callie made the comment as she walked into lane five of the shooting range.

"Not every woman would view a few hours working with a gun as the perfect date." Standing behind her, Ben took it all in.

The snug jeans and gentle swing of her hips as she moved around the three-by-five space. A hard shiny gun in direct contrast with her soft curves. The woman was so damn hot. Even the earphones hanging around her neck didn't turn him off.

"When you challenged me to a shoot-out, how could I say no?" She opened the box of ammo.

Excitement all but poured out of her. No question the woman knew how to handle a gun. Seemed to enjoy the smooth feel of the steel against her skin, because she kept caressing it. Kind of reminded him how she touched him, firm and knowing. She was a woman who had learned what she liked and went after it every chance she got.

Totally fucking sexy.

"Technically, you challenged me," he said.

She chuckled. "Because I said you were getting soft?"

That happened two hours ago after they finished the afternoon docket and she informed him that his job was "boring as shit." She then went on to tell him why, including plenty of profanity and complaints about lawyers in her explanation.

"Yeah, thanks again for that."

"Oh, please. Your ego is fine. Besides, it wasn't a comment on your fitness. It was a statement on how you spend your life in this unreal state where people agree with everything you say and want to make you happy." She checked the gun before lowering it to the shelf.

"You including yourself in that crowd?"

"Absolutely not."

"That's unfortunate."

She snorted. "You'd get bored with a woman who fell at your feet and treated you like you shit gold."

"That's an interesting visual image."

"You can be snide all you want. You know I'm right."

He did. Emma had said the same thing. Despite his burning need for privacy, the women in his life seemed to know a great deal about his likes and dislikes. That sensation pissed him off for some reason.

When her gaze wandered down his torso, he thought about skipping the shooting and dragging her down to the floor instead.

"Do you disapprove of my choice of clothes?" he asked.

She pointed at his face and wiggled her finger around. "See, you're doing it again."

"Talking?"

"No."

"Flirting?"

"Getting all hoity."

He'd never been accused of that until Callie came along. His background was as far from the rich kid ideal as possible. "What, no toity?"

"I've decided it's a defense mechanism."

Great, a psychological exam. Just what he wanted from her. "How about we start shooting now?"

The bullets jingled when she put her fingers in the small box and moved them around. "It's not true, you know?"

As usual, he had no damn idea what she was talking about. "Excuse me?"

"You know, you can just say 'what' without the other stuff. You don't need to pretend you're the king or something."

Only Callie could get away with talking to him like that. "I didn't—"

"My point is that you're not soft," she said

The quick change in conversation direction took him a second to adjust. "Okay."

"You look good."

"Uh-huh."

"Very good, actually. Spectacular even. It's one of the few things the sniping women in the courthouse get right."

"Thanks. I think."

Her eyes did that dipping thing again, leaving his face and going on an extended tour to his stomach, then lower. "You're actually in great shape."

"Okay, that's enough."

"And your stamina?" She smacked her lips together in a fake kiss. "It's like you're twenty."

His pants started to feel tight. "We can stop this conversation anytime now."

"Problem?"

"Only with my concentration."

"You worrying about misfiring?"

"I think we're off track here."

She treated his growing erection to an intense stare before getting back to work at the counter. Her fingers worked over the metal. "I'm just saying that if a man doesn't practice handling his weapon he gets rusty. You got to keep it primed and ready to go."

"Are we still talking about guns?"

She threw him a sexy smile over her shoulder. "What else would I be talking about?"

"Right."

She concentrated on loading the weapon and steadied her stance by separating her legs.

"You ever miss it?"

Ben forced his gaze away from her ass. "Excuse . . . huh?"

"A life that doesn't include sitting behind a desk. The military. The travel. You ever wish you were still there?"

He leaned against the wall to her right side so he could see her reactions play across her face as he spoke. "Since I served during a war, no."

"I'm sorry."

He barely thought about those years now. "It was a long time ago."

"Then what about the other parts? What happened in all of those years in between? I'm thinking nothing as exciting as what went before."

"Ah, I see. You're saying my current life is boring."

"Remember that I've sat in on the motions docket." She rolled her eyes. "That's some terrible stuff right there. Boring doesn't even come close to describing the brain-numbing nature of those hours."

"Yeah, I have to admit that's not a highlight of the job."

"Hardly."

A round of bangs echoed in the background. Ben stuck his head out of the lane and saw the light on six stalls away. That meant another shooter had come in. Between the hum of the lights and the shots, Ben figured this was as private as this building could get.

Callie didn't let something like an audience stop her hunt for information. She kept on making her list. "The adrenaline rush? The strategy sessions? The brotherhood bond of your unit?"

Without knowing it, she had touched on some of the reasons he joined. That, and he didn't have any other options. The army provided him with structure and a home when he desperately needed both. "You know a lot about the military?"

"No." She looked him in the eye this time. Her hand didn't move from the weapon, but he had her attention now. "I'm fascinated by the idea of people putting their lives on the line in that way. The honor and integrity angles are pretty irresistible."

"This sounds like some type of men-in-uniform fantasy."

"You gotta admit that level of courage is pretty damn sexy."

Getting women was about the only reason not on his "pro" listed for signing up for the army all of those years ago. "And here I thought the ladies liked the judge's robe."

"That's only because they're all trying to figure out what you have on under there. Me, on the other hand, I'm trying to figure out what's under here." She laid her palm over his heart.

The touch sparked something warm inside him. He tended to balk at oversharing and ploys to get him to talk about his past. Women always wanted to know what happened before, but he was a live-in-the-now kind of guy. But with Callie, the questions came with such a genuine zeal, without any agenda, that his inner wall holding her out crumbled slightly.

He slid his palm over hers. "You worried I'm empty under all the judge stuff?"

"No."

Not the most convincing response he'd ever heard. "Then?"

She dropped her arm, breaking the contact, and stepped back. "You've raced through several careers and landed a gig as the top banana. You're protective of Emma and wary of Mark. You're a monster in the sack and a star in the courtroom."

"That's quite a rundown."

She tapped her forehead. "A smart woman finds out all she can before hitting the sheets with a man."

A red flag went up in his mind. That comment sounded more real and less flip than he expected. "I suspected it before, but now I know. You checked on my past."

She shrugged. "I read the file Mark gave me."

There was more. The churning in Ben's gut told him that much. "And?"

Her head fell to the side. "And poked around a bit."

Now that scared the hell out of him. "After all that investigating, what do you think now?"

"I'm not sure."

He knew the thoughtful look on her face was a bad sign. "Tell me what that means."

"I want to know if there's more to you."

"Like what?"

"You tell me."

Ben had no idea what she was searching for. "Is this a test of some sort?"

"Yeah, I think it is." She finally dropped the gun and fully turned to face him. "Let's try it this way. We'll play a game of twenty questions."

"Isn't that what we were just doing?"

"An actual game this time. One with rules."

"Most people stick to shooting targets here."

"Not us." She ticked off the instructions to her makeshift game on her fingers. "If you want to answer, you answer. Otherwise, you shoot. But without a big number shot—I'm talking a plug to the head or the heart—you have to answer anyway. You only get one chance to evade the uncomfortable question and nothing is off limits."

"You do know I was a sharpshooter in the army, right?"

"And I was top in my class at Quantico." She petted the gun again. "You in?"

"I'm going to regret this."

She motioned for him to step up to the bar. "You can even go first."

He sensed a trap. The scenario she outlined sounded good. They'd both have an equal shot at finding out what they wanted to know, but he could see her fixing the game. Her lax stance suggested she didn't care much about what happened in the next few minutes.

The look was total bullshit. He'd bet she was ready to pop. Hell, he could see it in the way she shifted her weight from foot to foot. Calm outside. A ball of nerves inside. But what was life without risks?

"So, how does smart-mouthed Callie Robbins end up in the stiff FBI, earning high marks in gunplay?" He could have reached out to her or slipped his foot an inch or two to the left and touched her. He stood still instead.

She leaned back against the wall across from him. The move put them less than two feet apart. The tight area made the personal subject matter even more intimate. "I grew up in a small town. The type where girls got married at eighteen and pregnant right around then, usually before. College wasn't a priority. Excitement amounted to smoking behind the gas station and sex in the back of the movie theater. I went away to school, escaped really, worked my butt off, and joined the FBI. All of that because I wanted a real challenge."

"I never would have taken you for a farm girl."

"No farm, just small town. Stifling, really." She smiled. "Now it's my turn."

"I'm ready."

She snorted. "Right."

"Try me."

"Okay, smart boy like you with all of those opportunities. Why the military? Not that I think it's beneath you or anything. You just strike me as the college scholarship type."

He didn't realize he was holding his breath until it escaped his lungs in a rush of relief. Of all the questions she could ask, this one was the safest. "No money and mediocre grades."

"You, the judge, weren't an academic wonder?"

"I spent more time getting into trouble than opening books."

"Trouble as in you couldn't stay out of high school girls' panties?"

"Among other things. Truth is the army was really good for me. Gave me focus. I couldn't be more grateful for the chance I got there."

"Impressive."

"Without it, I don't know where I would have ended up."

That wasn't a lie. He had spent many years defending his mother and trying to understand his parents' choices. His father cheated. His mother, seeing the love of her life having sex with someone else in her bed, lost her mind and found the only gun in the house. Ben understood now that he dealt with the numbing loss back then with the quick use of his fists. He punched as a way of releasing his unspoken grief.

The draining loss lessened with the short move away from his hometown. Something about those extra thirty miles of distance let him focus his energy on sports instead of pounding people. The inevitable name change helped, too.

But he knew all about his secrets. He had lived with them for years, explaining the truth only when he had to and even then in small pieces, like to the governor's staff and committees who interviewed him for the judicial position. All of that was done in confidence. Still, the truth could seep out at any time. Ben actually waited for the day to come.

He wasn't worried about that now. No. All the question marks in his head right now related to Callie. He wasn't about to let this opportunity to really know her pass by.

"Who did you have to shoot?" he asked in a whisper, even though shots rang out from the other stall and echoed throughout the enclosed space.

By the way her eyes narrowed, she heard him just fine. "How did you know that?"

"You said it once in passing."

"I guess that means you do listen. Good to know. Most men aren't so good at that."

"You're stalling."

She looked down at her feet and then back up again. "I shot my former boss at the FBI. In the leg. One shot, but it did the trick."

Then she went silent. Actually looked up at him with those big eyes and an innocent smile.

"That's it? No story."

She chuckled. "You asked; I answered."

"Gee, I wonder what my next question will be."

"Doesn't matter because it's my turn. Why do people think you broke up Emma's engagement?" The words rushed out of Callie as if she'd been holding them in forever.

"Because I did."

Callie's eyes bulged at the fast response.

The question wasn't exactly a surprise. He knew Callie would hear the courthouse gossip about that one eventually.

"And?" she asked.

"I answered you." When her eyes darkened and mouth fell, he shot her a smile. "Hey, just following your interpretation of the rules."

"Oh, come on."

What the hell. "Emma was in love with Mark and the fiancé was a total ass. All wrong for her. A law partner with no personality. I just helped her to see it. Everyone assumes the rest. All of that untrue, as I've said about a million times."

"Which is why you're so sensitive about infidelity."

That was part of it, but he didn't plan on answering that question—ever—so he ducked it. "Isn't everyone?"

"That's not my experience with men."

"Want to talk about that?"

"Depends. Is that your next question?"

"No." Since she was now parsing out the questions, he tried to be more careful. "Under what circumstance did you leave the FBI?"

She hesitated for a second. Stared at the gun on the counter and then at Ben. Time passed without her saying anything. Then she picked up the weapon and fired a single booming shot.

The loud clap bounced around in his head. That would teach him to skip wearing the headphones before they started this game.

He didn't have to move the target to see where she hit. The bullet tore right into the paper guy's heart. "Interesting," he whispered.

"Not really."

He wondered why she was so sensitive about this subject. They had been all over each other, spent hours together without a break, and she refused to fess up on this subject. Now that he thought about it, she didn't talk much about herself at all. He didn't, either, but he had good reason, so he had an excuse. He knew the reasoning was convoluted and more than a little hypocritical, but he didn't care. The part of his brain tasked with rational thinking fizzled around her.

"Ready for the next one?" she asked.

"I doubt it."

She let her head fall to the side again in that pose she used right before she dropped a bomb or tried to seduce him.

He was hoping for the latter.

If possible, her eyes grew darker. "What's your real last name?"

Shots rang out from the other stall, but Ben barely heard them. "What?"

"Your. Real. Name."

This exercise officially had gone too far. "Callie—"

"Your background. The missing pieces are obvious. The fact your past starts somewhere in middle school and there's not a record of you anywhere before then gave me a hint."

The options zipped around his brain. He could lie. Walk out.

Or he could tell her the truth.

He cleared his throat. "It's not Walker."

"I know that much."

His mind kept reeling from the topic. "Then why ask?"

"You didn't give me a full answer." She didn't even flinch. Didn't run in panic when she fished around and came up with a correct theory about his name change.

Made Ben wonder, again, why he found smart women so damn attractive. If this were any indication about what she could uncover with just a few resources, she was nothing but trouble. "Yeah, it is."

"Did you ever think that it might feel good to share the hard parts of your life?"

"No."

"Why the change?" Her look of determination and set

chin gave way to a certain softness around her eyes. "What happened to you and your family?"

He didn't hesitate. He picked up the gun and aimed. With little more than a brief glance at the end of the stall, the shot ripped through the circle in the target's head.

She stared down the lane and gnawed on her lower lip. "I guess that's my answer."

"It's the only one you're going to get. And I appreciate if you kept the information you do know to yourself."

"You can trust me."

He thought so once. Now he wasn't so sure.

Chapter Fourteen

"The people in this courthouse need to grow the fuck up." Callie made that observation the next day the second after she closed Ben's office door and started stalking toward him.

Not that her anger did any good. Nope. He just sat at his desk with his head down and his pen out.

"Have a good time in the bathroom?" he asked with more than a little amusement in his voice.

She stopped on the other side of his desk. Even tapped the tip of her fingers against the wood to get his attention. "This wouldn't have happened if you had let me use your private bathroom."

He kept right on signing the papers in the stack in front of him. "I believe I was using it at the time you banged on the door and insisted I get out."

"You always have an excuse."

"I get exactly two seconds of privacy a day. I'm not giving that up, too."

She balanced her fists on his desk and leaned in close enough to smell the peppery shampoo scent in his hair. "Well, does it bother you that you're starring in the building's rumors?"

"Not particularly."

"Why?"

"It's not a new problem. That's been the case since I started here."

"Being named one of the metro area's most eligible bachelors must be a real hardship."

His pen hesitated. "Let's not talk about that."

The man was ignoring her concerns. That pissed her off almost as much as the chatter about her love life. He wasn't even taking a minute out of his busy important morning of signing orders to glance at her. The whole thing made her miss the shooting range. Lots of weapons to threaten him with there.

"Apparently this time everyone thinks we're sleeping together." She grabbed the pen out of his hand and threw it behind her.

He finally lifted his head. "I was using that."

"And do they shut up about it? Nope. They hide in the bathroom, standing around the sinks and chattering like gossipy old women with nothing better to do." She used her hands to demonstrate the yammering. "Idiots."

Ben rifled through his desk drawer and pulled out a second pen. No surprise that it looked just like the first one. He clicked the top. "Did they see you?"

"They did when I slammed the stall door open. Nobody said a damn thing then." Callie smiled at the memory. "Well, the younger one yelped like a puppy. Then they both pretended I was deaf and ran out of there. I thought about chasing them but refrained."

"Good to hear you didn't overreact."

Ben refused to understand her point. She decided to rap her knuckles against his precious desk to get his attention. "The two I caught were in there trying to guess when we hooked up."

"Old women used that term?"

"They wanted to know why *you* would bother with someone like me. Which means what, by the way?" When he didn't respond, she tried again. "Well?"

He slowly lowered his pen. "I'm not taking that bait. There is no way for me to answer that without you getting . . ."

"What?"

"Bitchy."

"See, that's more of the jackassery thing you do." She pointed at his big brainy head. "Pure jackassery."

He leaned back in his chair. "Callie, let's be reasonable."

He looked nice and relaxed, but she guessed the move was meant to put as much space as possible between them. She had to give him credit for that. The man was not stupid. Well, not entirely.

"Why?" she asked.

His pretty eyes narrowed at her in that way he had of saying "what the hell" without actually using the words. "That's not a logical response to my statement."

Frustration boiled up inside her.

"Did you just growl at me?" he asked.

"It was either that or bite you."

"May I ask why?"

"*May I ask why?*" She sang more than said the words. "You jumped right back into hoity land."

"If we're really going to argue about this you might want to look at the facts."

"Which are?"

"First, some of the women in question really are old women." When Callie tried to butt in, he held up a finger and made that annoying *tsk-tsk* sound. "Second, we are sleeping together."

"That's not the point."

"I actually think it is."

"The issue is their pathological nosiness." Theirs. Rod's.

Scott's. The whole damn building worried about who was with her when her panties came off. Never mind the cases on their desks. Ben's bedroom antics were the main topic on the e-mail loops these days.

A look between a smile and a smirk fell across his lips. "You sure you're not embarrassed?"

"More like ticked off."

"Callie?"

Ben had a way of saying her name that made him sound like a condescending professor. Not that she had all that much experience with those. "About sleeping with you? No. I don't have a reason to lie about us being together. Well, except for incurring Mark's wrath again and potentially blowing my cover. You're not the kind of guy a woman has to hide from people."

"I guess that's good to know."

"You're a judge, after all."

"I'm impressed you remembered that."

She drummed her fingers against his desk, ignoring the way he grimaced with each tap. "Why aren't you angry about this?"

"The gossip?"

"What else are we talking about?"

"Indeed." He held up a palm before she could harass him about his word choice. "Yeah, I know. Too hoity."

Now that was progress. "At least you're finally recognizing it."

"Not really." He laid a hand over hers and stopped her mad thumping against the desk.

She should have pulled away, but his warm skin gave her comfort. With Ben she could be herself, not worry about how each word could be perceived. She stepped into danger territory now and then by calling him names and questioning his background, but she felt safe in saying the words that kicked around in her brain. He'd fight back without demeaning or threatening her. It was a fair and equal debate. That level of security didn't come around that often, and she enjoyed it.

She even liked that hoity talk of his. Sometimes.

"You make me sound unreasonable," she said, knowing she was being a bit irrational.

"No." He made the word last for about six syllables. Sounded about as convincing as some of the criminal defendants who appeared before him.

She didn't really care what women who didn't know her thought. She worried about Ben's reputation. When she left, he'd still be there. Leaving . . . yeah, she didn't want to think about that at all. Spending hours with him each day sure beat the mindless days of dialing around on the television remote as she waited for someone to call to offer her a job.

"Get back to the part where you don't care about the gossip," she said.

"It's because—and don't jump down my throat—" He smiled as he talked. "The rumors are true."

"You're not worried about your reputation."

"No."

She didn't understand how that was possible. Having been in a position that demanded a certain level of public responsibility, and nowhere near the amount Ben's required, she knew every action had a reaction. Ben's relative calm in the face of another wave of woman-related gossip seemed off.

There was only one explanation. "Because you're a man."

He tapped his pen against the desk. "See, that's a word trap. I now know better than to react to that comment."

She slid her hand out from under his. "I'm the slut and you're the conquering male hero."

"Someone called you that?" His seat shot forward and so

did he. He morphed from lazy listening to furious in less than a second. Any redder and his face might catch fire.

"It was implied."

He eased up on the death grip on his chair's armrests but the dents in the leather from his fingernails took longer to fade. "It's not true and saying it is out of line."

"Agreed."

"If you hear that sort of name-calling, let me know."

She actually thought his protective streak was kind of cute. She decided to tweak him anyway. "What are you going to do, choke some old lady with her cardigan sweater?"

His shoulders lowered back to normal height instead of hovering around his ears. "Hopefully it won't come to that."

"Remember that I can shoot any person who bugs me. And feel free to take that as a warning for your own idiocy."

"That's not too extreme or anything."

"You don't want to test me."

He made a clicking noise with his tongue. "Got it."

"I hate when you say that."

"Good to know."

Great. Now he'd be saying it in every other sentence. Just what she needed.

He curled a finger at her. "Come here."

Uh-oh. He shot her one of those sexy smiles and her control took a lunch break. "What are you doing?"

"Trying to lure you to my lap."

That sounded so damned good.

But she was on a job . . . or something. There had to be a rule against office lap dances. Mark might not have spelled that out, but she was pretty sure it existed. "Absolutely not."

"Why?"

"We're at work."

"So?" The question sounded serious.

"You," she circled her hand in front of his face, "are a no-fly-zone when we're here."

"Since when?"

"Forever."

"So, if I wanted you to climb onto my lap, you'd say no." He pushed his chair back on its rollers and she got a good long look at the part of his anatomy he referenced.

The man chipped away at her common sense. "I have to stay on this side of the desk with my clothes on."

"Even if I let you wear the judge's robe."

A pretty graphic image flashed through her dirty, unprofessional mind. "What would you be wearing?"

"Hopefully?"—he tapped on his upper thighs as if inviting her to sit down—"nothing but you."

"I like the way you think, but I'm still not taking one more step toward you."

"What if I tell you all the things I want to do to you?"

She was two seconds away from doing a flying leap onto his legs. "I'm not going to be tempted."

"Really?"

She turned back to her desk. Papers sat there, right in front of her, but the black ink blurred. "But you have work to do, so let's—"

"I would start with opening the buttons of that slim shirt. Let my tongue wander over your breasts."

She froze, refusing to look at him. Her thoughts were bad enough. "Ben."

"I'd slip those pants off and see what you have underneath. I'm betting a lacy black thong. A tiny scrap of a thing that barely covers you. It will only take a flip of my finger to move it to the side and taste your bare skin underneath."

"That's cheating, since you saw me put it on this morning."

The chair squeaked, but she refused to turn around and see what made that interesting noise. Once she did, it would be all over. Like, her all over him.

"And just think of how much fun we could have while I strip it off and throw it on the floor."

The papers crumpled in her fist. She didn't even realize she had grabbed them until she heard the crunching sound. "You don't play fair."

"I warned you."

She looked at him then.

The signs were right there. Pulsing tension. A glimmer of heat in those eyes. Fingers that stretched and curled as if getting ready for something.

"Do the other judges know about your nasty side?" she asked.

"Only you, babe."

"Would you settle for a kiss?"

He stared at the ceiling and pretended to think about it. "Depends on the type of kiss."

"One that turns your hair gray."

"Now you're talking."

"No lap."

"Your loss."

Oh, that much she knew.

She shifted around his desk. Sat her butt down on the edge, right in front of him, with her hands balanced behind her. The position put her warm body between his open thighs. She tried very hard not to focus on the bulge she saw there.

"Are you going to behave?" she asked, hoping he'd say no.

"I hadn't planned on it."

Good man. "Well? Aren't you going to come up here and kiss me?"

He shook his head. "It's up to you."

Looked like the lap part was inevitable. She slid onto one knee, trying to keep her feet steady on the floor in case she needed to jump back up again.

He was having none of it. He scooped his arm under her knee and brought her in close to his chest. She threw an arm around his neck to keep from falling against him in a heap. In that position, every inch of her pressed against him. Her mouth lingered just inches from his.

"I like this position." He whispered the admission against her cheek.

"Stop talking."

Her mouth slid over his, tasting and caressing. Lips against lips, she brought him into her. Pressed her nails into his back with one hand and cupped his cheek with the other. A low rumble sounded around them, the mix of his moan and her blinding need. She wanted to brush her palms all over him, but she kept her touches light. Let her long, hot kiss speak for her.

"Excuse me." The familiar words rang out in the room.

Wrong voice.

She pulled her mouth away from Ben's and swiveled around to stare at the office door. Rod stood there with a smug air about him. His stance telegraphed a mix of contempt and disgust.

She searched her mind for something smart to say. Even something dumb would have been welcome, but her mouth refused to work. Her brain didn't exactly whirl to life, either.

"You need to knock before you come in," Ben said, his voice exploding through the room with the force of cannon fire.

Callie tried to jump off his lap, but Ben anchored her there.

"Sorry." But there was nothing in Rod's tone to suggest a genuine apology. And he hadn't made a move to get out, either.

Ben cleared his throat twice before talking again. "Rod, go to your office. I'll be there in a few minutes."

"Yes, sir." Rod shot her a victorious smile and then left without closing the door.

"I hate that kid," she grumbled.

"He's not my favorite person at the moment, either." Ben gentled his grip on her thighs. "I'm guessing you forgot to lock the door."

"Clearly. Although, in my defense, I wasn't expecting a slap and tickle session."

"Me, either. I was thinking of a kiss."

She smoothed her hand down the buttons of her shirt. "Let me up."

"I wasn't done." Ben had the nerve to look sulky when he said it.

"Are you kidding me? I have to break this off and go strangle the interfering little pisher before he runs blabbing all over the courthouse." She thought about cramming a case folder down Rod's throat while she was at it. That would keep him from talking.

No way was that interruption a mistake. Rod timed the whole scene perfectly. He wanted to catch them together. And did.

"What exactly is a pisher?" Ben asked.

"Nothing good." She noticed he didn't look the least bit upset about being caught in midstrip. "Not that you were all that helpful."

"Did you want me to beat Rod up?"

"Yes."

"I thought I'd try talking to him instead." The practical

judge persona was firmly back in place. His hands had moved from her ass to his chair.

Callie wasn't impressed with the sudden professionalism. "Wrong."

"Excuse me?"

"That kid has been gunning for me." She couldn't exactly tell Ben all about how she tracked most of the nastier courthouse rumors back to Rod's door. Well, she could, but she didn't want to be one of those women who needed a big strong man to fight her battles for her. "Just trust me on this, but my point was about you not letting go when the door swung open. You could have, at least, let me jump up and demand an explanation for why he walked in."

"Couldn't."

"Why?"

"My erection would have given us away."

She felt the press against her butt. "Oh."

"Yeah, oh."

"So now what?"

"I say the alphabet backward a few hundred times, get myself together, and then go kick Rod's ass."

"I'm all for the last part of that plan. About time."

"I was kidding." Ben pushed her to her feet and then stood up next to her. "I'm going to talk with Rod. No ass kicking needed."

"That's never going to work. The kid doesn't understand rational conversation. He responds to threats."

Ben placed a hard, fast kiss on her lips. "This is an office protocol issue. Frankly, I violated a few rules over the last week as well. But you're going to stay out of this conversation."

"Sorry. Can't." She tried to sound contrite, but she wasn't. Not one bit. "I need to be where you are at all times."

"You can wait in the hall."

Good Lord, he was serious. "That's not going to happen, Ben."

"You'll be able to listen in without Rod knowing. Think of the rush of power you'll get from that."

"I'd rather punch him."

"Maybe next time."

Chapter Fifteen

A half hour later, Ben left a fuming Callie leaning against the wall in the hallway as he knocked on Rod's door. Ben wasn't waiting for a formal invitation to come in. He was trying to show how the whole knocking thing worked. Callie could take a lesson on that as well.

Rod put down the phone and shot out of his seat the second Ben entered. Ben appreciated the quick attention and show of deference. Not that either of those reactions would make the next few minutes more comfortable. Talking propriety after getting caught with his hands under Callie's blouse seemed a bit hypocritical. But this was his office and with or without the death threats, whether Callie worked there or not, he would run it and do it his way. He was the boss. Being out of control of the situation had gone on long enough. He'd get things back on track. Somehow.

"Sir, I'm sorry." This time Rod sounded contrite.

"Sit down." Ben shut the door and took the seat across from Rod in the claustrophobic office.

The stark white walls didn't do anything to make the windowless room feel bigger or one ounce more comfortable. No personal items littered the surfaces. Only a desk, a computer, and a small bookcase with rows of legal resource materials. A sort of lawyer's prison cell.

Ben had only been in there a few minutes, and the place already depressed him. "We have a problem, Rod."

"I should have knocked."

"True."

"I thought you were alone."

"Obviously." Ben shifted, trying to find a position that didn't cramp his legs. "I could have been in a private meeting with lawyers, or with another judge. It is not appropriate for you to barge in. By my count, you've done that twice in the past week. This had better be the last time."

"Yes, sir."

Ben folded his hands together in his most serious judge pose. "Are we clear on the expectations and rules?"

Rod gave Ben a nervous nod. "Yes."

"Good."

"Again, I'm sorry."

"Understood." With the angry boss man stuff out of the way, Ben turned to the part he dreaded. The personal, no-one's-business stuff he had hoped would never creep into the workplace.

When it came to the rumors about Emma, Ben had chosen to ignore them. Explaining the true nature of their relationship to anyone who would listen would only have highlighted the whispers and made her life more difficult. She had answered enough questions about her failed engagement. Having him defect and publicly deny the romance would only shine the light back on her, and he wasn't about to do that.

But Callie was a different story. The rumors on this one were true, and that made all the difference.

Ben sat up straighter with his back tight against the chair. "Look, about what you saw in my office earlier—"

"I won't say anything."

Rod's man-to-man tone didn't make the situation any

easier for Ben. The clerk was about fifteen years younger, still filled with enthusiasm for the legal career ahead of him. He took pride in his job and did it well. The anything-to-please attitude made Ben feel about ninety. He half expected his bones to creak when he crossed his legs.

"While I appreciate you keeping this between us, for Callie's sake more than anything—" At the mention of her name Ben saw Rod's face fall. "What's wrong?"

Rod shook off the anger hovering around him. "Nothing."

"It's something." It looked to Ben as if Callie wasn't so paranoid after all. "You don't like her very much, do you?"

"She's not my business."

Ben agreed with that assessment, but it really didn't answer the simple question on the table. "She is part of a trial courthouse program implemented by the administrative judge."

"Sir, you don't have to explain."

But he couldn't stop himself. It was as if he needed to make sure Rod got the point that Callie wasn't just some bed warmer. Ben knew that. He wanted the courthouse gossip train to tell the story right. Callie wasn't using him. If anything, he was using her. He wanted to be with her and couldn't turn that desire switch off.

Ben drew in a long intake of breath. "I do, because I need you to understand the facts. My personal life is private. It should not be the topic in the lunchroom or anywhere else. But it was my responsibility to keep what should have been a non-work moment out of the office. I failed in that. From now on, I will do better."

Rod's mouth flatlined. "This wasn't your fault."

"It wasn't Callie's, either."

"If you say so."

No waffling there. Rod blamed Callie. Ben didn't know

how to fix that so he went around it. "We still haven't re-solved our issue."

"Sir?"

"You've been disrespectful to Callie."

Rod's eyes popped open. "Did she tell you that? She's lying, because that's not true."

"She didn't say anything. I'm going by what I see. Frankly, you don't hide your dislike very well. You frown and pout. For the record, that behavior is not professional."

"I haven't said anything."

"It's your attitude. Rod, you're going to meet all types in your law practice. You have to figure out how to get along with people you don't like whether those people be fellow lawyers, judges, or your clients. Trust me, you'll hate a lot of them."

"Yes, sir."

"You need to be less obvious about your feelings so that no one confuses your affect with a lack of respect. Do you understand what I'm saying?"

"Definitely."

Rod didn't. Ben could see the anger right there, festering. Could hear it in the clipped tone of Rod's voice. Instead of making the situation tolerable, Ben feared he had just made it worse. Rod would blame Callie for the dressing-down.

Hell, Callie would probably have a word or two about how he said it all wrong. Ben thought about sneaking out of the building to avoid that conversation. He might have if Rod's office had a window and a stalker didn't lurk around waiting to pounce.

"If there's nothing else . . ." Ben started to rise.

"Sir, can I be frank?"

The comment made Ben wonder what they'd been doing up until that point. He plopped back down in the hard wooden chair. "Of course."

"It's about Callie."

Ben swallowed a sigh. "I figured as much."

"See . . . it's . . ."

"Just spit it out, Rod."

"Her past is not a secret."

The need to get up and out of there stopped whipping around inside of Ben. Everything stopped. "What past?"

"With her former boss."

"Excuse me?"

Rod's frown eased slightly. "In the FBI."

How the hell did the kid know about the FBI? Ben tried to imagine Mark's reaction to that information leak. When Callie started working for Mark her FBI file got buried. Ben knew because he had tried to find it.

"Okay, why don't you tell me what you think you know?" Ben asked.

"This isn't important."

The kid was playing now. He practically vibrated with the need to spill his news. Ben could see the energy, feel it humming through the small room. "Just tell me."

"Not to be abrupt or rude, but she slept with her boss, got him in trouble with his wife, and then claimed harassment when the whole thing blew up in her face." Rod raced through the explanation, almost bounced in his seat with excitement.

Ben waited for the buzzing in his ears to stop before he talked again. "Where did you hear all that?"

Rod shrugged. "Around."

"Not good enough. I need a source." The idea that this pisher—Callie's name fit at the moment—tracked down her background pissed Ben off.

Then there was the actual information. Callie screwing around with a married guy? Ben hated the thought of that.

Deep down he knew her life before him wasn't his business. But this issue touched parts of him, parts he'd rather keep buried. She knew his feelings on the subject. He'd made his position on fidelity quite clear.

Ben's mind raced with the possibilities. Maybe this was why she took the shot at the gun range rather than explain her days at the Bureau. Or maybe Rod was the little weasel Callie proclaimed him to be and it was all a bunch of lies. Either way, Ben had a twinge of doubt now. And he hated that.

"I can't really say, sir. I was told on the condition of anonymity that I not share the information with anyone. I'm only telling you because I admire you and don't want to see your legal reputation squandered in a similar situation."

Ben wasn't impressed with the show of loyalty. "You have ten seconds to tell me the truth."

Rod's mouth dropped open. "But . . ."

The bullying came with the robe. Ben said that reminder in his head several times as he watched Rod shift around in his chair. Rod brought this on by launching into the story. He deserved to be called out on it, no matter how sickly pale his face grew.

"Eight, Rod."

"Sir, I'm not comfortable talking about this."

"You were perfectly fine a second ago when you were saying negative things about Callie." Ben made a show of glancing at his watch. "Five."

"I promised."

"Four."

"People could get in a lot of trouble." Rod all but pleaded now.

The whiny begging got through to Ben. The truth crashed over him. The kid had all sorts of money and tons of contacts. His friends worked in congressional offices. His father wielded a lot of power. Rich with resources—a very dangerous combination.

"You paid someone to check her background. Maybe dig around where they shouldn't be digging." Ben knew he got it on the first try when Rod's skin turned from pale to green.

"Only because I was concerned."

Damn, even twenty-somethings were trying to protect him. "You broke the law, Rod."

The kid froze to his seat. "What?"

"If Callie was in the FBI, and I'm not confirming that fact, and you were poking around in her private employment records—"

Rod started shaking his head. "I wouldn't."

"Someone did."

"No one got hurt."

"I'm not sure the FBI would agree that's the test." Ben knew Mark sure wouldn't think so. "Who else knows about this?"

"No one. I promise." The words tripped out of Rod's mouth.

"It had better stay that way, Rod. If I hear one more bit of gossip about Callie on any issue, FBI or not, I am holding you responsible. Got that?"

"But—"

"Do we understand each other?" Ben asked the question in a near shout and kept at it. "Well?"

"Yes, sir."

"Good."

Chapter Sixteen

Callie passed great and hovered on the brink of exceptional.

Air hiccupped in her lungs as she glanced down her bare body to the top of her thighs and Ben's dark head between. Just then his tongue licked over her in the most delicious way that sent her ankles digging into the mattress.

Her body continued to dampen from the inside out. The deeper he worked his fingers into her, the more her hips clenched. "Ben, now."

But his mouth and hands kept caressing, making her hotter . . . wetter.

They had started on this sensual journey an hour earlier. After getting all worked up in his office and not being able to finish, the rest of the day passed with a dull ache. Her skin itched, and her clothes felt tight. Sitting through an afternoon of lawyer boredom nearly killed her. Looking up at Ben and knowing the power of those hands made concentration impossible. Good thing she spent most of the time on that seat daydreaming anyway. Today those mind wanderings were of the X-rated variety.

When the last suit finally had left the courtroom, Ben suggested they leave right then, and she didn't argue. The clock barely hit five when he grabbed up his briefcase and headed for the door. A short car ride and a great deal of fumbling with shirts and pants later, and they lay naked and entwined on her soft sheets.

When he slipped down her stomach and then lower a few minutes after that she almost cheered. She went with groaning instead.

His tongue made another pass over her, causing her entire body to tighten. "Ben . . ."

This time he lifted his head. His wet mouth smiled up at her. "Yes?"

"Get the damn condom."

"Your bedroom talk needs some work."

She threw her arm to the side and patted the nightstand for the foil packet. Feeling it, she scooped it up and threw it on her stomach. Without missing a beat, her hand returned to the bottom of the headboard.

"Now," she said on a half breath.

"No arguments here."

But he took his time crawling up the length of her body. Muscles stretched. Long limbs moved in concert. His erection jutted out, easy for her to see and even closer for her to touch. If it were possible to stalk her in three feet of space, he did it.

With a sharp rip, he had the protection out and rolled it on. "Are you ready?"

"Way past that." Her head rolled from one side to another as her insides pulsed. "Please."

She was willing to beg. Thought about sliding her hand down his stomach and moving this along.

Then he picked up the pace. He slipped his hands under her knees and pushed her legs back toward her chest. The position opened her wider than before, free to his gaze and his body. This time he didn't wait. With one long push, he entered her. His cock went in smooth and deep until she couldn't tell if he was surrounding her or vice versa.

Leaning down, his mouth met hers in a soft, searching kiss so breathtakingly beautiful that her heart stopped for a second. When he lifted his head again, she saw the heat and determination. With his damp body over hers and his cock lodged inside, he began to move. This wasn't their usually frenzied mating. No, this one breathed with emotion and longing. Hours of wanting exploded in a rhythmic push and pull as he entered her and then retreated. The friction set off tiny fireworks behind her eyes.

Every part of her surrendered. She squeezed him from her legs to her tiny inner muscles. And when her body blew apart in orgasm, she took him along with her.

He panted and gasped as her chest heaved in an effort to suck in extra air. Her head fell back and her body shuddered. She came on a hard shout just as his body pressed inside a final time. While her hips rocked, his body jumped and twitched. With his eyes closed, he blew out a breath. As if his arms couldn't hold him, his shoulders fell and his full weight collapsed on top of her.

Except for rubbing her hand in gentle circles over his upper back, neither of them moved. Even after the last whispers of their lovemaking faded, they stayed in each other's arms. The room filled with the faint smell of sex. His harsh breathing hammered into her ear, but he quickly brought his body back under control.

After a few minutes he raised up on shaky elbows. "I should get you keyed up in the office more often," he said with a smile.

"Only if you want to have that conversation with Rod every day."

Smile—gone. Lazy banter stopped. The post-sex relaxation disappeared.

The mood broke that fast.

She immediately regretted raising the issue. They needed to talk about Rod and everything said in that room, but she rushed the timing. That much was obvious from Ben's sudden silence and severe frown.

"I guess I should have waited until the morning to bring this subject up," she said, hoping Ben wouldn't take the out.

He rolled off her and fell onto the mattress next to her. "Since when do you back down from a tough discussion?"

"I prefer being in control of them. Something tells me Rod is in the lead here."

Ben stared at the ceiling. "Thanks to you I'm starting to hate that kid."

Not the response she expected but still appreciated. "I told you."

"When I hired him he wasn't a . . . what did you call him?"

"Pisher." Loser, moron, twit. She had about a hundred names for Rod, each one more profane and nasty than the one before.

"Right. Well, Rod kept his pisher tendencies hidden until you came to the office."

She drew the sheets up to her chin. "Don't blame me. He's a parasite. Not that unusual in the legal world, from what I can tell."

Ben switched his gaze to her. "I'm hoping you're excluding me from that pile."

"Wouldn't let you go down on me if I did."

"I love your mouth." He brushed his thumb over her bottom lip as if to prove his statement.

"Funny but I was going to say the same thing about yours."

Her lower body still tingled, all sensitive and fiery, from his expert attention.

The tension swirling around the room broke. The easy bedroom calm returned.

Ben slipped an arm under her shoulder and pulled her close. "Happy to be of service."

The return to their usual post-sex cuddling eased the frustration running through her. Being there, in his arms, just felt right.

With her head on his chest, Callie fingered the sprinkling of hair on his chest. Working up the courage to talk about Rod and his accusations proved harder than she expected. She had heard every word, seen Ben's face when he walked out of the office. Sure, he covered his questioning frown with a small smile, but she saw the doubts lingering there. In only a few minutes Rod had inflicted some damage. Not enough to kill the sex, but enough to have an impact on everything else.

And suddenly the *everything else* mattered. She didn't want it to, but it did.

"Are we going to pretend it didn't happen?" Her voice came out so soft that she almost didn't recognize it.

"The sex?"

"Oh, no. We are most definitely going to remember that."

He chuckled, his warm breath blowing across her forehead. "I'll take that as a compliment."

"The highest, but I was talking about Rod."

Ben's arms tightened around her. "Is the goal here to kill the mood?"

She couldn't drop this. Suddenly the truth she tried to hide from him weighed down every part of her body. She wanted it out there. They could go through it and, hopefully, get around it.

Her palm rested against his thumping heart. "You can just ask me, you know."

"I already tried."

"At the gun range? Yeah, I know, but this time I'll answer."

"Why?"

She lifted her body and leaned on an elbow. She wanted to watch him, see his reaction. Test if he was the man she believed him to be. "Because the answer that's out there is wrong. So incredibly wrong."

"Tell me what's right."

"I want you to know the truth."

"Then I'll ask again." He curled an arm behind his head, lifting it slightly and bringing his face even with hers. "Why did you leave the FBI?"

"I worked for a jackass—"

"Wait." He closed his eyes for a beat and then opened them again. "Can you not use that term since you use it to refer to me all the time, and I have a feeling I'm not going to want to be associated with this guy in any way."

"You're nothing like him."

"Still."

She refused to get sidetracked with semantics. "He made a pass. Kept making passes. I deflected and ignored. After all, he ranked above me and had all the power. I was brand new and owed most of my career to him."

"This isn't 1950, Callie."

Blame. It hit her like a verbal slap. She expected more from Ben. Hoped for more.

"It is so easy for you to say if you're not the one sitting there," she said through a jaw locked to keep from screaming.

He wove his fingers through hers and drew them to his mouth for a kiss. "You're right. Knee-jerk jackassery. Sorry."

Callie wasn't ready to be soothed, so she pulled her hand away again. "I had dreamed of that job forever. It was my ticket out of Hickville. I didn't excel at school, never even thought about going to law school, which is what most FBI agents end up doing. I hadn't worked my way up through the law enforcement ranks. See, every way into the FBI was closed to me. It was pure luck that I got in. Or so I thought."

"Meaning?"

"The recruiter said he saw something in me."

"I can believe that."

"Then he became my boss. Turned out what he saw in me was an easy lay. A woman who would owe him." She waited for Ben to say something, but he kept listening. "He set me up perfectly. I got a promotion, a nice office. We weren't sleeping together, but everyone—and I mean everyone—thought we were. That was the only excuse anyone could come up with for why I even got in. Must have done it on a mattress or my knees."

"Jesus."

Ben rubbed her back. She doubted he even realized he was doing it, but it did calm the anger building inside her. Rather than fight him, she gave in and allowed her muscles to relax.

"I eventually found out I wasn't alone. There were two women before me. One got promoted and got out of his office. The other saw her career come to a full desk duty stop. Guess you can figure out which one took him up on his sex offers."

"Did he touch you?"

"He tried."

"What's his name?" The bed rocked from the force of Ben's fury.

Here she thought he judged her choices. Instead, he simmered. The rage rolled off him and knocked against her like being hit with a brick. She knew the feeling because it brewed inside her all the time. Some days, she could tamp it down and forget. Most others it rose up like an uncontrolled beast.

It was tempting to have a powerful judge take up her cause, but she had made her choice, good or bad, and refused to be one of those people who turned to rabid power to get her way. No matter how tempting.

That meant easing Ben from his superhuman pissed-off form back to normal. "It doesn't matter now."

"Of course it does. It just happened." Ben shimmied up higher on the stack of pillows behind his head. "When did you leave?"

"Not that long ago."

"Which means this is all still fresh." He switched into boss mode. "We'll get you a hearing and a superstar lawyer and—"

She kissed him to get him to stop. "Thank you."

"For what? I haven't done anything yet."

"Without knowing everything, for not assuming I brought this on myself or deserved it."

"Who the hell said that?"

Most of the people she worked with. Her friends who deserted her, leaving her alone and devastated. "There isn't going to be another hearing."

"Another?"

"The day he went too far, when he tried to take what I wasn't giving for free, I took out my gun and threatened him."

"He was lucky you didn't show off your gun skills and shoot him in the head. I would have been tempted."

"Well, he wasn't all that bright, because he tried again."

Ben's eyebrows shot up. "And that time you did unload on him."

"Right in the upper thigh, as close to his dick as I could get."

Ben didn't smile, but his fierce scowl relaxed. "I'm impressed."

"Well, don't be. The move started a horrific chain reaction. After a hospital stay, he got called in for questioning. To save his own sorry ass, he insisted we'd been having an affair. That I was the scorned woman who went nuts when he decided to stay with his wife over me."

"Fucking jerk."

"Exactly."

"He got in trouble for having sex with a subordinate. No more supervisory positions. Had to undergo some harassment classes."

"And you?"

"Paid administrative leave for six months, followed by a hearing on the improper firing of a firearm. My boss claimed I had tried to kill him and wanted criminal charges filed, but I was able to duck those. The FBI higher-ups didn't believe me, but the prosecutor did."

"But your FBI supervisors eventually realized you were innocent, right?"

That was the part that hurt the most. Everyone abandoned her. Sided with the guy with twenty years' service over her. Neither of the other women wanted to testify, and Callie didn't blame them, but she had expected more from the group she hung out with, drank beers with, and analyzed cases beside.

"My coworkers lined up to talk all about the perks I received. Everybody added two plus two and got thirty."

Ben wiped a hand over his eyes. "This ending is going to suck."

"Unfortunately, yes."

Ben let his hand fell against the mattress. "Say it so I can get furious all over again and then hunt this fucking moron down."

"I took a voluntary discharge. In return I was promised a good recommendation and the destruction of my personnel record. I didn't want the lies to follow me. This might be a city, but in many ways it's a small town. Having so many in the FBI know about me, or who they thought I was, stunk. And, really, I have to take some responsibility for the situation."

"You can't possibly think you should have slept with the guy."

"No, but losing my temper and shooting him was a huge mistake. Up until then I did everything right. Never mouthed off. Bet you can't believe that, huh?"

"It's hard to imagine."

"The FBI is a rules organization. You look a certain way, act a certain way, and don't bring unwanted attention to the workplace. I violated all of those unspoken mandates."

"I can't believe you had to deal with that. That no one stood by you."

"It's not over."

"Why?"

"I'm not independently wealthy. I have to work if I want to eat. That's why Mark's offer saved me. It gave me the chance to pay the mortgage and build my résumé outside of usual government service." Panic over what was ahead swamped her for a second, but she beat it back. "Now I have to figure out how Rod got his weaselly little hands on my file."

"I want to rip his fucking head off."

"I've been saying that about Rod since the day I met him."

"I mean your ex-boss."

Ben's anger fed her. Instead of getting her ramped up and ready for battle, it relieved her of months of pain and frustration. Knowing he believed her based only on her word, sided with her over the FBI and their pencil-necked investigators, took all of the anger balled up inside her and set it free.

"You know what I think?" she asked, ready to move on to a better subject. One that had nothing to do with her former career.

"We should call Mark and get him on this."

That one stopped her. "Since when do you willingly go to Mark looking for help?"

"I'd do it for you."

In that precious moment, her feelings and attraction for Ben came together in a thought both irrational and rational. She was falling for him. Not because of his robe or position. Certainly not because she wanted to land the guy other women wanted to bed. No, her heart grew and pounded because he was a good man, and when he looked at her like that, as if he could forget every responsibility for her, every ache inside her eased. He made the days better. He could take a verbal punch and light her world with his smile.

"I have a better idea," she said.

"We go to Rod's house and drag him out of bed?"

"Last thing I want to see is Rod naked. So, no thanks." She dropped a line of kisses from the dip at the base of Ben's throat to his nipples.

His fingers found her hair and held her there. "Callie?"

"I don't want to talk about the past."

"But I want to help."

"Oh, you do." She slipped lower and kissed his stomach. When it clenched at the touch of her lips, she kissed him again.

"We're not done with this conversation." The last syllable came out as a groan.

"Maybe, but first you're going to get soooo lucky."

Chapter Seventeen

Ben's good mood shattered early the next morning. Stepping out to get the paper counted as a pretty mundane activity, but not when a stalker roamed free and could come right up to the door to drop off a new threatening note.

Sitting on Callie's bar stool in the kitchen, Ben stared at the plain white envelope. Wished he had gone right to the shower and skipped his usual routine of checking the news. Mostly he regretted dragging Callie into the middle of this mess. All he wanted was for this sick bastard to make a move and get caught or go away. The middle ground, never knowing when or how the potential lunatic would make contact again, made Ben second-guess every move. Which Ben assumed was exactly the goal. Whoever this guy was, he toyed with them on purpose.

Ben glanced down again and saw his name scrawled across the front. He had seen the handwriting only once before but didn't need repetition to recognize it. The memory of that script was imprinted on his brain.

But what really bothered him was the location of this one. Callie's house.

Thanks to him, she wasn't safe.

"Damn it."

"I'd think a night of hot sex would put you in a good

mood." Callie walked in wearing nothing but her robe and headed straight for the coffeemaker. "Guess not."

"I was fine until ten seconds ago."

"What happened . . . ?" She turned around with a mug in one hand and the pot in the other. Her gaze bounced from his face to the counter. "Oh, shit."

"Different swearword but same conclusion."

She slowly lowered her arms, abandoning both forms of caffeine in favor of joining him in staring at the envelope. "Where was it?"

"Out front. On top of the paper."

"My paper comes right before six."

"Yeah, I know."

"That means the stalker, or whoever delivered on behalf of the stalker, came by within the last half hour."

"Figured that out, too." Ben thought about running around the neighborhood trying to find the guy, but he knew it wouldn't do any good. Condominiums lined the block. Anyone looking to hide would have about a thousand places to do it.

"Makes me sorry I didn't wake up earlier."

That made one of them. The idea of Callie running into the stalker unarmed and lazy from sleep chilled him. "I guess it's too much to hope that you have surveillance cameras hidden around this place."

"I could barely afford the building with the underground garage. The high-security one was out." She tapped her fingernails against the counter. "Mark is going to shit over this."

"Not if we don't tell him."

"We can do that."

Ben waited for the punch line. "Okay."

"But only if you have some big ol' desire to get killed."

"Not really."

"Then the note goes to Mark."

Ben didn't bother fighting her on this; he'd never win, and wasting time didn't strike him as particularly prudent at the moment. The stalker was already two steps ahead.

"Be warned, I'm going to open it." When he picked it up she slapped his hand. "Come on, Callie. Not this again."

"Exercise some of that impressive patience of yours." She opened the cabinet under her sink and took out a pair of yellow plastic gloves. The things were big enough to cover her skin up to her elbows. Once they were on, she held her hands up like a surgeon preparing for an operation. "There."

"Are you kidding with those?"

"They're practical."

"Do you get a lot of forensic emergencies in your house?"

"I use them to clean. These are new." She flipped her hands around. "Never been used."

"Got it."

"I doubt that." She grabbed a steak knife out of the drawer. "You know, for a judge you aren't all that astute about forensics."

Because he had already done the assessment in his head. "It's a cheap envelope you could buy anywhere."

"So?"

"We won't find any fingerprints or identifying marks."

"And you know this how?" She picked the paper up by the edge and cut open the top seal. Nothing fell out or exploded.

That was a triumph.

"I read the report from the last time around," he said.

"The stalker could have gotten sloppy. For your information, that's how we catch the bad guys. They make a dumb mistake and we swoop." She dumped the note onto the counter.

"We both know that's not true with this guy."

"Well, he certainly hasn't gotten any more chatty." They

both stared at the writing. "What does '*Time to pay*' mean?" she asked.

"Seems kind of obvious to me."

She drummed her fingers again. With the gloves on, the sound amounted to a dull thud. "Is it too much to hope you owe someone money? Someone with a strange sense of humor and significant boundary issues."

"I wish it were that easy." Ben pushed away from the counter. "I think we can agree that my stalker isn't a fan and wants revenge for something."

Looking at the note was only going to piss him off. He knew it would only be a minute or two before the hammering started in his head. Everything about this situation gave him a headache.

"You know what's next, right?" She peeled off the gloves and threw them in the sink. "I'll give you one guess and it starts with an M."

"Right. We go find my badass brother." Ben hated when that turned out to be the answer.

"And then we watch him stomp around, swearing like a madman." Callie did a quick impression of his brother's storming. "Can't hear enough of that. If I'm really lucky he'll blame me for not staying awake all night staring through my peephole."

"He's going to demand I take a vacation. That will set off another round of arguing and . . . what?"

She bit her lower lip. "Well."

That headache came on full force, thumping and pounding until Ben could barely hear. "Not you, too."

"This person is following you. Knows your habits and where you're sleeping, which you have to admit is disconcerting. This isn't a time for a testosterone rush or to lead with your overpumped ego."

"My what?"

"You need to be smart."

"I generally am."

"You're a stubborn bonehead. That's not the same thing."

Ben glanced at the clock on the wall behind her. "On that note, we need to get to work."

"If I didn't know better I'd say you were ignoring me."

"That doesn't sound like me."

An hour later, Callie and Ben sat next to each other on one side of Emma's small conference room table. Emma and Mark picked the other. From what Callie could tell, Mark turned out to be even less charming and understanding than predicted. He had bagged the note and called his office for a forensic team to show up at her house. Two seconds after that he launched into his lecture on how Ben needed to leave town, which Ben promptly ignored in his usual "me can stop bullet with my hand" way.

Callie wished they'd all disappear. She wanted to crawl back into bed with Ben and forget all about the notes and Mark's foul mood and Emma's concerned frown. She wasn't afraid, because she didn't really believe any of this was about her. The note was a message for Ben. But a woman should be able to have a little postcoital downtime.

Emma picked up the baggie with her perfectly manicured fingers. She looked at both sides of the envelope through the plastic. "Anyone notice anything unusual about these threats?"

Ben glanced at the note and then looked away just as fast. "Other than the fact they're all aimed at me."

"I'm talking about the wording. The comments are like a dare. Almost childish," Emma said.

"Have any five-year-olds who might be carrying a grudge?"

Callie asked, hoping to lighten the mood. Only Ben smiled. Emma was too busy studying the few pieces of evidence to respond.

Mark snapped his cell phone shut. "This is serious. Let's stay focused."

Callie ignored the brief dressing-down. Long or short, Mark was famous for them. Didn't make them any less annoying. Just meant they weren't a surprise when they came at you with the force of machine-gun fire.

Even though she planned to ignore Mark, she wasn't ready to let Emma's insight drop. "This guy, toddler or not, is hard to follow."

Mark looked at his cell when it vibrated against the tabletop but didn't get it. "Meaning?"

"The strategy here is incomprehensible." Callie decided to lay out the concerns spinning around in her mind. "The guy goes from blowing things up to playground taunts. I agree with Emma. The age or maturity level seems wrong. It's as if he's in a state of arrested development. I half expect the next note to be written in crayon."

"Exactly," Emma said. "This is strangely personal but not particularly adult in execution."

Mark shook his head. "But the bombing had professional overtones and the guy never leaves any forensics behind. That suggests a high level of competence. Information about bomb making is available to anyone with the Internet and a wallet, but putting it all together takes time and focus."

"Yet his reactions are more like those a teen would have. Running around behind people leaving cryptic notes. If he's smart and violent, why change strategy and leave threats?" The more she spoke, the more Callie sensed she was right. They were not looking for an unhinged radical or a person with a record. This was someone with a vendetta but limited experience with actual warfare. "Why take the risk if you know how to build a bomb that gets the job done from a distance? Why crawl right up close and risk detection?"

Mark slipped a pen out of his inside jacket pocket and grabbed for a yellow legal pad. "Now put all of those thoughts together. What do they suggest to you?"

The facts came back to the same place for Callie. "The person is already close to Ben. He's someone—and I do think it's a he—with a working knowledge of the legal system and access to the same."

"You mean someone at the courthouse? One of our colleagues?" Ben asked, suddenly interested in the conversation playing out in front of him.

About time.

"I'm thinking a lawyer or a person who studies the law. Maybe a guy who thinks he's smarter than everyone else and can't possibly get caught." Like a certain little pisher she knew and despised.

"We're going through your old cases." Mark pointed his pen at Ben and Emma. "Both of you. We're looking for anyone who could be holding on to anger and searching for a way to get even. That includes your time on the bench and when you practiced."

"But up until now you've been focusing on parties to the case, correct? If Callie is right, you need to add in the legal community as well." Emma blew out a breath. "That's a long list. It's also pretty upsetting to think that someone who appears before us could act like this. I just don't understand why that would be."

"Are you including Ben's time hearing family law cases?" Callie dipped her toe into the nosy end of the pool. Scott's comments on the issue had refused to leave her head. She had intended to ask Ben but then Rod walked in . . . and the sex. Mark and Emma likely knew the truth, but Callie didn't want to take the risk and drag a private issue into the room.

Emma jumped in her seat. "You think a divorcing parent is doing this? Maybe one who is also a lawyer? Several of them come through here, unfortunately. Lawyers are notorious for broken marriages."

Callie shrugged in what she hoped was a "no big deal" way, but she did note Emma's odd reaction. "Just want to be thorough."

If Ben was concerned about something from his family law days, he sure didn't show it. He slumped in his chair slipping into what looked like a boredom coma.

"Still nothing on Jenner?" Ben asked.

Mark's gaze darted to Emma. After her slight nod, Mark continued. "When questioned Jenner took great satisfaction in telling us how Emma should be in danger for what she said about him and how someone was going to take her out. Not him, of course. He's a law-abiding citizen who got framed by the police and ruined by Emma, in case you hadn't heard."

Ben scoffed. "Sounds as if the sociopath hasn't changed much in prison. Still blaming everyone else for the fact he got caught."

"He also wanted us to know that he saw the news and knew about the bombing. Went on to assure us that if he had built something to try to kill Emma it wouldn't have missed her," Mark said.

"Charming. I can see why his wife sticks by him. He's quite the prize." Callie knew about Jenner only from what she had read in the paper. That was enough to make her hate him and worry for Emma's safety.

"Some women can't figure out when to let go." Emma's statement earned a rough glance from Mark, but if she saw it she went out of her way to ignore it.

Callie wondered if Emma was thinking about her own circumstance. Now that Callie knew about Emma's feelings for Mark, Callie spent a lot of time trying to figure out why they weren't together.

"What is he waiting for?" Ben asked. "You'd think he would have made a move by now."

If she were into eye rolling, Callie would have done it right then. "You'd rather this Jenner monster go ahead and attack now?"

Ben looked ready to engage in an eye move of his own. "No. I'm wondering why he doesn't."

"I have a theory." She almost hated to mention it because it would send Mark flying off on another tangent. One that could result in her being moved to protective custody.

"What is it?" Mark asked.

Callie chose her words carefully. There was enough tension pressing on the room without her adding a new level of panic. "What if this isn't about Emma or Jenner at all? Let's go back to the proposition that this is an inside job by someone who works with Ben, sees Ben every day, and is friendly with him in a way that Ben would never expect a problem."

Mark nodded. "I'm with you so far."

"What if that friendliness hides hatred?" She swallowed. "What if Ben is the primary target but not the intended victim?"

"Wait, I'm confused. You still think it's me?" Emma shook her head. "I know that was the original theory, but I don't see it. I don't have anything to do with your condo. I don't even know where it is. It doesn't make sense that the stalker would come after me there?"

They all started talking at once. Make that yelling. Ben stuck to few words, not that Callie could actually hear them. Not with everyone rushing to shoot down her theory.

"Uh, hello?" When the low rumble continued, Callie whistled.

Three pairs of stunned eyes stared at her.

Ben whistled back. "Nicely done."

"I have skills. And if you'd all shut up for two seconds, I can show them to you." She let the scolding hang out there for a second. "I think the point is to test Ben. To keep him off balance and punish him for something we haven't figured out yet. But the stalker has found a means to hurt him that has the potential to torture Ben the most."

Understanding settled on Mark's face. Those intelligent eyes sparked to life. "By going after the women in his life."

Callie wasn't a fan of being lumped into categories, but that one was okay with her. "Exactly."

Ben made a "T" with his hands. "Stop a second."

Now that everyone listened to her, Callie wanted to push forward. "What's wrong with you?"

Ben scratched the back of his head. "Well, honestly, I'm lost."

Mark took over. "The stalker went after Emma because he thought she was your girlfriend. The bomb. Her guard. All attacks direct to Emma to either hurt her or scare her. Then the rumors started floating around about you and Callie."

"And the threats switched." Callie warmed to the theory the more they dug around in it. "We haven't experienced the personal attacks since. There is a detachment now, as if the stalker is trying to figure out what I mean to you. He's modifying his plans and changing his aim."

Ben's mouth dropped open. "You're the target."

"Technically you're still the target," Callie said.

Ben stood up. Anger pulled at every inch of his stiff body as he rounded on Mark. "Pull her off the case. Now."

"Wrong." Callie tugged on Ben's arm to get him to sit down.

"If you are in danger because of me"—he looked between

both women—"either of you, then I want you both out of here, as far away from me as possible."

Ben shifted into protective mode. He was using his best judge voice and making demands that would affect her life and potentially destroy her last chance at having a career. Cute and kind of endearing in a way, but not going to happen.

"This isn't your decision, Ben. Just because we're sleeping together doesn't mean you get to dictate to me."

Ben dropped back into his chair. "Is now the time for that discussion?"

"Stop it," Emma said in the nasty voice she had once used on Jenner. "We are grown women. We can make our own decisions."

Callie did not see that one coming. She almost spit when Emma jumped to the defense.

"You are the same women who are in danger because of me." Ben's eyes pleaded with his brother to step in. "Mark, help me here."

Instead of joining Ben in panic mode, Mark started scribbling on the pad in front of him. "We could spin this to our advantage."

"How?" Emma asked, cutting off whatever Ben was about to say.

"Callie is a trained operative. We can use her to draw out this guy."

Callie decided right then that Mark could yell all he liked. The guy knew when something had to be done and did it. "Perfect."

"No fucking way." Ben practically growled the words. "And that's final."

"It's a good solution, Ben. I'll come up with a plan that keeps her safe. My men can—"

Ben refused to listen. He shook his head. Even pounded on the table with his fist. "It's too damned dangerous."

Rather than offending her, the fierce show of concern impressed her. Ben wasn't questioning her skills. He was worried about her safety.

That distinction was the only reason she didn't kick him in the balls. "I carry a gun and know how to shoot it."

"That will be a great comfort when I'm calling your next of kin."

"I don't have anyone to call."

Her flip response made Ben's jaw tighten even more. "That's your argument to me?" he asked.

The vein in Ben's forehead pumped hard enough for Callie to see it. She thought her joke would slow him down. Instead, his anger kicked up a notch . . . or twelve.

Mark tapped his pen against his notepad. "Okay, let's settle down."

"If the gossip is the key, then our pool of suspects might have gotten smaller. That's a matter of internal politics," Callie said, hoping to get the conversation off her and onto a plan of action. "My name isn't in the paper. Ben and I haven't gone out in public together. Emma's right. This is someone who knows where I live, what hours you two keep, and how to get around the courthouse's security system. That screams inside job."

Mark stared at Emma. "Scott. He delivered the first note."

"That would be kind of a stupid thing to do if he were the stalker, wouldn't it?" Emma asked.

Callie hated to break the sisterhood bond she had going on with Emma, but . . . "Or brilliant. It's not as if he's at the top of the suspect list right now."

Ben threw Emma an apologetic half smile. "I do see him every day. He comes over and talks with Callie."

Callie knew Ben wasn't going to like it, but she had to say

it anyway. "Well, if Scott is on the list you need to put Rod on there, too."

Ben sighed in that condescending way only Ben could do. "Hating the kid doesn't make him a suspect."

Ben could engage in heavy breathing for all Callie cared. She refused to back down on this. "He's been digging into my background. Knows all about what happened to me at the FBI."

Mark's pen stopped moving. "He what?"

Callie winced inside and hoped it didn't show on her face. "Yeah, I meant to tell you about that."

"That's what your reports are for, Callie. This is exactly the kind of information that needs to cross my desk as soon as you have it."

"It just happened."

"I'll back her up on that," Ben said.

"Then it looks as if I have two new suspects." Mark stood up. "I'll get back to you as soon as I have more intel and a plan to put Callie out in the open to flush the stalker out."

"That is not going to happen." Ben rose to his feet and shot his brother an unreadable look. "I need to talk with you outside."

As if Callie didn't know what that subject would be. "No."

"You're telling me I can't have a conversation with my brother?" Ben's chilly tone stopped all movement in the room.

She ignored the bluster. "I think if you want to argue with someone about this, it should be me."

Mark let out a harsh chuckle. "Listen to your girlfriend."

Callie didn't hear anything after that. She was too busy dealing with the emotional punch of the word and the fact Ben didn't deny it.

Chapter Eighteen

"Ben is going to hate this." Emma offered that insight in the dark of her bedroom as she curled up on Mark's bare chest the next evening.

Their lives had fallen into a comfortable pattern. Eat, sleep, sex. Some women might find that hollow. She savored the step forward. It wasn't empty like before when he'd show up now and then, restless and ready to burn off energy by making love to her until her bones ached. That was their usual pattern. Now, with him by her side each day, their talk consisted of more than a few rushed conversations with the lights off.

With this assignment, Mark came to her each night worried about the threats, yes, but also talking about the day and news and other mundane nonsense couples customarily shared. It was so normal. Or as close to it as they had ever gotten.

"I'll worry about his happiness later. Right now I'm focused on his stalker and his safety. On Callie's safety. Hell, on your safety." Mark tucked one arm under his head, lifting his upper body higher on the pillow. "I'll be satisfied when this is all settled and I can sleep more than two hours at a time."

"When Ben finds out you convinced the administrative

judge to hold a reception announcing this fake new judge's assistant program as a way to lure lawyers and put Callie on display, he will have a brain aneurysm."

"Callie agreed with my plan."

"Not that you gave her a choice." Emma used her finger to trace the arrow of dark hair from Mark's chest down his stomach to the top of the sheet and back up again. "Temporary or not, you are her boss."

"She could have left the job."

"She would never do that. She's a good soldier."

Mark made a rough noise between a cough and a snort. "Not always."

Emma thought about the way Callie stood up to Ben over and over again. "Probably not, but you have to admit that she's desperate to keep Ben safe."

"We all are."

"She's good for him."

"Hmmm."

"What does that mean?"

"I didn't say anything."

Emma leaned up to get a better look at the facial expression behind that ominous half grunt. "But you disagree with me about Callie."

Mark drew the rumpled sheet down off her shoulder, exposing her breast to his seeking thumb. "She's in love with him."

The fact Mark picked up on a bit of personal information about other people shocked Emma. He missed every signal she threw him, but somehow he saw the caring and devotion behind Callie's smartass comments. Interesting.

Emma didn't know if she should praise the progress or be furious that it took him this long to acquire the basic skill of reading emotions. "Let me just say wow."

"You didn't know that?" His fingers tickled and caressed. "I thought you were the astute one of us."

"I saw it. I'm stunned you did. From what I can tell, Ben hasn't figured it out. It's not clear the truth has even hit Callie yet."

Emma hoped Callie and Ben would stop hiding behind the bickering soon. They were good for each other. He needed someone to love him for him, protect him, and not bend to his considerable will. Callie wasn't the woman Emma would have picked for Ben, but seeing them together the match made sense. Callie was perfect for Ben in every way. Together, they'd smooth out each other's rough spots.

"It's my job to notice things," Mark said.

"But this is emotional. About feelings and fancy romantic things. Honestly, not your strong suit."

His intense stare moved from her nipple to her face. "I do have a heart, you know."

She had spent decades believing that. "Of course."

"I understand women have needs and want to hear certain words. They expect promises and half the time don't care if there's no follow-through so long as the vow is made. Maybe I suck at showing all of that, but I do get it. You of all people should know that."

She kissed him then not for her but because he seemed to crave closeness, and she wasn't about to allow the opportunity to let him feel her love race by without grabbing it. She showed him with her mouth as it passed over his, soft and smooth at first and then strong and sure. Nibbling bites against his bottom lip. The sweep of her tongue when his mouth fell open. She kissed him with all the love bottled up inside her and felt his heart kick in faster in response.

When she broke off, he touched his nose to hers in a move so gentle tears threatened at the back of her eyes.

He palmed her breast. "If you're trying to change the

subject, it's working." His voice rumbled against her skin as he spoke.

Such a temptation. She thought about ending all civilized conversation right there. Rolling across the bed appealed to her, but she didn't want to lose the intimacy of sharing thoughts. Not when they burned inside her as if she had to get them out.

"Why is it bad for Callie to love Ben?"

Mark pressed a short kiss on the end of Emma's breast. "I like her."

She cradled his head against her. "Aren't those two ideas incompatible?"

"Not that I can see."

"If they end up together, you get Callie in the family."

"She's had a rough time. Had some unfair breaks." He kissed his way along Emma's throat as his lips made a trail up to her mouth. "I don't want to see her upset on a personal level."

"That's good to hear." What little she could comprehend. Mark's kisses wiped out her will to talk. To understand anything but the joy of being with him.

He shifted until she sprawled on her back with him hovering above her. From this position, he leaned in, letting his lips brush over the sensitive skin of her breasts.

She felt her eyes cross from the pleasure. "And?"

He lifted his head and searched her face with his heated gaze. "You want to talk about this now?"

"You started this with your half answers."

Being a master at multitasking, he returned to her body, licking her nipple and watching it pucker in response. "On a professional level this assignment is a test of sorts for Callie. She's smart and isn't afraid to give her opinion. She can do the work and do it well. I'd like to have her on my team, but that's going to be impossible after the fallout."

Emma struggled to keep up with the conversation even as the sensual torment threatened to overwhelm her ability to reason. "From?"

"The breakup."

The harsh finality of the words broke through. Her hands slid off his shoulders and fell to the bed instead of wandering down his body and under the sheet tenting him. "What?"

"Forget it."

She pinched his shoulder. "Talk to me."

"Hey!"

"How did you get from where they are now to being over?"

"No nails. Not that way."

"I'm serious. Why do you think that?"

Mark blinked a few times. "Because Ben won't love her back."

"What?"

"And she'll leave. I can't blame her, but it would still make working together awkward."

Emma pushed against Mark's shoulder until he leaned back and let her sit up. "You're acting as if this is all inevitable."

"It is."

His pure confidence on this question confused her. "Because?"

"Ben won't fall for her. His head will stop him. On the surface, maybe he'll toy with the idea. But as a forever-after thing? I can't see it."

"I thought you liked Callie."

"I do. I even agree she'd be good for him long term. Problem is he's not a long-term guy."

The words slashed through Emma. "You mean *you're* not a long-term guy."

Mark's mouth flattened even more. "I'm talking about Ben."

"You're talking about your relationship fears and imputing them to Ben. You are two very different people."

Mark's face closed up, as if on the verge of explosion. "I am not afraid."

She noticed that was the only part of her speech that bothered him. "Right. It's worse than that. You're terrified."

He stopped touching her. His back inched higher on the headboard as the physical and emotional space yawning between them increased. "What the fuck is that supposed to mean?"

"You're actually going to sit here, in my bed, and ask me that question?"

"I have a right to, don't you think?"

She grabbed the sheet and pulled it up to her breasts. Awkward and leaning half on her side, she refused to lie back down and be quiet. One thing she learned from Callie was that there were times when a woman needed to speak up. Emma knew her opportunity had come and passed several times over the years as Mark waded in and out of her life. There were a thousand points where she could have said no. Not granted easy access to her house or her body. In this instance, she wanted to grab him and hold on. Make him stake a claim.

"Mark, what do you think we've been doing all of these years?"

"Living."

"Existing." She hesitated, letting the reality sink in.

"Emma, I—"

"Why do you think I walked out on my engagement?" She saw the sarcastic comment coming and put on the brakes before he could say something that made her want to smack him. "And you better not say because of Ben or I will throw you out the window, I swear I will."

"Your fiancé was the wrong guy. You finally saw that. If you had asked me, I could have told you that from the beginning."

"Why didn't you tell me?" What she really wanted to know was why he refused to fight for her. Did the idea of her sleeping with another man really not eat at him? When it came to thinking of him with anyone else, she grew homicidal.

"It wasn't my decision."

She closed her eyes and counted to ten to keep from shouting. "You can't be this clueless."

Confusion warred with fury in Mark's eyes. "What do you want me to say?"

"How about something that doesn't piss me off?"

His mouth dropped open. "What's gotten into you?"

Backbone. The fear of losing him, of having him walk out and find someone else, no longer scared her as much as the idea of moving backward. She loved that he came to her house during the day, and without the emotional protection of darkness, like he belonged there. That he shared moments of his work with her. That he finally gave her hours beyond those filled with great sex.

She stood up with the sheet wrapped around her body. With her skin still warm from his knowing touch, she threw down a challenge she never planned to issue. "I handed back the ring to another man because I love you. I've always loved you. Not Ben. Not any other man. Just you."

Mark blinked but didn't give her anything else. Not a smile, not a frown. He just sat there staring at her as if he had no idea what to say or do.

Yeah, clueless.

She kept talking, hoping the sheer force of her desire

would win him over. "I can't live in neutral anymore. I want you here, with me, all the time. Sure, it won't be easy for you—"

"Emma, you know I can't. No matter how much I want it, it's impossible."

Grief pounded her from every direction. She stayed on her feet but only as a matter of pure will. "Why?"

"I'm not built that way." A note of longing sounded in his voice as he reached out a hand toward her. "Come back to bed."

She was falling apart, and he sat there as thick and frustrating as ever. "You are a coward."

His arm dropped. "What did you say?"

"You heard me."

The switch from bedroom Mark to secret agent Mark happened that fast. First, clenched muscles. Then the locked jaw.

"Just because Callie talks like that and engages in name-calling, that doesn't mean I'll tolerate it from you."

Waves of unending rage knocked the sadness right out of Emma. Heat flushed through every pore. '*Tolerate?*' I am a goddamn judge. A smart, capable, independent woman."

"I've always thought so, but how you're acting now . . ." He shook his head. "I don't get it."

"What you don't understand is that there is a woman standing in front of you who would do anything for you. Would wait until you grew up enough to love her back. Would sit here and take whatever you could give so long as you kept trying to give more."

The harsh lines at the corners of his eyes eased. "I feel the same way about you. You have to know that."

It was as close to a declaration of love as she would ever get.

And it wasn't good enough.

"That's where you're wrong, Mark. You will never give me the one thing I desperately need."

He had the nerve to look confused. "Which is?"

"You."

It was so simple and so damned difficult at the same time. She knew his heart belonged to her, but the constant uncertainty aged her in ways she never expected. Her belief in completing a journey of forever-after with him had taken a beating. Maybe it was naïve, but she wanted the chance at the fairy-tale dream. Kids, house, security—all of it.

But she could only do so much on her own.

A shocked silence filled the bedroom for almost a minute. Emma knew because she counted the seconds, at the turn of each one hoping he would open up and at least promise to try.

"There's no one but you. Ever," he said in a harsh whisper.

There was a time when that would have been good enough. It would have meant everything as she waited between visits. Now they deserved something bigger.

"And there's no one for me but you," she said, feeling the words with every cell inside her.

"Why can't you let that be good enough for now?"

The question came from a genuine place, filled with angst and a gruff tone that told her his mind refused to understand what was happening. But she knew.

"Because your idea of *now* never changes. You won't deal in a future, and that's what I want for us." With her heart crumbling, she leaned down and kissed him on the forehead.

When she tried to stand up again, he held her by the wrist and kept her close. "Don't do this."

"You know where to find me and what you need to say."

Pain showed on every line of his face. "I can't."

She blocked out his denial and his pleading. "Until then, you sleep downstairs."

"You're punishing me for not saying what you want."

"I'm doing what I've always done. Loving you and hoping you'll be brave enough to love me back."

Chapter Nineteen

Three days later Ben slipped on his silver dress tie and crossed the ends, pulling tight enough to pop his head off. He took his anger out on the silk. He wanted to unleash it on his brother.

Mark's mood had changed from dark to oppressive over the past few days. He dropped the bomb about the courthouse reception he had set up—the same one where Callie would be in danger every single second—and dared Ben to argue. Emma refused to talk. Mark refused to talk. Ben knew that meant one thing. That something very bad had happened between them. Something that threw Mark off stride, which is what terrified Ben the most.

Mark and Emma would work it out, whatever "it" was, but Callie's safety couldn't depend on Mark getting his head clear again. She needed Mark's full concentration. Every ounce of skill and every bit of experience earned over the years came down to this job. Callie's safety depended on it. Having Mark kick around like a lovesick teen didn't exactly engender a lot of trust.

"Are you done pouting?" Callie walked into her bedroom and stood behind Ben with her hands on her impressive hips.

A deep purple dress skimmed over her body, ending about

an inch above her knees. The color gave her cheeks a healthy pink glow. The thin straps holding the material on her shoulders showed off her toned arms and creamy shoulders.

And that neck. Exposed by the upsweep of her hair, long and lean and begging for his teeth to mark her as his. He wanted to peel the material off her. Let it fall to the floor at her feet. See what sexy tiny scraps of underwear she wore underneath . . . if any.

He settled for acting pissed off instead. "Judges don't pout."

"What would you call it?"

He concentrated on the tie. Looking at her would only distract him. "Worry."

She slipped her arms around his shoulders and let her fingers dangle right where he tried to work. Even with the temptation of her soft skin and sexy bedroom eyes, he tried to focus on the image of his hands in the mirror. To ignore the light scent of ginger that hovered around her and enveloped them both.

When he finished and lifted his hands, the lopsided knot resembled something a fifth grader might do. Getting dressed proved to be one more skill he lost around her. Rational thought and common sense being the two main others.

"Here, let me." She turned him to face her.

He wanted to resist, but saying no to her about anything grew harder each day. When they caught the stalker and life at the courthouse settled back into a manageable routine, she would leave. That reality burrowed into his head until it shook him.

"It looked fine," he grumbled.

She undid his pathetic excuse for handiwork. "If you were going to a Halloween party as a kid dressed in his daddy's suit, maybe."

Her knuckles brushed against the hollow of his throat.

With each pass, his body warmed and tightened. That's all it took these days—a knowing look, the lingering touch of her hand anywhere on his bare skin. His lower half stayed in the locked and loaded position at all times around her.

Hell, he hadn't had this many erections since high school. Proved that being a lawyer didn't have to suck the sexual life out of a guy. Good to know.

Make that great; however, they still had a problem. She would leave and soon. The courthouse sheriff, the administrative judge, the police, Mark—every able-bodied law enforcement person in the metro area on the case wanted it brought to closure. Many offices aimed significant resources at getting the stalker's identity and then putting him in jail.

All good things except for the part where his time with Callie would wind down with a surety that made him want to punch on the brakes. Hell, he hadn't even been in his own bed in more than a week. Suddenly his life revolved around Callie. He refused to let the stalker matter, but Callie definitely did.

The answer to the problem managed to be simple and difficult at the same time: the dating wouldn't stop. He'd ask her to stick with him even as her work commitments took her somewhere else. They'd find time in the evenings, on weekends, between work travel and personal issues. The important thing was for her to stay in his life.

She snapped her fingers in front of his face. "Ben? Come back to me."

He shook his head to clear out the image of him and Callie going on a weekend getaway to a place without the news and stalkers and courthouses and anything else that would get in the way of keeping them naked. "Excuse me?"

"No." She laughed as she said it.

"What?"

She pressed her palms against his cheeks. "You're not excused."

Her amusement caused the ramping up inside of him to unwind again. "Any reason in particular?"

"Well, Mr. Hoity, there's the part where you refuse to trust me."

Her perception sobered him. "That's not true."

She wrapped her arms around his neck. "Everything is going to be okay tonight. I promise."

He wanted to stay focused, but her sweet smile lured him in. Hands on her hips, he pulled her in close, letting her feel the attraction surging through him. "You can't be sure of that."

"I know I can shoot and kick when I have to."

He peeked down the scooped neck of the material and saw the inviting tops of her breasts. "In this dress?"

"You like it?"

"There isn't a man alive who wouldn't. I think you know that and that's why you wore it." No question she chose it to drive him fucking insane. Standing across from her in the courthouse lobby during the party, watching her hips swing and her toned legs move in perfect precision, would make every minute pass like a decade. She knew it and planned to torture him with it.

"I picked it because I wanted to see you drag it off of me."

"Sounds good to me." His hands found the zipper and started tugging.

She swatted at him. "Not now. After."

He tried one more shot at being reasonable. Even though Callie had developed an immunity to the strategy, he couldn't let the matter drop. Not yet. "I don't want you to do this."

"I'll be fine. Now shut that pretty mouth of yours and kiss me." She threw him off with her wistful smile.

"Why?"

"You need a reason?"

"No."

"Good answer."

She lifted her mouth to his and planted a long, wandering kiss on his lips. One that took his breath and started the countdown to clothes on the floor.

Just as the fire flared, she dropped her head on his shoulder. "Man, you're good at that."

"We could stay and see where this goes."

"Or we can go and see this other part to the end."

The end. Just the word he didn't want to hear.

"Do we all understand the plan?" Mark asked at the small gathering around the sofa in Ben's office.

Mark insisted they all arrive an hour before the reception to go over details. On his fourth run-through, Callie started dozing off. She could only hear a plan so many times before her internal radio switched on.

Having worked cases, she knew things rarely went as projected. Her goal was to stay alive and make sure Ben stayed that way, too. If she got a glass of champagne and caught a stalker out there, well, those would just be bonuses.

Emma nodded in response to Mark's latest rehash. She stood by the door, her eyes downcast, looking ready to bolt.

Callie hoped to maneuver Emma into a quiet corner later and see what was wrong. Her face looked drawn, and the sparkle in her eyes, the one that appeared whenever she saw Mark, had been extinguished. They walked in like robots earlier, side by side, not touching or talking. They had taken serious steps not to look at each other since. Only ten feet separated the two, but Callie had a feeling she could put the entire courthouse between them when it came to their emotional divide.

"Got it," Ben said from beside her on the couch. "We're good."

As far as Callie was concerned he certainly ranked better than good. His black suit highlighted his muscular frame. In a robe, a suit, or even naked, the man looked mighty fine. Being seen on his arm wouldn't be a hardship. Well, it would in terms of the gossip grind. People already believed they slept together. Tonight, when she walked in as his date, they would know what they only now assume. Mail loops would jump to life. The stares and whispers would overwhelm on Monday.

She wasn't sure she even cared anymore. Spending days together taught her to respect and appreciate him. The laughter, the sex, the closeness gave way to something else. Like it or not, she was falling for him. The deep and stupid type of falling. Where the initial physical attraction struck from out of nowhere, this love snuck up quiet and soft. She tried to block it, even joke it away as a by-product of a great time in bed. None of that got the job done. Ben had worked his way into her head and her heart, finding a home there, and now refused to budge.

Ben leaned over and whispered, "You okay? You don't have to do this."

"Yes, she does." Mark's stern tone begged for a fight. The way his hands curled into fists, he was ready to go.

"I wasn't talking to you," Ben said in an equally rough voice.

Callie was not about to engage in any male silliness. Not when both men looked so nice and proper in their dressy business suits. "I'm set."

Mark nodded. "Then let me catch you all up on the Rod and Scott situations."

Callie looked around the room. "There are situations?"

"Is this necessary?" Emma asked.

"If you want to stay alive it is." Mark didn't even glance in Emma's direction as he spoke. "I have men posted around the party. Two are with the food service folks. Two will be stationed in the crowd. The sheriff has his men on alert."

"What does this have to do with the clerks?" Ben adjusted his sleeve as his gaze traveled between Emma and his brother.

Callie gave Ben credit for sensing the tension. It descended on the room until it choked her. Even though he claimed to "get" most things, she doubted he truly understood what happened. She sure as hell didn't. A relationship explosion of some sort was her guess.

Mark stood behind one of the chairs, tapping his pen against the cloth. "Rod has a degree in science."

"So?" Ben asked.

"Wouldn't be hard for him to build a bomb or oversee it being done."

Callie thought this would be the perfect place for the eye roll, only it didn't really go with her dress, so she refrained. "Even I have to say that's a tenuous link, and I hate that kid. He's a pompous ass. Being able to handle beakers doesn't turn him into a crazed attacker."

"Well, the feeling is mutual." The pen disappeared into Mark's jacket pocket and out came a small notepad. He flipped through the pages. "From our courthouse sources it's clear Rod is making a stink about you. He hasn't mentioned the FBI, but he has made other nasty comments. Also has quite the e-mail campaign going, and some of the websites he's searched are questionable. I'd read you this list but it'd scare the hell out of you."

"What does that mean?" Ben asked.

"The information he would need for the bomb, to go around undetected on a stalking campaign, it's all on there."

"I told you that kid was a shit." Pisher no longer seemed strong enough, so Callie changed nicknames for him.

"He's been investigating dangerous subjects—all of them perfect for getting rid of people he didn't like."

Ben leaned forward with his elbows balanced on his knees. "Doesn't make sense. Why the grudge against me? I've never been anything but decent to him. Other than the Callie situation, we've gotten along fine."

One thing Callie did know. Men are idiots. "I'm a situation now?"

Ben smiled. "You know what I mean."

Mark snapped the notebook shut. "We're still digging on that one."

"And Scott?" Emma asked. Her gaze skipped around the room before finally landing on Mark. "Are you still on a rampage about him?"

Callie decided to back Emma up on this one since the vein on Mark's forehead looked ready to pop. "I have to admit that I don't see it."

"Both of you ladies have a soft spot for Scott." Marked hitched his chin in his brother's direction. "But he has a history with Ben."

Ben froze. "He does?"

"Ben presided over Scott's parents' divorce." From his curled lower lip to the clipped tone, Mark was almost smug as he dropped that one.

Emma gave a little snort. "That is not news."

Callie felt as if she kept running toward the bus, but it just moved farther away. These three had shared so much that she got cast in the role of permanent outsider. It annoyed the crap out of her. She wanted to be part of the inside jokes and in on the stories from the past. Instead, she had to play catch-up all the damn time.

Instead of screaming, she settled for a calm question. "So everyone knows about Scott's tie to Ben but me?"

Ben dropped his hands in front of him. "I didn't."

For some reason, that admission beat back the frustrated longing growing in Callie. For once in her life she wasn't stuck on the outside looking for a way in.

Emma waved them all off. "It's not a surprise to me. Scott told me all about the history when he interviewed for the clerk position. Said he got interested in the law because of his parents' divorce."

"You didn't think to tell me that before now?" Mark's anger thumped like a caged beast.

Emma didn't even spare him a glance. "No."

Whatever had passed between them, the fight had been a killer. Callie could see that in the stiff way Emma held her body as if waiting for the blows from Mark to land. "Anything else, Emma?"

"Scott said the divorce ripped the family apart. He talked about the way Ben handled everything. Scott insisted that had a huge impact on the choices he made from there."

Mark nodded. "Sounds ominous."

Emma shot him a don't-be-a-moron scowl. "Well, it wasn't. It was flattering to Ben."

"I don't remember the kid at all." Ben shook his head. "Or his parents, for that matter."

"It was a long time ago," Mark said.

Callie gnawed on her bottom lip. When the opportunity came before, she let it go. This time, she had to put Scott's odd comments on the table. "And a bad time for Ben and his career."

Ben eased back against the couch, his shoulder touching hers. "What do you mean?"

No way she could back down now. "You had to leave the family law bench, right?"

All three stared at her, but only Ben answered. "No."

She felt as if she were breaking a confidence, but his safety mattered more than his discomfort. If this held true to the rest of their relationship, Emma and Mark already knew the details. "Ben, look, I know this isn't the time to bring this up, but—"

If it was possible for three mouths to drop in unison, it happened. Callie couldn't help but be awed by the sight.

"What are you talking about?" Ben asked, the confusion obvious in his voice.

Nowhere to run now. "Scott told me you had to be removed from hearing family law cases. That the administrative judge, someone, took you off those cases."

"That's not true. There's a mandatory one-year rotation hearing family law cases when you join the court." Ben looked to Emma who nodded in agreement. "I did my time and asked to get off as soon as my time was over."

Callie knew him well enough to see a half story when he dumped one right in her lap. "But something did happen, right?"

"He's not hiding anything. It's not a secret," Emma said in her best Momma Bear protective tone.

"It's not very pleasant, either." With each word slow and measured, Ben started talking. "An angry husband killed his wife and kid after I ruled on alimony and child support. He preferred to see them dead rather than to pay them money."

The shock came fast and hard. Callie heard stories on the news all the time with that ending. Knowing Ben stood in the middle of one made her heart bleed for him. "That's awful."

"I wish I could say it never happens, but it does." He studied the back of his hands as if they were the most interesting things ever. "Emotions run high; people are at their worst. This one drew a lot of attention because a child was involved."

"I actually prefer hearing criminal cases to the divorce matters, or I did before the Jenner disaster." Emma talked into the air as if lost in thought. "Contested custody cases amount to pure bloodbaths."

Ben tried to brush off the horror by making it into something ordinary, but Callie knew better. Such a devastating act would touch him, torment him, until he figured out a way to handle the misplaced guilt. Intellectually he moved on, but Callie wondered how much stayed with him. "Was Scott related to the dad who—?"

"No."

Mark didn't look convinced. "Could he be associated with the case?"

"If so, he sure as hell hides it well." Ben's hands moved faster. "I've never had a problem with the kid. Hell, I barely talk to him most days. Just pleasantries in the morning. That sort of thing."

Callie had seen that and knew Ben's perception was dead on. "But why does he think you were forced out of family law cases?"

"No idea. Maybe he got some old gossip confused."

"He knew about you and Emma and her . . ." Callie looked at Mark then Emma.

"Fiancé. You can say the word." Emma's tight smile looked as if it cost her something to offer it.

"I was trying to be tactful," Callie grumbled under her breath, knowing she had failed pretty big on that score.

"Really?" Ben feigned shock. "Are you trying to learn new skills?"

"You're hysterical."

Ben held out his hands. "Just call me the funny judge."

"Maybe that's why you got that most eligible bachelor thing."

Ben dropped his arms back to his sides. "You can't stop yourself. You just have to keep bringing that up."

"Yes, I do."

Mark cleared his throat. "Okay, that's it. I'll look into the Scott angle. I've had trouble with him ever since I saw him on the security tape sliding the note under Ben's door. His explanation checked out, but it could have been part of his plan. In the meantime, you guys stay sharp." Mark headed for the door, pausing only for Emma to shift out of the way so he could pivot around her without them touching.

Callie saw Emma flinch at Mark's coldness. Standing up, Callie walked over to the other woman. She'd never been all that good at the comfort thing, or the sisterhood thing, or most other girlie things, but she could see the hurt and betrayal in every line of Emma's face. She almost doubled over from the pain of whatever passed with Mark.

"Are you okay?"

Emma flashed an overly bright smile. "Of course."

Callie looked to Ben for reinforcement. When he didn't immediately join in, she threw him a bug-eyed, stop-being-a-dumbass look and he jumped to his feet.

"Can we help?" Callie asked, not knowing what she would do if Emma said yes.

"With what?"

Ben stood in front of Emma with his arms crossed and stared down at one of his oldest friends. "What did he do?"

Callie liked the stern, kicking-butt look. She wanted him to step up and help and he did. He didn't merely play the role of the rock-solid guy who rarely disappointed. He lived it. Even before she really knew him she could see it. The integrity and focus. He could be thick and stubborn, but under that outer layer of potential jackassery, he was a good man. The best. He loved and protected people. He felt things much deeper than he wanted to admit, as evidenced by his rough time as a family law judge.

She might not be all that smart, but when she fell for a guy she was freaking brilliant about her choice.

Emma stopped hiding behind the blank stare. Sadness flooded her features. "The strange thing is that he didn't do anything but be his usual Mark self."

Callie cringed at the thought. Relationship Mark seemed downright dense to her.

"Tell me what that means." Ben stood next to Emma and wrapped a gentle arm around her shoulders.

"I gave him an ultimatum."

Ben gave her a squeeze. " 'Bout time."

Callie tried to figure out what the female equivalent of a high five was for situations like this. She settled for an empty phrase instead. "Good for you."

Emma's hand shook as she touched her fingers to her forehead. "You're both wrong."

Ben glanced at Callie. They stared a stupid stare that suggested neither of them knew what to do or say in a situation like this. Callie wasn't even sure she should be here, since she barely knew Emma.

Then Emma lifted her chin and threw back her head as if conquering some inner challenge. "Know what he did?"

"I'm almost afraid to ask," Callie said.

"He chose to leave me. I offered him my love and he slept on the couch downstairs instead."

"Damn," Callie whispered. Poor, deluded dumbass Mark.

Ben took the news in stride. "He'll come to his senses. He always does."

Callie didn't find Ben's words all that comforting, but she kept the thought quiet.

"Some relationships aren't meant to be." Emma reached over and covered Ben's hand where it lay on her shoulder. "Promise me you'll do better."

Ben nodded. "Sure."

Callie heard the flat tone and wondered for the first time if she was headed down Emma's sorry path. "We better go downstairs. Party's starting."

Emma threw her false smile back on. "Showtime."

Chapter Twenty

The plan called for them to enter in a big couple scene and then mingle separately, leaving Callie covered but seemingly alone for periods of time. Ben wanted to hold her hand, throw an arm around her—something. She insisted on a more subtle approach of fingers on his elbow.

With their bodies close together, they emerged from the security screening Mark had set up. The second they entered, the talk in the two-story courthouse atrium room grew quiet. Glasses clinked and a low rumble of mumbled voices bounced off the marble surfaces as the topic turned from polite cocktail party chat to their first outing as a couple.

Callie glanced at the crowd, flashing an in-control smile. "Quite a turnout."

"I never knew I worked with so many subtlety-impaired people." It was as if every person turned and looked at them at the same time. Two hundred pairs of eyes, some shocked and some knowing, all focused on Callie's possessive hold on Ben.

"You gonna refrain from your usual jackassery tonight?" She didn't hide her amusement.

"Probably not."

"I don't have time to babysit you. I have a job to do."

He noticed she continued to scan the crowd. "How do you smile like that and growl at me at the same time?"

"Years of training."

The not-so-quiet whispers of the group joined and almost drowned out the music playing in the background. He was waiting for people to start pointing. The shift of attention and general interest in seeing them together was that obvious.

"I could kiss you and really give them something to talk about," he said as he waved to a few fellow judges.

"That would be overkill, don't you think?"

"I'm always in favor of kissing you."

She gave him a squeeze. "That's sweet, but poor Rod might throw himself down the elevator shaft." She actually smiled over her idea.

"Bloodthirsty tonight, aren't we?" He steered her to the open bar on the far side of the room. Just in case anyone missed the grand entrance.

The sweep took them right past the clerks and several lawyers. The administrative judge nodded in acknowledgment. Callie smiled and said her hellos to everyone as they passed. Most gawked and none seemed to get that Callie was taunting them with the swing of her hips and sassy smile.

Ben only wanted the dangerous parade to end.

He turned his back on the audience and ordered. "Two white wines."

Leaning over his shoulder with the intimacy of lovers, she spoke in a voice low enough for only him to hear. "I shouldn't drink."

"They're both for me." He handed her a glass anyway.

"Where is Rod? Certainly don't want him to miss the show." She took a small sip and continued her surveillance over the rim. "I need him keyed up and out of control."

"So he can kill you?"

"It will never get that far."

Ben sputtered as he drank, sending the liquid flowing over his hand. "That's comforting."

"Smooth." She winked.

"Just so you know for this acting thing, a real girlfriend would be concerned I was choking and not laugh."

She shot him an odd look. "No, she wouldn't."

He didn't know what that meant. Whatever title she wanted to use, girlfriend or no, he had his ideas of where she fit in his life. Convincing her to agree could be the problem.

They had to get through tonight first.

"Promise me you won't do anything stupid," he said, knowing it would be more effective to talk to the wall.

"Like?"

"Wrestle Rod to the floor and cuff him."

"Oh, I can't promise you that." She slipped her glass into Ben's open hand. "There's the little rat."

Ben tried to follow her gaze. "Who?"

"Target number one."

Rod stood slump-shouldered, nursing a drink by the bar on the other side of the room. "I thought you were calling him a pisher now."

"Was. Then I switched to shit. I'm pretty much just throwing out the names as they come to me."

Plotting. He could see her eyes widen as the thoughts moved through her head. "Stop."

She dragged her gaze away from Rod. "What?"

"You can't just go up to him."

"No, but I can walk by him six or seven hundred times and see if he takes the bait."

"There's this legal concept called entrapment."

"It's called walking, lawyer boy."

"Callie—"

Distracted, she gave Ben a quick kiss on the lips and then took off. The public show of affection kept him rooted to the spot. It was so sudden and out of character that his body froze. He couldn't even reach for her with the two glasses in his hands, which he assumed was part of Callie's plan to get away fast.

He doubted she even realized she'd kissed him in front of everyone. But others picked up on it. More than one male lawyer gave him an *atta boy* nod and smarmy smile. No wonder Callie thought men were idiots. Times like this, Ben thought she had it about right.

Fifteen minutes later, Ben hovered on the verge of exploding. If Scott or any other man sniffed around Callie one more time Ben vowed to drown them in the punch bowl.

He could spot her purple dress anywhere in the marble courthouse lobby. The flowers and tables lined with silver serving trays, the busboys and the hundreds of people gathered in the two-story space, none of it hid her from his view. She walked with such assurance and a grace that clashed sharply with her foul mouth. That mouth he worshipped just a few hours ago and planned to taste again soon.

For the first time in days he had more than five inches of space between them. The freedom weighed him down. Seeing men run around her in circles, staring at her chest and admiring her legs, sent his temper soaring. The gossip, the gawking. She dealt with all of it because of him. He had no idea how to pay back that kind of debt.

"Rod is not a happy young man," Mark said as he signaled the bartender for a drink of water.

Ben kept his attention on Callie. He didn't want to lose her in the crowd. He noticed he was not alone. Rod stood near the security entrance, sipping on a glass of something.

He usually mingled, getting along with everyone except Callie. Tonight he sulked, his laserlike stare beaming directly into her back.

"Find out anything?" Ben asked.

"He's stepped up the angry diatribes against Callie. Where he sent e-mail and implied before, his hints have gotten harsher. He's suggesting she has a sordid past but refuses to give any details."

"He's probably afraid I'll kill him."

"That's the impression most people have." Mark rolled his shoulders back. "Walking in together made quite an impression. The room is buzzing. I heard more than one told-you-so as I marched through the crowd."

Ben spent his time ducking conversations. He's been unsuccessful several times. There was no shortage of colleagues eager to offer both congratulations and advice. "Another judge took me aside and questioned the propriety of dating someone who works for me."

The older man's warnings rang in Ben's head. This judge had questioned Ben's integrity and good sense and was not all that shy about giving a long lecture on the matter. When everyone thought Ben was sleeping with Emma, they stayed quiet. Even if he messed up her engagement it was his private business, but with Callie everyone had an opinion.

"It will all blow over once we ferret out the stalker. Everyone will understand, and your office can get back to normal."

Sounded boring. "Unless my clerk is indicted in the process."

"Admittedly, that will not be great PR for you, but you'll survive."

Knocks to his reputation didn't concern Ben that much. He had lived long enough and survived the devastating and very public loss of his parents. Harmless finger-pointing was the least of his worries. After the initial excitement about having a potential killer in their midst, life in the hallways and small offices would calm down. Memories would fade. To the extent they didn't and the whispers continued he'd ignore them.

But none of that made up for the idea of having someone hate him enough to hurt Emma and Callie. To think he could sit there on the edge of violence day after day, not knowing what someone he hired planned behind his back, stunned Ben. He took pride in his ability to read people. Now he wasn't so sure.

His stare stayed on the most likely offender. "Little shit."

"Rod?"

"How could I not see what was going on in his head?" Ben thought he'd picked up that skill long ago. Finding out he failed—again—had him questioning how he handled the people in his life.

Mark shifted his body to block Ben's view of Rod. "Don't."

"What?"

"We don't know anything yet. Let's follow the evidence and not Callie's intuition on this one. We go off too early or you lose your shit on him, and we could risk our only chance to catch him off guard."

"This is not my first day."

"Just keep in mind that as soon as he thinks he's lost your loyalty, we're done. No telling what he'll do at that point."

"Could it be worse than the last few weeks?"

"Yeah, Ben, it could. His bomb could go off and take someone with it next time. He could follow through on his threats." Mark lowered his voice as a group of lawyers edged closer. "People could actually die this time, including you or someone you care about."

Ben knew he deserved the lecture. His temper kept spiking. Heat flushed through him. It was all part of the fight mechanism that burned inside him, ready to blow at any second. It had always been this way. His body prepared to fight while his mind wrestled with the details.

Mark was right. There was too much to lose.

"I know it's not fair, but I see Rod and I want to shove his head up his ass." Ben hid his mouth behind his glass as he talked. A few curt nods and an unwelcoming scowl to passing attorneys were enough to ensure they didn't stop to chat.

"Now you sound like her."

"She's rubbing off on me." He liked that idea.

"That's surprising."

Ben broke his informal surveillance on Rod to look at his brother's face because the sharp cadence to his words meant trouble. "Why?"

Mark shrugged. "Didn't see you letting a woman matter that much."

"Is this your way of telling me what happened with Emma yesterday? Where is she anyway?" Ben asked, feeling a flash of guilt for not checking on her sooner.

Mark nodded in the direction of a group of lawyers. Emma stood tall and proud at the center. "The guy next to her is an undercover bodyguard."

Now Ben knew what, or who, Mark had been staring at so intently while they talked about Rod. "Why aren't you with her?"

"I can watch her from here."

"Is that good enough?"

Mark slowly lowered his glass. "Did she say something to you?"

"I was hoping my brother would fill me in."

"Nothing."

"Come on, Mark. You look like hell. The only person who looks worse is Emma. She almost dropped on the floor when you left my office."

Mark's jaw locked. "She'll be fine."

"I'm not convinced, but my bigger concern right now is you." Ben watched Scott move closer to Callie. "And don't bother to tell me you're fine. You're not."

Shock flashed across his face, but Mark quickly hid it. "We fought. It will blow over."

"And she'll let you back into her bed?"

"Yeah." Mark glanced at Emma. The longing was there in his eyes. "I sure as hell hope so."

"There's a way you can make sure that happens."

"A commitment." Mark's face pinched even more. "She made that clear."

Ben blew out the breath he was holding. At least he didn't have to baby-step Mark through the conversation. He clearly knew what Emma needed. He understood her ultimatum. But living with it, acting on it, required something from Mark. Ben wasn't sure his brother could pay the price.

"Is it that hard? You've loved Emma forever."

"Let me ask you this." Mark's hard stare focused on Callie. "You ready to give her what she wants?"

The words sat there. Ben didn't answer because the comment came from nowhere, hitting him with the force of a baseball bat. Here he was thinking about dating. Mark had them dancing down the aisle. The idea of that, of walking through life with anyone, shut down Ben's brain.

Mark nodded. "That's what I thought."

"It's not the same thing."

"You keep telling yourself that."

Callie smiled as she watched Mark and Ben talk. She hoped Ben yelled some sense into his big brother. Heaven knew the guy needed a romantic wake-up call. A strong, lovely woman stood by his side and he kept walking away. Proved that jackassery ran in the Walker family . . . or whatever their real name was.

She still hadn't gotten the full story. A voice in her head egged her on, shouting for her to confront Ben about the issue. They exchanged so much, but he held back this bit. The story sat between them as a barrier to moving forward. But he wasn't Mark. Ben didn't suffer from relationship panic and romantic stupidity. She hoped he would soon knock down the wall and confide to her the whole story.

"That was quite an entrance," Elaine said from behind Callie.

Callie turned around expecting to see judgment even though the tone of the welcome held none. Instead, Elaine wore a huge smile. Her amusement proved contagious, because within seconds, Callie couldn't hide her grin.

"I bet there are more than a few women working in the courthouse and here tonight who would disagree with you."

Elaine snorted. "If Judge Walker wanted any of those women, he'd be with them. He's choosy and private, but when he wants something he goes after it."

Curiosity pricked at Callie. "Something as in women?"

"Women, baseball tickets, a plum case. Judge Walker can be very persuasive."

And that was with his clothes on. Callie knew he worked best naked. "That's the only reason I agreed to throw on a dress and come tonight."

"Well, I must admit I didn't expect the public show. That's not really the judge's style." Elaine frowned. "But a lot has changed recently."

"What?" Callie followed Elaine's stare to Rod. He stood next to a potted plant pretending he belonged there.

"I've never known Rod to drink to excess."

"Maybe you don't know him all that well."

Mother-hen instincts on full display, Elaine's eyebrows lowered and her demeanor took on a haughty feel. "Meaning what?"

"Just seems to me he's angry all the time."

"Lately, yes." Elaine squared her shoulders. "I'll go talk to him."

She was off before Callie could call her back. Last thing Callie wanted was someone calming the kid down. She needed him out of control and acting stupid.

"Can I get you something to drink?" Scott slid up beside her.

She was so engrossed in analyzing Rod that she almost missed target number two when he crossed right into her path. With Elaine consoling the pisher, Callie took on the not-quite pisher.

"I'm good. How are you enjoying the big feast?" she asked, making stupid conversation in the hope of getting him comfortable and off his game.

Scott smiled at her over his glass. "The entertainment sure was interesting."

"The music?"

"You and Judge Walker."

Always good when a plan came together. "Ah, well, you did predict that one."

"To be fair, I had an inside track on your relationship."

Something about the way he said that made her skin prickle, and not in a good way.

"How so?"

"Some of it was obvious. I mean, his office door stayed shut once you arrived. You were always in there. Not a day went by without Rod complaining about being locked out."

"Oh." Callie didn't really know what else to say to that since despite Ben's attempts to the contrary, nothing all that interesting happened while they were alone at work. At home was a different story.

"And Rod talked a lot about what was happening between you and Judge Walker."

Of course he did. The kid didn't know how to keep his big yap shut. "I can only imagine the kind of things he said."

"Nothing good."

"That's not a surprise."

"Something about you threatens him. Is it . . . ?" Scott shook his head. "Forget it."

Scott obviously wanted to be begged into talking. She let him have his way. "What? Go ahead and say it."

"It's almost as if Rod has a crush on Judge Walker."

Her drink sloshed around in her stomach. "A sexual crush?"

Her mind rebelled at the idea. The thought made sense on some levels, but she hadn't gotten an attraction vibe from Rod about Ben. It was much more of a parasitic follower vibe.

Scott waved the thoughts away. "It's strange. Forget I said anything."

Like that was going to happen. "Tell me how you came to that conclusion."

"First, Rod said negative things about Judge Blanton. As her clerk, I cautioned him about it. Warned him about the talk getting him in trouble. Then when you arrived Rod switched his anger from my boss to you." Scott's hands kept moving as he talked. "I joked with Rod about wanting to get rid of the competition and he got furious."

"What did he do?"

"Made some threats about shutting me up."

"What?"

"It was dumb-guy stuff, then he stomped around."

Sounded like her typical day with Rod. "How could you tell the difference from his usual demeanor?"

Scott gave her a sad smile. "Rod's actually a pretty decent guy. I know he can act jerky, but he means well."

"Uh-huh."

"There's just something about Judge Walker that makes Rod jumpy. Being moved out of the courtroom and replaced by you brought out the worst in him. He started spending all of his time at the computer."

The more Scott talked, the less sure she felt about . . . Scott. He struck her as awful eager to spill the goods on Rod. Either Rod was unraveling in some kind of sick spiral, or Scott was invested in making her think so. Either way, she didn't trust the law clerks in the building. Made her think law schools needed a better screening process.

She decided to poke around. "Do you remember telling me about Ben's time in the family law rotation?"

Scott's lazy camaraderie disappeared. "Sure."

"Did Rod tell you about that?"

Scott hesitated. "It's pretty well known."

"What is the 'it's' you're referring to?"

"A lady who appeared before him was murdered and people tied it back to the judge's handling of the case. There were some complaints about how the judge handled cases. He got pulled off the rotation right after." Scott smacked his lips together. "Doesn't matter."

A good explanation since it connected to a traceable reality. Whether she bought it was a different question. She'd think about that later.

Scott made a show of looking around. "Where is he?"

"Ben?"

"Rod."

She scanned the room looking for the little shit. She didn't spot him anywhere. But she did see Mark heading for the elevator bank with one of the undercover lawyers right behind. Ben stepped right into her line of view.

"What's going on?" she asked.

Ben wrapped his hand around her elbow and smiled down at Scott. "Can I steal her for a second?"

Scott toasted Ben with his glass. "Of course."

Ben pulled Callie over to the side. The move probably came off as a bit of romantic flair to anyone watching, and everyone seemed to be watching every move. She knew he was in superprotector mode.

She waited until another random clerk said hello and then scurried away when Ben didn't respond. "Growling at people is not the best plan for getting them close enough to find out information."

"We have movement with Rod."

Seeing the way Ben's eyebrows drew together, she ignored the stupid spy speak. "I'm guessing this has something to do with Rod being missing."

"He's in my office. Mark's people are following him on the security cameras." Ben motioned for Emma to come over and join them.

The move by Rod, the tracking, it all felt wrong to Callie. "But we don't know what he's doing inside the office. It could be innocent. He does work up there, after all."

"Mark added cameras to the inside after the first note. We kept that quiet."

She remembered the day Ben made a play from his desk chair. How he wanted to break the separation of work and bed rule. "Wait, didn't we—"

He shook his head. "Nothing happened, so there isn't video."

"As if that's a good enough answer." She shot him her best you're-an-idiot look. "You should tell a woman about such things before you start offering your sexual services, if you know what I mean."

"Got it, but the point is about Rod. He's being watched every second." With each word, Ben's cheeks hollowed out further.

She dropped the relationship lecture because she knew something really bad was coming. "And?"

"He's at my desk. They're concerned he's planting something."

Her stomach dropped down to her spiky heels. "Another bomb."

"We'll find out in a second when they arrest him."

Chapter Twenty-one

"I don't care what she said." Rod looked around Emma's conference room, his eyes wide and wild. "I didn't do anything."

Ben stood by the door and listened to Rod's fifth denial. He looked at Sheriff Danbury, then at Mark. The kid even had the nerve to look at Ben for support.

No fucking way that was going to happen.

"Ben, why don't you step outside for a few minutes and let us talk with Rod here," Mark said as he slid into the seat across from the kid.

Nice try, but that wasn't going to happen, either. "I'm good where I am."

Sheriff Danbury gave Ben a solid man-to-man look. "This is a law enforcement matter now."

"It's personal."

"Ben." Mark's voice carried a warning.

Ben ignored it. "I'm not moving."

He wanted to beat the kid to death. This time Rod went after Callie. This note was written to her. Left for her to find. An invasion of her space and it didn't mince words— *"You're next."*

When the sheriff and Mark's men converged on Rod a half hour earlier, he had his hands in Callie's desk drawer.

The white envelope sat on the blotter. Rod had been blaming Callie for framing him and whining about fairness ever since. Ben thought it was interesting how guilty people always cried about how unfair and biased the process was.

"I didn't do anything. I know my rights, and you can't keep me here." When Rod tried to get up, Sheriff Danbury shoved him back in his seat.

"Sit down, son. And stay there."

"You're on the hook for threatening a judge, for assault. Attempted murder." Mark ticked off the list of offenses.

Shock raced across Rod's face. He lifted out of his seat again despite the firm hand on his shoulder. "No. Never."

"You hate Callie." Realizing he never supported her on that claim brought guilt crashing down on Ben.

"Not enough to hurt her."

"What about Judge Blanton?" Mark seethed with rage. "You could have killed her with that bomb. And why go after her bodyguard? Was that just to prove your toughness?"

All of the color leached out of Rod's face. "I didn't have anything to do with any of those things. You can't put them on me."

"You have no idea what I've collected on you," Mark said in what Ben assumed was a wild embellishment or the kid would have been locked up long before now.

With his training, Rod should recognize the tactic. Ben hoped in the advanced state of panic he didn't.

"There can't be any evidence because I didn't do anything."

Mark tapped his pen against the table. "Nothing, Rod?"

The kid's mouth moved, but no sound came out. Finally he sputtered out a few words. "I talked about her. It wasn't anything big. Everyone's talking about her. That's not proof of anything but gossip. Last I checked, that's not illegal."

Ben feared Rod might be right about that. Getting caught

running his mouth and hating Callie was one thing. Finding evidence for the bombing was another. Ben hoped the police would search Rod's apartment and find something to link him to the bigger plot.

From the sour look on Mark's face, he didn't buy into the kid's story at all. "You're going to get cocky now?"

"I'm just stating a fact."

"You want to talk facts? Sounds good to me. What about this?" Mark waved the bagged new note in front of Rod's face.

"I don't know where that came from."

Mark kept right on grinding. "Tell me something. What exactly was your plan for Callie?"

Ben tensed as he waited for the answer that was sure to break his tenuous hold on his control.

"Nothing. Look, she's setting me up. Don't you understand?" Rod scanned the office looking for support from anyone who would listen. When no one jumped in to help him beat up on Callie, he rubbed his hands hard enough to turn them bright red. "She told me to come up here and meet her."

Mark shook his head. "Not true."

"Yes!"

"Try again."

"She did. I'm telling you. It just happened downstairs."

It took all of Ben's control to keep his body still. He wanted to launch across the table and shake the kid until he stopped lying. But once he started he might not stop, so Ben rooted his feet to the ground.

Mark slammed his fist against the table. "She's one of us, you idiot."

All the bluster left Rod. "What?"

"She works for me. Following your stunt with the bomb, I planted here her to protect Ben. She's his bodyguard and has been shadowing him to make sure he stays alive. At the same time, she's been conducting a bit of surveillance. Can you guess her target? Let me fill you in. It wasn't Elaine."

Rod's face turned green around his mouth. "No, that can't be true."

"Is it sinking in now, Rod?" Mark tapped the side of his head. "Is that legal brain of yours kicking into gear? Do you get how much trouble you're in?"

"But, I . . ." Rod turned his pleading eyes to Ben. "Judge Walker, you know I respect you. I would never do anything to hurt you or Judge Blanton."

Conveniently left out Callie. Ben felt his brain explode. He came off the wall, ready to strangle the kid. Ben wanted Rod on the floor and barely breathing. "You little shit."

Mark stood up and threw a last-minute body block. "Ben!" Mark grabbed Ben by the forearms and pushed back.

Rod dug his fingernails into the arms of his chair and slid in his seat as if trying to get as far as possible away from Ben's attack. "Sir, I didn't—"

"You could have killed us with that sick stunt," Ben shouted around Mark's shoulders.

"That's enough." Mark nodded to Danbury. "Watch the suspect."

Over Rod's yelling excuses and the sheriff's threats to keep quiet, Mark pulled Ben outside. Ben fought every step. He tried to move around Mark, but his brother was too big, too pissed off.

Mark got them into the hallway and shoved Ben against the far wall. "Calm the fuck down."

The brain knew he deserved to be removed from the action, but Ben depended on other parts of his body right now. He wanted to use his fists and unleash the energy pumping through him. "Let me back in there."

"You had one chance and you blew it when you lost your cool."

"I need to hear this."

"You need to get out of here. Go home." Mark pointed over Ben's head. "You."

"You better not think you can throw me around like that." Callie's heels clicked against the floor as she came to stand next to Ben.

"Take him home." Mark shot an angrier frown at Emma. "And there is no reason at all for you to stick around. One of my men will take you to your house. I want you to stay there until I know Rod's our man. That goes for all of you."

They all started talking at once. Ben didn't care what anyone else had to say. He sure as hell wasn't leaving. "Callie can take Emma. I'm sticking around here until I know what set Rod off."

Callie sighed. "I am not in the mood to be ordered around like the hired help."

"Me, either," Emma said.

"Enough." Mark's scream bounced down the hall. Ben bet it could be heard above the music and celebrating of the clueless folks downstairs. "I can't do my job with an audience."

"This affects us, Mark," Emma said.

He exhaled. "As soon as I know something I'll call."

Chapter Twenty-two

Ben paced fast and furious across Callie's living room rug. She waited for him to wear a path right through to the cement underneath. She understood. When the adrenaline pumped that hard and every cell in the body got that keyed up, coming down took something extra. Good thing her body volunteered for the duty of helping Ben relax.

"Ben?"

He spun around and snapped. "What?"

Well, not until he knocked that shit off. "Okay, I know you're upset, but yelling at me is only going to get my shoe in your shin."

"Sorry."

"Speaking of which." She kicked off her high heels, and her arches sighed in relief. "Much better."

Ben's hands went to his hips. "Why are you so calm about this?"

"The dress looked bad with flats."

"What?"

"Aren't we talking about my shoes?" She knew they weren't, but Ben needed idle conversation to help him deal with the emotions surging through him.

"Rod threatened you. Twice."

So much for subterfuge. "I'm aware of that."

"Most people would be pissed off about something like this."

Callie was . . . sort of. The whole Rod-as-stalker spiel wouldn't compute in her head. Until she saw the compelling evidence, she refused to jump on the conviction bandwagon. The kid made hating him easy and believing in him hard. But nothing about him said killer to her.

"Would you like me to get all huffy and puffy like you are?" she asked.

"Actually, yeah."

"Not going to happen."

"Maybe you're used to people treating you like shit, but I don't like it."

Since she had zero idea what that meant, she ignored it. "I see you're not ready to stop fuming."

"No."

The man made it hard to seduce him. Right now she toyed with the idea of smacking him. "How about being an ass? You almost done with that part?"

"Don't you want to figure out what's going on?" Ben asked, his judge voice clicking into place. "You are the one who pegged him as the stalker."

"I offered his name as a possible suspect."

"Oh, please. You all but dragged him down to the jail. Shouldn't you be celebrating? Maybe bombarding me with a round or two of 'I told you so' or something?"

"Would that really make you feel better?"

"I just want to see some kind of reaction. Hell, I almost twisted that kid's head off in that room. And why? Because of you. Because he threatened to hurt you."

The simple honesty gave her hope. She'd never heard anyone say something so lovely in such a hard voice before, but she got the underlying meaning. He gave a shit about her. She mattered to him.

Yeah, she wanted a piece of Rod, too. She burned with the need to punch the crap out of him but not until after she understood the story. In her mind, none of this made sense. Rod as the overwrought kid with an outsized ego problem? Oh, yeah. She noticed that about ten seconds after she met him. But running around blowing things up to get Ben's attention? She didn't see that at all. The kid idolized Ben in a butt-kissing way, not a psychopath way.

Peeking in on Mark's interrogation would give her a chance to dig into all of her theories and concerns, but she knew Ben couldn't be there. So, she slipped from work mode into girlfriend mode. Earlier Ben tried to lecture her on how the species acted. Even though the girlie gene missed her, Callie didn't need a lesson in partner behavior. She knew exactly how someone who loved Ben would act, because she did.

Quiet and without warning, the falling thing fell. This wasn't just a matter of being attracted and wanting to spend time with him. Their relationship had progressed far past that for her. She wanted him, loved him, ached for him.

The quick trust was so foreign to her. She waited and dissected in relationships. She didn't give up her dreams for a roll in the sack nor did she back off from what she believed in to satisfy any man's tender ego. With Ben she wanted to dive in, body and mind. To share her hopes and unload her burdens.

In such a short time, he'd taken her messed-up world and offered her a purpose again. She loved him, his life, his decency, and even his jackassery.

For now, though, she'd soothe him the best way she knew how. Until she knew he returned her feelings, she'd use her body to take away the edge of his temper. "Sit."

His eyes narrowed. "Excuse me?"

She smiled at his natural fall back into hoity-toity land and pointed to the couch. "You. There. Now."

"I don't want to sit, Callie. I want to—" His voice cut off when she hiked her dress up right to the edge of her panty line. Or what would have been her panty line if she were wearing any, which she wasn't.

"Yes, Ben?"

He swallowed hard enough for her to see it. "What are you doing?"

"I'm getting ready to climb on your lap, but you're going to have to sit down and make a lap for my plan to work."

"My lap?"

The poor man lost the power of speech. Now that was pretty damn flattering. "Right on your legs. Yes."

"Now?" He tried to play it cool, but the anger in his voice morphed into pure heat. The tight fists uncurled, and his hands slid down his sides.

"It's the only way for you to see what I have on under this dress."

His gaze shot to the shadowed junction where her thighs met. And didn't wander away again. He squinted as if trying to see what she hid under the bunched material.

Exactly according to plan.

She stripped, and his mind focused solely on her. On this, Ben proved wonderfully predictable.

"You need to burn off some energy. I need you inside me." She scrunched the silk in her palms and lifted the dress another half inch. Any higher and the mystery would be gone because a great deal of her would be out in the open.

"Wow."

"I see you're finally getting me."

"The plan sounds good." His stare locked on her legs.

"Then I need you to touch me."

"Really?"

"Actually, I'm going to make that a requirement of this exercise."

"Fine." He threw off his jacket and dropped down on the couch.

"That's a good boy." She straddled him, placing one knee and then the other on the outsides of his thighs. The position put them eyes to breasts. With her hands braced against the top of the couch, she eased down and pressed his erection against her through his dress pants.

With his hands on her sides just under her breasts, he leaned his head back and stared up at her. "When do I get to see underneath the dress?"

"You're an action type of guy. Why don't you let those long fingers go exploring and find out?" She dragged his hand to the very heat of her.

"You're naked." The second his fingers touched her bare wetness his body hummed with excitement. Shaking overtook his hands. He shifted to get a better angle, to ease two up inside her.

"Not completely. I'm still wearing the dress."

"But that's it." He slid his fingers higher.

"You are quick."

"Please tell me you took your underwear off when we got home. That you weren't walking around the courthouse in this state."

"Well, no. This is my reception outfit. Except for the soaking-wet part, of course."

"Male lawyers were drooling over you. If they had known . . ."

"This is only for you." She leaned down and brushed her lips against his ear to calm him back down when his mood got all riled. "Watching you made me hot. I knew I'd be ready the second we walked in the door."

"Jesus."

She drew her dress up higher so she could watch his hand, see his fingers disappear inside her and then pull out slick before entering again. The back and forth mesmerized her. She watched him touch her. Felt the insistent caresses. The combination took her body from ready to flaming fire.

"You feel so good." Her groan of satisfaction filled the room.

"I was about to say the same thing about you." His free hand slipped around to her lower back, guiding her as she rode his hand.

The moment was for him, but she stole some time for her. With her head thrown back, she closed her eyes and gave in to the sensations rolling through her from his probing. It wouldn't take much for him to set her off. The promise lured her.

She inhaled a few times before dropping her mouth to his. The kiss lingered as his fingers worked. He pumped. His lips conquered.

She lost the battle.

Giving up the fight to the rhythm, she let her building orgasm rock her hips. Her body sucked his fingers deep inside as she gasped for breath. Then her lower half bucked. Waves of pleasure crashed over her until he gentled his touch against her sensitive folds.

When she finally fell against his chest, her mouth pressed against his neck. Her muscles turned to soup.

"Beautiful woman." He whispered the word against her forehead.

"Talented man."

He chuckled. "One who's hard as hell and sick from wanting you."

"That's sweet."

"I didn't mean it to be. Kind of was asking you to hurry up before my underwear catches fire."

"Let me take care of that for you." He didn't argue as she slid off his lap to sit on the floor in front of him. "My, those pants do look mighty tight."

He plowed his fingers through her hair. "They sure are now."

"You poor thing."

"I've had a rough night."

"Maybe this will help." She cupped him through his pants and felt his cock jerk in response.

"Definitely."

With his deep breaths as an invitation, she eased the zipper down, listening to the steady clicks as the front of his pants came undone. "Where were you hiding this at the party?"

He brushed her hair off her neck and stared down at her fingers. "I was too busy trying not to kill the men who tried to get a peek down your dress."

"Mmmm." She lifted his penis out of his boxer briefs and squeezed her palm around him.

He groaned as his hips shifted forward on the couch to meet her mouth. "Yes. Just like that."

She gave him what he needed. Her tongue circled his tip as her hand moved up and down on him.

The torment had his hand clenching in her hair. "Harder."

Her pace stayed steady as she took him deep into her mouth. Warm and hard, he slid down the back of her throat, growing thicker with each stroke. She caressed and licked, pumped and enticed. When his body tightened and his words shifted to grunts instead of words, she knew she had succeeded in making him forget about anything but her.

*   *   *

Two hours later Rod sat with his very high-powered father across from Mark at the conference table. With the accusations shooting at him, the kid had been smart enough to ask for a lawyer. Unfortunately, the lawyer in this case meant his wealthy dad, Dale. Which was even worse.

The only good part was that Dale wanted Emma in the room. If it wasn't for the request and the very real possibility the kid would have stopped talking if Mark refused, Emma knew she'd be at home. Alone. Mark never would have let her stay. Acquiescing grated on him. She could see it in the hard edge to his jaw. As it was, he agreed but limited her access to standing and keeping quiet.

"I was set up." Gone was the panic and yelling. Rod acted calm and in control now. Having Daddy right there ready to pull the plug on the questioning made Rod's chest puff up.

"You were caught on camera." Mark's smile promised retribution. "Didn't know we put those in, did you?"

"You saw him standing in a room. In an office he works in, I might add." Dale looked at Emma. "We all know that is not evidence of anything. And I suspect if you watch the full video, you'll find your real suspect walk in and out before Rod ever got there."

Mark tapped his pen against the table. "Why were you in there, Rod?"

"I was told Callie wanted to see me. To have it out over some of our disagreements. Once she arrived at the party, I went upstairs to wait. Figured she'd flirt and mingle before joining me."

"You're changing your story."

Rod looked at his dad. "That's not true."

"Earlier you said Callie was the one who told you to go upstairs."

Rod traced an invisible pattern on the table. "I thought the message was from her."

Dale put a firm hand on his son's shoulder. "Just tell them who gave you the message."

Rod glanced at Emma. "I'm sorry."

She knew the accusation was coming. Felt it before he said the name. "Don't play games. Just tell me."

"Scott," Rod said.

Dale stood up. "There you go. As you can see, you have the wrong clerk. Now, if you don't mind, I would like to take my son home and forget this evening ever happened."

"Not quite." Mark motioned for Dale to sit back down.

The man balanced his palms against the table and stared down Mark instead. "Mr. Walker, it's time you admit you made a mistake here. Rod is willing to move on, with apologies from you and Judge Walker, of course, along with some other concessions, including a stellar recommendation and some help with landing him an associate position wherever Rod thinks is best after his clerkship. This questioning, however, must stop right now."

Mark screwed up his mouth. "How nice of him to let us set up his life for him."

"Mark—" Emma stopped talking when he sent her a look of pure fury.

He turned back to Dale. "I'm not convinced of Rod's innocence, so I think you can imagine how long he'll need to wait for those apologies."

"You were wrong about me," Rod said.

"We have your computer records and know what you've been checking out, Rod."

"Nothing bad."

"Bomb making websites. Combine that with your background in science and we have a problem. An exploding kind." Mark leaned back, his demeanor cooler and more in control. "I'm just trying to figure out the motive."

"For his degree?" Dale asked, obviously stunned that Mark had added the facts together and come up with attempted murder.

"I planned to go to med school." Rod's voice grew louder with each syllable. "And the website stuff is not true. You can't lay that on me."

Dale touched his son's arm, opting for maturity over Rod's hot temper. "That's enough."

"You sure? It was just getting interesting," Mark said.

Dale smoothed down his tie. "If I were you I'd be worried about Scott's background, not Rod's."

Emma jumped in the conversation. Couldn't help herself and ignored Mark's scowl to do it. "What does that mean?"

Relief showed in Dale's eyes at dealing with her instead of Mark. "You have the wrong clerk. Scott lured Rod up here. Scott is obsessed with Judge Walker. Scott has access to the offices and computers just like Rod does. It would appear Scott has fooled everyone and tried to frame Rod."

The thought sent Emma's mind reeling. What if she had introduced the craziness into all of their lives? What if, once again, her instincts had failed her.

Mark looked to Sheriff Danbury. "Where is Scott now?"

"I'll find him." The officer took off at a near run.

Emma hoped Dale was wrong. And that it wasn't too late.

Chapter Twenty-three

Callie woke up from her sex-induced doze an hour later. She lay on her side with her arm thrown across Ben's bare chest. Somehow they ended up in the dead center of her bed with the sheets bunched underneath them. Not comfortable, but he didn't utter a complaint. Probably because he was too busy drifting off to sleep.

She curled into him and felt his breath blow against her forehead. Her hand rose and fell on his stomach with each intake of air. Slowing the longer she touched him.

Comfortable but not okay. She needed him awake and talking.

She poked his side. "Are you asleep?"

His shoulders jumped off the pillow as his eyes popped open. "What?"

"Having trouble sleeping?"

He groaned. "Am now."

"I need to ask you something."

He hid his eyes under his free arm, the one she wasn't crushing under her. "This is almost unfair."

Talking to his forearm was not her idea of a good time, so she pushed it over his head and stared at him. "How do you figure?"

"You jostle a guy out of—"

"Who the hell uses the word jostle before his eyes are even open?"

"—and expect him to have an intelligent conversation."

"You're the one who's supposed to be so freaking brilliant."

"When I'm awake, maybe."

"You're fine." She drummed her fingers on his stomach. "So, do you think Rod did all of this?"

Ben's face crunched up in disbelief. "Are you kidding me?"

"No."

"I thought we settled this issue last night."

She scooted up until her elbow rested on the pillow next to his head. From this angle, she could watch his eyes . . . and poke them if needed. "I don't see a motive."

"We're really going to talk about this now." He spun the alarm clock around until the green lit numbers beamed across the bed. "At midnight. That's your plan?"

Time for the big guns. "Should I have talked about this before I got down on my knees and took you into my mouth?"

"I can see I'm not going to win this battle."

"Of course not."

He pretended to bang his head against the pillow. "Go ahead."

"Rod as the stalker. Does that work for you?"

"He hates you, remember?"

"Oh, thanks for blaming me for everything that's happened."

"Just playing along." Ben stretched out both arms wide to the side and yawned.

"Don't think you can ignore me by pretending you're tired."

"I don't think you appreciate how much energy it takes to keep a woman like you satisfied." His fingers brushed up and down on her arm. "Not just any man could keep up with you."

That was good since she only wanted one man. "Are you looking for a compliment?"

He closed one eye and pretended to think about the question. "I think I am."

She leaned down, her mouth hovering over his. "You rocked my world."

"Nice one."

Her thumb skimmed along his lower lip. "If you were any hotter I'd be in the hospital."

"Right back at ya, sweetheart."

He lifted his head and stunned her with a soul-burning kiss. Warm, wet, and wild. It teased and caressed, stole her breath, and then replaced it with his. Just when it wound down and she thought about pulling back, he speared his fingers through her hair and held her close.

The second round wiped out all memory of the first. His mouth met hers, slanting and exploring, convincing her that dropping her defenses and letting him in had been the right move.

When she finally lifted her head, a happy dizziness assailed her. "Talk about impressive."

He flashed a cocky smile. "I aim to please."

Being silly, she used her finger to trace a heart on his skin. "It didn't work, you know."

"And here I thought I could control you with sex." He closed his eyes, but the big grin stayed put.

The quiet allowed her to study his strong features. So handsome and powerful. Just seeing him turned her bones to jelly.

"You can but only for short periods of time," she said.

One eye shot open. "That better not be a knock on my stamina, woman."

"Wouldn't dream of it." She waited until he drifted back into a state of sexual bliss. "But I still haven't forgotten about the Rod issue."

Ben let out a long, labored groan as he sat up, propping his back against the headboard. The move brought her up on her knees at his side.

"Women."

"You love women."

"The quiet ones." He rushed on before she could smack him for that. "But I can see I'm not going to get any more sex or even post-sex flirting until we talk about this. Go ahead."

"That's using your big brain."

He gestured for her to continue. "Hit me."

"I'm pretty good at reading people." When he stayed quiet, she continued. "The Rod connection doesn't make sense."

"You're the one who put him on Mark's radar."

She bit her lower lip, trying to think of a way to make someone as smart as Ben ignore the obvious and rely on her instincts instead. "I put Elaine on there, too, but I never thought she wanted to hurt you. Everyone near you, close to you, talking about you, or mooning after you went on my list of possibles."

His eyes widened. "Mooning?"

"Got a problem with my verb?"

His fingers explored the side of her arm, raising goose bumps as he went. "And you complain about my word usage."

"I complain when you say stupid things like 'word usage,' but that's not the point."

"What is it then?"

"I know the evidence is pointing that way, to Rod, but don't you think it's a bit convenient?"

"Having my law clerk try to kill me? No. There's nothing convenient about that. Trust me."

It never dawned on her that Ben might view the whole situation as a knock against him. That he would read the signs and figure he failed Rod in some way. "It's not your fault."

Ben didn't pretend to misunderstand. "I hired him. That means I put Emma in danger. Made you a target. There's no one to blame but me for this one."

Feeling the need to soothe him, she snuggled against his chest and inhaled his musky scent. She reveled in the comfort of having him wrap his strong arms around her waist. "You can't predict crazy, Ben."

"I know."

The wistful note in his voice made her look up. "Does this have something to do with your name change?"

His arms stiffened around her. "We're talking about Rod."

The verbal smackdown packed as much force as a physical one. Disappointment streamed through her. She craved intimacy, and he refused to talk about something so important and basic about his life. A true unloading and sharing of the past. For her, for the first time, it came easy. Seemed right. But he still refused to open that door and let her in.

Rather than let the push back destroy her, she focused on her thoughts about Rod. Sitting up, she pulled the sheet over her lap, leaving her bare breasts open to his view but cutting off his access to anything else. "It's really Scott."

Ben blinked several times. "You lost me."

"I was so sure about him being the one."

"Because he dropped the first note off at my office? He had an explanation for that. It made sense. Even Mark had to admit that much."

"Explaining this is tough." She tried to put something as

fleeting and uncertain as her uneasy feeling into words. "He was almost desperate to have me see Rod's faults."

"That sounds familiar," Ben mumbled.

"I'm choosing to ignore that."

"Got it."

She wound the edge of the sheet around her finger and pulled tight enough to cut off the circulation. "And then there's the thing about your family law judge days."

"For the record, I'm still lost."

The slow and halting speech gave him away. Ben had no idea what she wanted him to say.

She tried the direct approach. "Scott insists you got kicked out of divorce cases."

"Didn't happen."

The cotton sheet bit into her skin as the tip of her forefinger turned purple. "But something did."

"Honestly?"

She was two seconds away from wrapping the sheet around his neck and forcing him to talk. "Uh, yeah, you should always assume I want the truth."

"It was not my strength."

He said something. She had no idea what. "In English and without the judge bullshit."

"I sucked at it."

The chuckle escaped before Callie could stop it.

Ben shot her a dry look. "Thank you for being so supportive."

"I'm sorry." Or she would be as soon as she the doubling over in laughter thing went away. When his scowl deepened, she snorted her amusement to a halt. "Lost control there."

"Really?"

"It's just so ridiculous. You are the judge stud. The idea of you not being up to the job doesn't make much sense."

"The cases took me by surprise. I expected negotiations over the silver. I got multiday trials about who should have the kids ten minutes more than the other parent and how to divide holidays I'd never even heard of."

"Sounds hideous."

He folded his arms across his stomach. "And I'm making it sound good."

"But you're talking about the type of cases, not how you were at making those decisions."

She tried to imagine him failing at his job and her mind shut off. She'd seen him in action. He controlled the people, the arguments, even the break times. The docket ran according to schedule and his demand for respect from everyone who appeared before him rang clear despite being the youngest judge on the bench.

"I wasn't married. Didn't have kids. What the hell made me qualified to sit in judgment, dividing up stuff and time with kids and then forgetting all about the poor people the next day?"

The man underestimated his skills. Most people would fall asleep or bang lawyers' heads together. Not Ben. He remained cool at all times. "You can't possibly know about all the stupid subjects that come before you now. I swear two lawyers argued about carpet for four hours the other day. You know a lot about carpet, do you?"

Ben sighed in a way he viewed as indulgent and she viewed as condescending. "That was a contracts case about an expensive real estate development program."

She dropped the sheet from her hand. "Like I give a shit. I'm making a point here."

"So am I. I didn't know shit about being in a family, so when it came time to deal with them I messed up. Every night I went home thinking I had sent kids to the wrong house or gave too much money here or there. Poor Emma got a near-daily earful about my hatred for the cases."

Callie heard every word. She focused on one. "You have a brother."

"What?"

"How could you not know about being a family?"

His mouth slammed shut. The free flow of words cut off. "You know what I mean."

"No, I don't. I was an only child raised by a single mom with a dad who moved on before I was five, but I get family."

"This was about making decisions." He tried to wave his hand in dismissal, but she caught it and held it to her chest.

"Ben."

"What?" The snappy retorts returned.

"What happened?"

"I just told you I wasn't good at the job." Throwing his feet over the side of the mattress, he stood up and reached for his boxer briefs.

The sudden distance echoed through every part of her. That wall of silence kept getting higher and thicker. Much more and she wouldn't be able to see any part of him.

"What are you doing?" she asked, dreading the answer.

"I thought I'd go to the kitchen and—"

Her heart detached from her chest and spun into free fall. "Run away."

His head shot up. "Excuse me?"

She didn't even have the emotional strength to poke at him. It took all her concentration not to curl into a ball. "Why won't you tell me the truth? After everything that's happened and all that we've shared, I don't get it."

"Some things aren't up for discussion."

The words battered and beat her. With careful movements

she stood up, hoping her shaking legs would hold her. From the opposite side of the bed, she broached the one subject she hoped could be taken for granted.

"What do you think we're doing here, Ben?"

His response came brisk and sure. "Dating."

That was a good start, but she had to be clear. Her heart staked everything on him. The risk of confusion and pain was just too great. "And?"

He lifted his hands out to the side. "What?"

"So, in your world we have sex and see how it goes."

His shoulders relaxed. "Exactly."

"That's all I get."

"What else do you expect?"

A future. A promise to try. A whisper of hope for something more. "Well not a proposal or—"

"Good."

The punch knocked her off her feet. She sat down hard on the mattress before her knees collapsed. "Is this how you operate?"

"I said I want to date you."

Shock gave way to bubbling fury. "Lucky me."

"What is the matter with you?"

"Do you really want to know?" That flat affect suggested he didn't, so she rushed to fill him in. "I love you, you dumbass. Through your stupid hoity talk and criminal stubbornness, I fell for you. I'm sitting here, for the first time ever, thinking about tomorrow and how you fit into that, and you're talking about a few informal meetings for you to get your rocks off."

"That's not fair."

Maybe it wasn't, but she didn't care. "Have you ever stayed with a woman past the initial sex stage?"

He stood there, fallen mouth and dead eyes.

"I'm guessing a woman starts making claims and getting to know you, and you move the fuck on."

"We've known each other for about two weeks and you want me to declare my undying devotion."

She did. Damn her, she did. "I want you to admit that I mean something to you."

"I said I wanted to date." He made the pathetic offer through clenched teeth.

Every day he showed her he cared. When it came to telling her his heart and letting her see how he became the man who stood before her, however, he backed off. It would always be like this. That's the guy he really was. She would push and he would balk. If she wasn't careful she'd be looking decades later for a tiny crumb of a commitment. She'd be Emma.

"You're worse than Mark." Each word cut into her. "He doesn't pretend to give a shit."

"That's enough." Ben whispered his order.

"You give off the available vibe, but you are anything but. Whatever happened in your past, this precious information you can't dare share, it's warped you. Ruined you for a normal future."

"I said stop." He rubbed his forehead as his voice increased in strength.

Harsh accusations poured out of her. Every inch of her grew numb, but her mind threw out words and comments almost faster than she could say them. "You walk around seemingly together and complete, but inside you are in more pieces than Mark."

"Enough!"

His wild shout rattled the walls.

She clapped. "At last, a real emotion."

"This isn't funny."

"No, Ben. It's heartbreaking."

If possible his face closed up even more. "I don't know what you want me to say."

The last tie of hope slipped away. Her stomach felt as if it had been carved out and handed to her. "You said it. Only left one thing out."

His look became guarded. "What?"

"Good-bye."

Chapter Twenty-four

Mark burst into Ben's office the next morning without knocking. "Why aren't you answering your cell?"

Not the person Ben wanted to see. Despite the nuclear fallout of an argument yesterday, Ben counted on Callie showing up with a cooler head. Act like a grown-up and talk the situation out. He had no idea what he'd say in response, but he'd forgive her. They could move on. They could get the relationship—yeah, he admitted there was one—back on track. Dating made sense. Proclamations of love he couldn't handle. She loved an idea. One that existed for him in fairy tales but not in reality. His parents taught him that firsthand.

In his head, all the pieces fit together in a neat bundle. But that didn't explain why going even one day without seeing her ripped him apart. Two hours in, and he had not accomplished a single bit of work this morning. At every noise in the hallway he looked up expecting to see her in his doorway. When Elaine buzzed him with a call, he waited for Callie's voice on the line. He never expected to miss that snide voice calling him names, but he did.

She had spun a kind of web around him. No doubt about that. She had him wondering and questioning. Enjoying time together made sense to him. Love never entered the picture.

Not that he consciously said no to the possibility. Ben wasn't afraid of commitment and wasn't the type of guy who needed a harem hanging on every word to stay happy. The thought of forever simply had never made sense to him. As a kid he saw the two people he trusted most betray each other. As an adult, he saw love rip Emma and Mark apart.

Violence and pain. No wonder he never felt the temptation and tug of what others called love.

None of that changed the facts, however. He missed Callie's ridiculous comments. Hell, after just a few hours away he missed her to the point where his chest ached.

And was not at all in the mood to deal with Mark's barking. "The case is over. I can turn off my ringer and enjoy ten minutes of quiet if I want."

"Wrong."

Biting back a slam, Ben studied his brother's face. For a guy who solved a huge case, he looked panicked. "What's going on?"

Mark stopped in front of Ben's desk. "I'm not fucking around here. Where is she?"

"Who?"

Panic gave way to red-faced anger on Mark's face. "Don't be dumb. I'm talking about Callie. Your girlfriend. The woman you can't seem to live without."

Mark's assessment, even though he yelled it, brought Ben's mental wanderings to a halt. "What the hell does that mean?"

"Where. Is. Callie?"

Damn, hearing her name made Ben's stomach burn with the pain of loss. "I have no idea."

"Ben, now isn't the time to play games. We have a serious problem."

He leaned back in his chair. "Tell me."

"It's Scott."

Ben turned the phrase over, but it still didn't make sense. "I need more than that to catch up here."

Exhaling two or three times, Mark visibly controlled his anger. "We took the security tapes back. Scott dropped off the note. Not just the first one. The second one."

The enormity of the words sunk in. "Scott threatened Callie?"

"Scott is the one who convinced Rod to go upstairs to the office and wait for Callie. It looks like Scott set Rod up."

"That doesn't make any sense." Not that the Rod connection fit together, either. Callie was right about that. Thinking about it, she seemed to be right about everything. He feared she saw through him, understood him better than he did.

He couldn't worry about that now. He had to focus in.

Mark rested his hip against the side of Ben's desk. "Does the last name MacAllister mean anything to you?"

"Not other than it being Scott's last name. Should it?"

"Yes."

"Mark, just say what you have to say. If you have a clear question, ask it."

"You had a case when you started with the family law court. An ugly divorce. The dad had to pay a lot of money, claimed he couldn't, and you threw him in jail for contempt."

"That happened more than once." Memories of sad stories played out in Ben's mind. Some fathers turned to lies to keep from paying alimony and child support. Never mind their kids didn't have food or a safe place to live. These men just couldn't tolerate the idea of giving over what they viewed as their money alone to their ex-wives.

"Well, this time the guy was Scott's dad. He claims the divorce broke him."

Ben searched his mind for details but couldn't grab them. Except for the murder, no individual case stuck out. He had blocked out so much of that part of the job. Seeing pain in kids' eyes reminded him of his own tortured childhood, and his mind shut off. He crammed down on his compassion and rushed decisions for fear of growing to care too much about the people who moved in and out of his courtroom with painful tales that grew worse with each hearing.

When the administrative judge had offered a new assignment, Ben said yes before knowing what it was. "I hated that work."

"I'm not saying you did anything wrong. From a quick look at the file it appears Scott's dad hid assets so the mother would get nothing. He cried poor, bankrupted his own company, and blamed his wife for ruining him."

"You mean his wife and me."

Mark rapped his knuckles against the desk. "My concern is Scott."

"Where is he?"

"That's the problem. I don't know. When we stormed the elevators to grab Rod, Scott slipped out of the courthouse. No one has seen him since."

Ben sensed Mark held something back. Something huge and potentially awful. "Okay."

"No, it's not, because I can't reach Callie. Not at home. Not here. She was his final target, and she's not responding to messages. Could she be at your place?"

Guilt fell over him like a blanket. "She's never been to my house."

Everything inside Ben slammed to a halt. Breathing. Thinking. Stupid worries about how to describe their relationship, what title to give it, slid away. All that mattered was her safety. He wanted her right there, with him, fighting and kicking. Suddenly, on the verge of losing her, he wanted her forever.

"Ben, do you know where she is?"

Ben looked at his brother, letting him see all of the pain and self-hatred there. "No."

Mark blew out a long breath. "Okay."

"You think . . ." The words stuck in Ben's throat, refusing to form into the rest of the sentence.

"Yeah, she's in trouble. Big trouble."

Chapter Twenty-five

For more than an hour, Callie ignored the constant ring-ing, first the home phone and then the cell. To get some needed peace, she threw her work phone in the toilet. Seeing Mark's number in the window was just a reminder of all she'd lost. Like a kick to the stomach, she'd think of Mark and her mind would wander to Ben. Then the tears would start. She knew she'd move to the anger stage eventually. She was too busy drowning in loss and sorrow to get there just yet.

Then she heard the insistent knocking. In her desperate haze, she stumbled to the door and opened it without think-ing. Despite her vow to not care, she secretly hoped Ben would appear. That he had come to his senses and returned to grovel.

She'd make him do it, too. Even if it turned out to be a fraction of her blinding pain, that worked for her.

Instead, Scott. Door open. Her without a gun. Her brain in a funk. Tears still clogging her throat. She'd never been this vulnerable.

Her mind scrambled to come up with a strategy. She pushed out thoughts of Ben and his stupidity, of her lonely future and the stretch of unemployment ahead of her. Everything, every second and ounce of strength, turned to Scott.

Forget Rod. Her instincts had been right. Scott was the

stalker. She saw the truth stamped across his face. From the thin line of his lips to the madness in his eyes, she knew with a dead certainty he wanted to hurt her so as to hurt Ben.

She forced a lightness she didn't feel into her voice. "Hi."

Scott looked older, meaner. More self-assured and less like the dedicated clerk who liked to chat with her in the afternoons between dockets. "May I come in?"

She judged the distance between, then figured out slamming the door on his face wouldn't work. Running past him screaming into the hall didn't have much of a shot, either. Not before he lunged and she lost.

"Of course." She gestured for him to come inside.

He took two steps and then turned to face her, his back to the door and his body blocking her exit. "You were a surprise."

"I'm sorry, what?"

"His ties to Emma were pretty obvious." He stood with his hands behind his back. The stance seemed casual, vulnerable even, but something in it telegraphed a preparedness for battle. A desire to engage and fight.

"I don't know what you're talking about."

"They came to work together, went to dinner. Hell, good old Ben even chased away her fiancé to make room for himself. The stud judge was in fine form there. I know because I watched it all go down from the safety of my law school a few blocks away."

Not judge. Ben and Emma. From the timeline he referenced, Scott was coming unglued right before her eyes. It was as if evil walked in and wiped out everything good and decent. He sneered. His voice dripped with disgust. Even being younger, he scared the hell out of her. Crazy was hard to beat no matter the age and height.

Callie decided to play dumb. Stall for time while she forced her head into the moment to come up with a solid plan.

Maybe she could steer him toward the kitchen and make a run at the knives.

Since she didn't have anything else, she went for it. "I don't know what you're talking about."

Scott's head fell to the side. Then came the *tsk-tsk* sound. "We're past this, don't you think?"

A chill ran through her at his dead tone. Gone was the light banter and the deference he'd always shown. The act disappeared and in its place stood a twisted young man with a motivation immune to common sense and rational argument. That left brute strength. She'd have to beat down the churning inside her, that tightening sensation that might freeze her to the floor, and go after him on a physical level. Get the jump and hope it was enough to combat whatever superior strength or nasty weapon he might have.

She shifted slightly. As he talked, she pivoted, moving even with his side. One step closer to a mad dash to the wood block on the counter.

"Do you want something to drink?" she asked, trying to throw him off balance emotionally.

Instead, he grabbed her arm and squeezed hard enough to drive her to her knees. "You ruined everything."

"Scott, you're hurting me."

"You brought this on. You know, I actually liked you until you started staring at Ben like he meant something to you."

She struggled to break free, but Scott only held on harder. "He doesn't."

"Once you started sleeping with him, you became my plan."

She tried going limp to give Scott a false sense of being in charge. "For what?"

"Revenge." Scott dropped her arm. From inside his jacket, he took out a knife of his own and slid his finger along the blade. A small bead of blood appeared on his skin. If Scott felt the cut, he didn't show it. "I've been plotting and waiting. Taking my time and getting close."

"To Ben?"

"Of course, you dumb bitch." The snarl, the rabid anger, took over. The knife cut through the air and far too close to her face.

She held up her hands, letting him think she'd surrender. Pleading with him seemed to be what he wanted, so she gave it to him. "I'm sorry. I just don't get it. Can you tell me why?"

"You know."

"I don't." She had a guess, but not the actual answer. "Tell me."

"He destroyed my family. Put Dad away and left me with that crazy slut."

Bile rushed up the back of Callie's throat. This anger festered and grew. Now it was a living, breathing beast fueling all this uncertainty and destruction.

"You mean, your mother?"

Scott shook his knife at Callie. "She gave birth to me. She was never a mother. My dad took care of me. He went to my games. He helped with homework and got me to school. She sat around spending his money."

Hate spewed out of Scott. It was as if the venom and rage had been locked away, building, and now flailed around trying to get out. Anger filled the room, sucking the air right out.

"Ben was the judge."

"You're damn right." The blade whipped right in front of her face.

The move gave her the perfect out. She backed up closer to the counter. "Listen to me."

"Setting up Rod was the easy part. He despised you. When

he realized you were sleeping with Ben, he went out of his head crazy with it. He thought you pushed him out, took away his star mentor. A few well-timed comments and I could set him off anytime I wanted. Made it easy to get into his office and poke around on the computer."

Her foot slipped closer to the kitchen. "And the bomb?"

Scott was too engrossed in his story to notice she was within an arm's reach of grabbing the knife. "I found the information, built it. It's not hard to get the right people to take care of jobs like that. You pay some money to plant it by making them think it's something other than a bomb and keep your identity quiet. They panic when they realize what they've done and stay quiet. I don't even know the guy's last name but he did me a favor."

"But your unknown partner missed."

Scott leaned in, his lip curling up in a sneer. "No. The plan was just to scare the judge. To let him know someone was watching, someone who knew the kind of weak man he really was. I did it, too. Hell, the former military hero couldn't sit at his desk without a security detail. What kind of man is that?"

"So you wrote the notes." Tramping down on the fear racing through her, she put her hands behind her, searching with small movements for the edge of the counter.

"I wanted Ben to know how it felt to lose something. Someone. My plan was to toy with him and then take Emma out. Watch him buckle without her there for him."

"But I messed everything up." Out of the corner of her eye she saw her front door move. The slight waver could be a dream. Blinking, she cleared her sight line and saw it happen again.

Either the adrenaline caused her vision to bounce, or someone was out there. She'd bet on Mark. She knew she couldn't count on Ben, but for this—law enforcement stuff—the Walkers were solid. She needed seconds only. A diversion and a good throw and Scott would go down without incident. The energy flowing through her would get the job done. The crash later would be a bitch, but after the fight with Ben, she didn't see many bright days ahead.

"He fell for you." Scott said it as an accusation.

She shook her head. "He didn't."

Scott's mouth pulled tight at the edges. "Yes. He. Did."

Her finger touched the cool marble behind her. With a quick mental inventory, she placed the knives without seeing them. "Is your plan to kill me?"

"I feel bad about that, but the judge needs to know how it feels. He can't destroy people, the cocky bastard, and expect to go on as if nothing has happened." Scott stepped in front of her, only inches away. "You're different."

"I'm not."

"I see the way he looks at you. Taking you out will break him. With you I can accomplish more than I ever hoped to gain with Emma."

"Scott." Mark's firm voice rang through the room.

Scott jerked toward the door just as Mark stormed in with Ben right behind him.

She'd never get a better chance. Reaching around blind, she grabbed for a handle. The cool plastic hit her palm and she kept moving. She brought the blade down in an arc just as Scott shifted to the side. His voice an insane cry, he thrust his body toward her. Off balance and shifting his wild gaze between her and Mark, Scott missed his aim. The knife slipped passed her close enough for her to feel the whoosh of movement.

But her tip made contact. As his body moved through the air, flying in front of her, she went for his shoulder. Unable to stop his momentum, he came down right on her knife.

The stab went into the space where his arm met his neck. Blood spurted as Scott's eyes flew open in stunned surprise. Just as he reached up to touch his injury, Ben came out of nowhere and clipped Scott from behind. The tumbling tackle sent the men crashing to the floor.

Mark yelled. Police flooded the room. Chaos reigned as sirens screamed in the distance and people filed in and out, stopping to talk to her. All the words ran together. In a fog, she had no idea what anyone said or why.

Everything moved in slow motion. She saw the flash of Ben's stern face as he made his move. Then she saw Scott pinned to the floor with Ben looming above him.

"Ben, stop." Mark yelled the order as he pulled Ben from behind.

It took two men to wrestle Ben off Scott and another one to hold Mark back from taking a turn at going after the kid. The surreal scene of blood and violence played out before Callie like a movie. She'd taken Scott out and then the cavalry arrived to finish the job in a wild frenzy.

"Are you okay?" Ben held on to her arms and shook her until she looked at him.

The confused haze refused to clear her mind. Scott. Ben. Everyone here, and none of it made sense.

"Callie?"

She ignored Ben's pleas to get through to her and concentrated only on the medic who knelt on the floor tending to Scott's injuries. That mental image was safe. It wouldn't break her heart or leave her weeping on her bathroom floor. Looking at Ben, seeing his loving face, knowing he would never give her what she needed or what they both deserved, would shake the last of her tenuous control.

She stood seconds from falling apart. Seconds from slumping at his feet. The shock, the emotional drain of watching

Ben walk out—it all backed up on her. She wanted to crack a joke and act like none of it mattered. But it did.

"I caused all of this." Ben said the words over and over.

He pulled her close, his arms closing around her as she stood still and tried to hold her body from his. She clenched her palms into fists to keep from touching him.

"God, Callie, talk to me."

"This was all about a divorce case. A stupid, bitter case that ended years ago." The neutral thought comforted her. She didn't even realize she said it out loud until she heard her strained voice.

She would focus on that. On the reason, no matter how insane, rather than on the pain lancing through her when she inhaled Ben's familiar scent.

"Ben, let me." Mark pried Ben's hands off her and stared into her eyes. "Are you okay?"

The numbness eased. She could talk to Mark. He wouldn't destroy her or use her. "Yes."

Ben's face crumpled. But she knew the way his shoulders slumped and his eyes darkened with sadness, none of that was real. It would all go away as soon as he got over his feelings of having failed to protect her. That was stupid. None of what happened with Scott was Ben's fault. Scott was a messed-up kid, fed a steady diet of hate by his father, and grew to be a vengeful, confused young man. They had all prevented a horrible tragedy that day.

No, the guilt beating down on Ben was misplaced. He made many mistakes, but not that.

"I want everyone to leave." She needed to build up her resistance. To find a place where she didn't see Ben's face every time she closed her eyes. She needed to act like she didn't care, but right now she didn't have that sort of strength.

"You can't stay here." Mark's voice was strangely gentle. "This is a crime scene."

"She can come home with me," Ben said, his voice eager for the possibility.

The time for her to play the role of his sexual plaything had passed. "No."

Anguish radiated off Ben. "Callie, I know you're mad at me, but be reasonable."

She ignored his words and his desperate pleading. "Mark will take me to a hotel."

Mark nodded. "Of course."

"Are you fucking crazy?" Medics and policemen turned to Ben at his outburst. "She can't be alone."

"I need space." Somewhere without Ben and without memories, where she could work it all out in her head and figure out how a kid like Scott had gotten so confused and dangerous. She'd never understand Ben's choice, but she could learn from Scott's.

"Can I talk with you?" Mark didn't give Ben a choice. He dragged him back into the kitchen. "You've got to back off."

Ben's throat burned with the need to throw up. Hearing Scott's words as he flashed the knife at Callie stole the last bit of peace Ben would ever feel in his life.

Seeing her broken and pale almost killed him.

Desperate to get back to her, he nodded. Ignoring Mark was the only way around him at this point.

Mark shoved against Ben's shoulder to get his attention. "I'm serious here. Whatever you did to fuck this up so bad with her, you need to fix it. But later."

"I can't wait."

"I'm not giving you a choice."

The despair overtook him. Ben hated himself for being so damned stupid. He wanted her. Missed her. Didn't want to see anyone else and couldn't imagine a life without her. When she talked about love and the future, he'd been too dumb or too scared to realize he'd already fallen for her. Admitting it made it real, and once it was real he could lose it all. He had anyway.

Call it by whatever name, the dull ache inside him wasn't going away. Within a short time he met the one who could mean everything.

And now he had to tell her. To break through that blank stare and make her listen. He just hoped he hadn't blown it by pushing her away emotionally one time too many.

"She left me, Mark." Ben couldn't believe how much it hurt to say it.

The stern frown left Mark's face. "I figured, but damn, I'm sorry."

"She said I was like you."

Sadness fell over Mark's eyes. "Man, don't be like me."

"Let me go to her then."

Mark shook his head. "I can't."

"Why?"

"It's too late. She just left with one of my men."

Emma heard her front door open. Since the alarm didn't go off and the earlier call from Mark was to report that Scott was in jail, she didn't panic. But she did get pissed off. She had laid down her requirements and Mark had walked out. Now he thought he could return to his old ways. Breeze in after a brush with danger and make love to her.

Every cell in her body wanted him to come in, hold her, give her those few moments of love before he gave in to the less permanent state of passion. She deserved better.

She wrapped her robe around her, holding it at her middle with one arm, and met him at the top of the steps.

"What are you doing here?" She asked in her most detached voice.

He glanced up. The light from the entry lit his tired face. "What do you think?"

"We're not doing this again." A sob rushed up on her from out of nowhere and caught in her throat. "I can't do it."

"You told me to make a decision."

"And you did."

"No, you assumed I did."

Her heartbeat took off. "What are you saying?"

Without a word, he dropped two suitcases at the bottom of the staircase. Then he turned around and walked out of the house, leaving the front door wide open.

Cool air rushed in from the dark night, but she didn't hear a sound. "Mark?"

He came back with two more suitcases and another bag thrown over his shoulder. Glancing up, his eyes met hers. With bags in his hands and weighing him down, he put his foot on the bottom step.

"What is this?" She dared to hope.

"Me moving in."

"You're telling, not asking?"

He climbed a few more steps. "Yes."

Blood pounded through her. "I don't remember inviting you."

"Maybe not with your mouth, but you asked." He stood a few stairs away now, dragging luggage behind him.

She closed her eyes in relief. Somehow, some way, he had read that signal. For years he missed every single one. This time, when it mattered and her will held firm, he came back. He was the one to concede.

"I don't know what kind of man I'll be to live with full time, or why you would want to find out, but I know one thing." He dropped the bags in his hands and let them fall back down, thumping against each step as they went.

"What?" she asked, more than a little breathless.

"I want to figure it out with you." He trailed his fingers down her cheek. "If you'll have me."

"You're sure?"

"Not about much but about you, yes." His gaze never left her face. "Still love me?"

Emma smiled through tears. "Always."

He smiled right back. "Good."

Chapter Twenty-six

"What do you want?" Callie asked the question from the doorway of his office. She didn't come in. Didn't close the door. Just stood there fuming in her proper navy pantsuit.

Three days had passed. After the time apart, Ben was so damn happy to see her that he didn't even care about the off-the-charts attitude.

Relief spread through him. Safe and in one piece just as Mark promised.

Ben lowered his pen to the desk to keep from snapping it in two. With a wave of his fingers he motioned for her. "Come in."

She didn't move.

"Problem?" he asked, half worried that she'd give him a list.

"I don't appreciate being summoned to your office."

"I left a voice mail."

She crossed her arms over her chest. "You told me to come or you'd hunt me down."

"That might have been unnecessarily dramatic." Inside he knew the vow rung true. He would find her and make her listen. Drive anywhere and say anything to get her back.

"Sounds like your typical jackassery to me."

He never thought he'd miss her name-calling, but he had. As sure as he'd missed the floral scent of her perfume and the soft touch of her skin against his, he missed that mouth and all she could do with it. That included both her bedroom skills and her sharp wit.

She pushed him, challenged him. Even through the bickering and fighting, being near her made his day brighter. The dark hours of the past few nights had taught him that. He finally had a name for the feeling—love. Took him a long time and a lot of hurt to get there, but he made it. He loved her and wanted to keep loving her, starting right now.

He pointed at the seat on the other side of his desk. "This would be easier if you came into my office and sat down."

Her hands didn't even twitch. "In case you're not clear, I don't work for you anymore."

"According to you, you never did."

"True."

They finally agreed on something. At this rate, he might have found the only thing. "So, then . . . ?"

"My point is that the days of following your endless orders are over."

"What did I order you to do exactly?" He searched his mind for one instance of bossing her around and came up blank.

Her snorting and rolling her eyes? Interesting to see that she still excelled at those skills. He was smart enough not to reciprocate. She'd likely have kicked him in the balls if he tried.

After a few seconds, she glanced around the room. Her stare settled on her desk, which still sat next to his. Elaine had tried to move it out. He refused. Holding on to some part of Callie was imperative until he could hold all of her. Ben didn't tell Elaine that, but he sensed the older woman understood the issue.

"I didn't come here today so you could stare at me with that stupid look on your face," Callie said.

She had him wishing for a mirror. "Didn't realize I was doing anything strange."

"Yeah, well, you are." She sighed in a way dramatic enough to make the Hollywood crowd jealous. "So, spill it. What's the emergency?"

"I'd like to talk to you in a civilized manner."

She dropped her head to the side. "Back to using your big words, I see."

"Your preference is that we scream across the office at each other?"

"I'd rather go home."

"And do what?"

Her eyes narrowed into nasty little slits. "Is that your way of asking if I found a job?"

"Did you?"

Her chin lifted. "Yes."

He was happy for her as long as the job was in the D.C. metro area. If he had to move to get to her, he would. But, damn, he wanted her right where she was. Scratch that. He wanted her with him and he didn't care where that happened so long as it happened soon.

"Where?" he asked.

"Where what?"

"The job."

She dropped her hands as her attitude kicked up. "As much as I enjoy mindless chatter, and I don't in case that's not clear, I'd rather you just say what you have to say so I can go."

The idea of her leaving broke something inside him. To stall the inevitable he said the first thing that popped into his mind. "Mark gave you a job."

"If you knew, why'd you ask?" She frowned as she spit out the question.

"It was a guess."

"Once again your big brain fed you the right answer."

A harsh chuckle escaped his mouth before he could stop it. "Snotty as ever."

"Good-bye, Ben." She turned around and headed for the door.

Desperate to stop her, he stood up and launched into the one thing sure to get her to stay. The door was open. There were lawyers in the hallway. There would never be a less private or less appropriate time, but he was running out of options.

"It was a murder-suicide."

She froze in place with her back to him.

"You want to know the details, right? That's what this is about. Sharing." When she didn't answer, he kept going. He figured if he talked she couldn't leave. "My father had been fooling around with Emma's mother for months. Maybe longer, I don't really know. At one time that fact mattered, but it doesn't now."

He saw Callie's shoulders relax. Maybe she had locked her heart off to him, but that didn't stop her from being nosy. Now that he finally offered her the information she'd been seeking, she listened.

"Emma remembers when her mom started to leave during the afternoons. She'd go out, make some excuse, and then come home hours later. Since my father worked all the time, I never noticed the change in pattern." Ben hated that part. The idea that their collective lives ran uncontrolled to this terrifying point in time while he played sports and argued about eating fish. He'd always hated fish.

Callie shifted until Ben could see the side of her face.

He decided not to squander this opportunity. No matter how much the words hurt, he'd say them. Relive each moment as if it unfolded in his mind and somehow stay on his feet as the memories battered him. "One Saturday while my father was supposed to be working on some random work project, Mom took us to soccer practice. She forgot something, which she never did. She was anal to the point of obsession. The car didn't move into reverse until she ran through her mental checklist several times."

"What was so important?"

My fault. The words from his childhood bounced around in his mind. *My fault.*

"My extra shirt. She always brought a change of clothing for after the games and practices. Thought it was unsanitary to run around and then go ride in a car to dinner without changing."

Callie turned the whole way around until she stood facing him, her sad eyes growing darker by the second.

If she tried to comfort him now he'd never make it through this. The voice in his head screamed at him to get it all out. "With us being watched by coaches and other parents, she ran back home. The expected hours away from the house watching us run around and then getting us dinner turned into minutes."

Callie took a few steps into the room. "You don't have to say anything else."

"Yeah, I do." He inhaled, fighting off the anxiety that welled up when he thought about that day. That soccer practice. If she had just stayed on the bleachers with the other moms.

At some point she may have found out about the affair, but it might not have happened in her own bed, right in front of her like some sick punishment. They could all still be alive.

"The rest is speculation," he said. "It's pretty clear she drove up, saw my father's car, and went in. Neighbors heard the shots."

Callie's tough-gal face fell. "Ben . . ."

"My dad was a former military man. Kept a gun in the house for protection and taught us all how to use it. That it wasn't a toy and should be respected. How's that for the ultimate irony?" In an act meant to teach responsibility, his father handed his mother the knowledge to end everything.

"Ben, I'm so sorry."

"Moving in with our grandparents, changing schools and names—that all came later. A bunch of mental health people suggested we erase our parents from our lives and move on."

"Did you?"

"Mark is sick in love with Emma and can't figure out how to spend three days in a row with her before he has to bolt." Ben shook his head. "Yeah, it sticks with you. Molds and ruins everything it touches."

"What about you?"

"I thought I came through it without any visible scars." He came around to stand at the front of his desk. He needed her to bridge the remaining gap between them.

"Now?"

"I was wrong."

She walked across his carpet and came to a stop two feet away. "How?"

With one sweep of his arm, he could hold her as he'd been dreaming about for days. To keep from acting on the impulse, he grabbed the edge of the desk behind him. "It never dawned on me I had an issue. I love women. Dated and had fun. Sure, I moved on but the breakups were mostly mutual."

"I'm guessing you came to your senses at some point?" she asked.

For the first time in days she hoped. The sensation built, block upon block. He needed to unburden and let her in. If he could give her something, then maybe this wasn't a fluke or an ego thing.

"I was running."

"From?"

"Commitment, risk." He took her hand then. Lifted it to his mouth for a quick kiss. "If I didn't get entangled, if I convinced myself I just hadn't found the right woman yet, life made sense. I could look at Mark's life with a reserved superiority, knowing that I had gotten through the madness that still held him."

The barrier she set up around her heart cracked. The promise she made to hate him forever fell away. "This is deeper than being afraid of commitment, which is lame, by the way."

He nodded. "Thanks for the support."

"You didn't break up, you escaped. Anything meaningful threatened your comfortable solitude, including me. Rather than take any risk or go back to being insecure, you destroyed and moved on."

His life appeared so solid and stable on the outside. She now saw the crumbling. Never was there a man more in need of love. Her heart sat right there ready to give it if he would only reach out and take it.

"Yes."

"Sounds kind of empty," she pointed out, hoping he would agree.

"I didn't think so at the time."

Emotionally, he kept walking backward. She bent her head so he wouldn't see the disappointment and longing. "Okay."

He tipped her chin up. "Until you."

A rush of relief fizzled as soon as it came. What if this was part of the protectiveness, of not wanting to be the bad guy or hurt anyone? That was a cycle she refused to join. "Oh, Ben. You never let me in. We had great sex and fun conversation. The intimacy level never passed what you could get from a friend with benefits."

His thumb slid over her lips. "I don't want one of those."

She searched her eyes. "What do you want? Do you even know?"

"You."

A gulp of need hung in her throat. She wanted so badly to surrender. But the man was good at words, brilliant at winning arguments. She couldn't stand to be one more fight, a trophy, and nothing more.

She stepped back, trying to get a little space and keep her perspective. Being so close to him and to everything she wanted was a seductive lure. "Ben, I can't be the plaything or office sex toy. I mean, I could for a few months. It'd be fun, but I deserve more."

"I never asked for that."

"That's the point. You didn't ask for anything. You gave even less."

He gulped in air. When she tried to explain, he nodded. "That's okay. I deserved that."

"The words aren't meant as an insult. Not really. But I need something else. Any woman worth having is going to demand more."

"I get that now."

"Probably not."

His eyebrow lifted in question. "Excuse me?"

She had to smile at the timing. "There are those hoity words again."

"Then let me try saying it another way." He slipped his hands into hers. "I love you."

He could have called her a chicken and left her less surprised. "What?"

He kissed her knuckles, smoothing her skin with his tongue. "I love you."

She could feel him trying to convince her, willing her to give him another chance. With his hands and his eyes he made a promise. She couldn't believe it, but she started to see it.

"It crept up on me and knocked me blind, but there it is. I didn't want it, and fought every last drop of feeling, believe me." He brought her in closer, and this time she didn't fight it. "My brain insisted the feelings amounted to nothing more than a physical attraction. See, if it's lust or sex you don't have to worry about spilling your secrets, about baring it all."

The crushing weight lifted off her chest. It was as if the past few days of torment and anguish hadn't happened. Every dark nook and tiny crevice flooded with light.

"You love me?"

"Did you really not know that?"

She wanted to believe it, but no. Until he said the words, pleading and holding as if letting go of her would destroy him, she didn't believe. "Ben, you've held on to every bit of information, forcing me to beg for scraps here and there. You're only talking now because you need to."

"Right."

"You admit it?"

"I'll tell you every last detail of my life. Share every minute of the pain that nearly crippled me, that turned Mark into an emotional pile of crap. I've done so many things I'm not proud of. The man standing before you now is a huge turn from where he started."

She pressed a hand against his heart. "The man I see seems pretty good to me."

"I'm not perfect."

"Yeah, no kidding."

"But for you I'd try to be." He took her face in his hands. "I will be."

The power of his vow and strength of his commitment made her heart burst with happiness. "No one has ever offered to change for me before."

"I do love you and will do anything to make you happy."

His feelings hovered right there at the surface. He did love her. She saw it in every cell, every pore, and every muscle. He wasn't hiding it or renaming it or being a clueless guy seaching for the right words. He opened his heart and let his emotions pour out and surround them.

"How do you know it's not a bad case of heartburn?" she asked, half in jest.

For the first time since she walked in, he smiled. "I want heartburn to go away. This, what I feel for you, I want to last."

"Sweet talker."

He treated her to a long kiss, one that chased away every fear and doubt. One that apologized and stole her soul. When he lifted his head, she tried to pull him back down to her.

"I'm not sure I'm a forever type of guy—"

Oh, he was so very wrong about that. "Yes, you are. Any man who is so adamant about fidelity is a long-haul sort."

"I don't know about that. I just know that you crave a home and stability."

"So, you do listen."

"To you? I wouldn't dare not to." He grew serious again. "You want a man who will believe in you and support you. Someone to fight with and name-call. I can be all of those things for you."

He threw everything she wanted right at her feet. Only a stupid woman would walk away. And she was not dumb.

"I just want you to be yourself." She threw her arms around his neck. "I love you."

His face lit up. That stupid grin almost swallowed his entire head. "Never thought I'd hear that again."

A giddiness took over her whole body. She wanted to laugh and giggle, and those girlie things were not her. With him, she felt free . . . and loved.

"Get used to it, Your Honor, because I plan to tell you every single day."

He nuzzled her cheek. "Forever?"

"Forever for my forever man."

Their lips met and the kiss quickly turned hot. Hands, tongue. They were about to break a sacred office rule.

Ben pointed at the camera in the far corner of the room. "Let's get out of here."

"I thought you liked to work."

He winked at her. "With you, I much prefer to play."

"I always said you were a smart man."

If you liked this book, try Bianca D'Arc's
ONCE BITTEN, TWICE DEAD,
available now from Brava!

"Unit twelve," the dispatcher's voice crackled over the radio. Sarah perked up. That was her. She listened as the report rolled over the radio. A disturbance in a vacant building out on Wheeler Road, near the big medical center. Probably kids, she thought, responding to dispatch and turning her patrol car around.

Since the budget cuts, she rolled alone. She hadn't had a partner in a long time, but she was good at her job and confident in her abilities. She could handle a couple of kids messing around in an empty building.

Sarah stepped into the gloomy concrete interior of the building. The metal door hung off the its hinges and old boards covered the windows. Broken glass littered the floor and graffiti decorated the walls.

The latest decorators had been junkies and kids looking for a secret place to either get high or drink beer where no one could see. There didn't appear to be anyone home at the moment. They'd probably cleared out in a hurry when they'd seen Sarah's cruiser pull up outside. Still, she had to check the place.

Nightstick in one hand, flashlight in the other, Sarah made her way into the gloom of the building. Electricity was a thing of the past in this place. Light fixtures dangled brokenly from the remnants of a dropped ceiling as Sarah advanced into the dark interior.

She heard a scurrying sound that could have been footsteps or could have been rodents. Either way, her heartbeat sped up.

"Police," she identified herself in a loud, firm voice. "Show yourself."

She directed the flashlight into the dark corners of the room as she crept inside. The place had a vast outer warehouse type area with halls and doors leading even farther inside the big structure. She didn't really want to go in there, but saw no alternative. She decided to advance slowly at first, then zip through the rest of the building, hoping no one got behind her to cut off her retreat.

She had her sidearm, but she'd rather not have to shoot anyone today. Especially not some kids out for a lark. They liked to test their limits and hers. She'd been up against more than one teenage bully who thought because she was a woman, she'd be a pushover. They'd learned the hard way not to mess with Sarah Petit.

She heard that sort of brushing sound again. Her heart raced as adrenaline surged. She'd learned to channel fear into something more useful. Fear became strength if you knew how to use it.

"This is the police," she repeated in a loud, carrying voice. "Step into the light and show yourself."

More shuffling. It sounded from down the corridor on the left. Sarah approached, her nightstick at the ready. The flashlight illuminated the corner of the opening, not showing her much. The sounds were growing louder. There was definitely someone—or something—there. Perhaps waiting to ambush her, down that dark hallway.

She wouldn't fall for that. Sarah approached from a good ten feet out, maneuvering so that her flashlight could penetrate farther down the black hall. With each step, more of the corridor became visible to her.

Squinting to see better, Sarah stepped fully in front of the opening to the long hallway. There. Near the end. There was a person standing.

"I'm a police officer. Come out of there immediately." Her voice was firm and as loud as she could project it. The figure at the end of the hallway didn't respond. She couldn't even tell if it was male or female.

It sort of swayed as it tried to move. Maybe a junkie so high they were completely out of it? Sarah wasn't sure. She edged closer.

"Are you all right?"

She heard a weird moaning sound. It didn't sound human, but the shape at the end of the long hall was definitely standing on two feet with two arms braced against the wall as if for balance. The inhuman moan came again. It was coming from that shadowy person.

Sarah stepped cautiously closer to the mouth of the hallway. It was about four feet across. Not a lot of room to maneuver.

She didn't like this setup, but she had to see if that person needed help. Sarah grabbed the radio mic clipped to her shoulder.

"This is Unit Twelve. I'm at the location. There appears to be a person in distress in the interior of the building."

"What kind of distress, Unit Twelve?"

"Uncertain. Subject seems unable to speak. I'm going to get closer to see if I can give you more information."

"Should we dispatch an ambulance?"

Sarah thought about it for a half a second. No matter what, this person would need a medical check. Worst-case scenario, it was a junkie in the throes of a really bad trip.

"Affirmative. Dispatch medical to this location. I'm going to see if I can get them to come out, but I may need some backup."

"Dispatching paramedics and another unit to your location. ETA ten minutes on the backup, fifteen on the paramedics."

"Roger that."

With backup and medical help on the way, Sarah felt a little better about taking the next step. She walked closer to the corridor's mouth. The person was still there, still mostly unrecognizable in the harsh light of the flashlight beam.

"Help is coming," she called to the figure. From its height, she thought it was probably a male. He moved a little closer. Wild hair hung in limp hanks around his face. It was longer than most men's, but junkies weren't best known for their grooming and personal hygiene.

"That's it," she coaxed as the man shuffled forward on unsteady feet. "Come on out of there. Help is on the way. No one's going to hurt you."

Sarah stepped into the corridor, just a few feet, hoping to coax the man forward. He was definitely out of it. He made small noises. Sort of grunting, moaning sounds that weren't intelligible. It gave her the creeps, as did the way the man moved. He shuffled like Frankenstein's assistant in those old horror movies, keeping his head down, and his clothes were in tatters.

This dude had to be on one hell of a bender. Sarah lowered the flashlight beam off his head as he moved closer, trying to get a better look at the rest of him. His clothes were shredded like he'd been in a fight with a bear—or something else with sharp claws. His shirt hung off him in strips of fabric and his pants weren't much better.

The dark brown of bloodstains could be seen all over his clothing. Sarah grew more concerned. He had to be in really bad shape from the look of the blood that had been spilled. She wondered if that was all his blood or if there was another victim lying around here somewhere in even worse shape.

His head was still down as he approached and Sarah backed up a step. His hair hung in what looked like greasy clumps. Only as he drew closer did he realize his hair wasn't matted with oil and dirt. It was stuck together by dried blood.

Then he looked up.

Sarah stifled a scream. Half his face was . . . gone. Just gone.

It looked like something had gnawed on his flesh. Blank eyes stared out at her from a ruined face. The tip of his nose was gone, as were his lips and the flesh of one side of his jaw and cheek.

Sarah gasped and turned to run, but something came up behind her and tripped her. She fell backward with a resounding thud, cracking her skull on the hard cement floor.

She fought against the hands that tried to grab her, but they were too strong, and her head spun from the concussion she'd no doubt just received. She felt sick to her stomach. The adrenaline of fear pushed her to keep going. Keep moving. Get away. Survive until her backup arrived.

Thank God she'd already called for backup.

Not one, but two men—if she could call them that—were holding her down. The one with the ruined face had her feet and the other had hold of her arms, even as she struggled against him.

She looked into the first one's eyes and saw . . . nothing. They were blank. No emotion. No feeling. No nothing.

Just hunger.

Fear clutched her heart in its icy grip. The second man looked wild in the dim light from her flashlight. It had rolled to the side, but was still on and lancing into the darkness of the building's interior nearby. Faint light shone on her two assailants.

They both looked like something out of a horror movie. The one from the hallway was, by far, the more gruesome of the two, but the one who wrestled with her arms was frightening, too. His skin was cold to the touch and it looked almost gray, though she couldn't be sure in the uncertain light. Neither spoke, but both made those inhuman moaning sounds.

Even as she kicked and struggled, she felt teeth rip into her thigh. Sarah screamed for all she was worth as the first man broke through her skin and blood welled. The second man dove onto her prone form, knocking her flat and bashing her head on the concrete a second time. Stunned, she was still aware when his teeth sank into her shoulder.

She was going to die here. Eaten alive by these cannibals.

Something inside Sarah rebelled at the thought. No way in hell was she going down like this.

Help was on the way. All she had to do was hold on until her backup arrived. She could do that. She *had* to do that.

Channeling the adrenaline, Sarah ignored the pain and used every last bit of her strength to kick the man off her legs. She bucked like a crazy woman, dislodging the first man.

Once her legs were free, she used them to leverage her upper body at an angle, forcing the second man to move. The slight change in position freed one hand. She grasped around for anything on the floor next to her and came up with a hard, cylindrical object. Her nightstick.

Praise the Lord.

Putting all her remaining strength behind it, she aimed for the man's head, raining blows on him with the stick. When that didn't work, she changed targets, looking for anything that might hurt him. She whacked at his body with the hard wood of the stick. She heard a few of the bones in his hand crack at one point, but this guy was tough. Nothing seemed to faze him.

Finally, she used the pointy end of the stick to push at his neck. That seemed to get some results, as he shifted away. He moved enough for her to use the rest of her body for leverage, crawling out from under him.

His friend was up and coming back as she crabwalked away on her hands and feet, toward the door and the sunshine beyond. Her backup was coming. She just had to hold on until they could find her.

The two men followed her, moving as if they had all the time in the world. Their pace was steady and measured as she crawled as fast as she could toward the door. It didn't make any sense. They could have easily overtaken her but they kept to their slow, walking pace.

Sarah hit the door and practically threw herself over the threshold. She had to get out in the open where her backup would see her right away. She was losing blood fast and her vision was dancing, tunneling down to a single dim spot. She was going to pass out any second. She had to do all she could to save herself before that happened.

Backup was coming. That thought kept her going. They'd be here any second. She just had to hold on.

She crawled into the sunlight, near her cruiser. Leaning against the side of her car, she tried for her radio, but the mic was long gone—probably a victim of the struggle with those two men. They were coming for her. They had to be.

But when she looked up, she saw them hesitate at the doorway to the building. The second man stepped through, but the first stayed behind, cowering in the darkness. The second man's skin was gray in the outdoor light. He looked like some kind of walking corpse, with grisly brown stains of dried blood all around his mouth. Some of it was bright red. That was *her* blood. The sick bastard had bitten her.

The man walked calmly forward, under the trees that shaded the walkway to the old building. Sarah had parked on the street, out in the open. She watched in dread as the man walked steadily toward her, death in his flat gaze.

Then something odd happened. He stopped where the tree cover ended. He seemed reluctant to step into the sun.

Sarah blinked, but there wasn't any other explanation she could think of. Then she heard the sound of an approaching vehicle. Her backup.

With salvation in sight, she finally passed out.

Things are getting dangerous in TAMING THE MOON,
the latest from Sherrill Quinn, out now from Brava!

"Look at me."

She raised heavy lids and stared into dark eyes glinting with the knowledge that she'd gotten the message. He dropped his hand and strutted away from her, confident that she'd stay put.

She watched him, loathing him with each shaky breath she drew. When the bastard had moved in next door, fate had dealt her a dead man's hand. He'd seen her, had wanted her, so he'd taken her, turning her into a monster. Six weeks ago he'd told her he had a special job for her, a job that could elevate her from Omega to something . . . well, something more than the bottom of the pack.

She'd perked up, as he'd known she would. But when he'd told her the job was to murder someone, she'd refused. She was a middle school phys ed teacher, for crying out loud. Not an assassin.

But then he'd taken Zoe, threatened to kill her if Olivia didn't do as she was told. She'd seen him act with swift ruthlessness where disobedience and defiance were concerned. Just a few months ago he'd broken the neck of another pack member's son as casually as if he were flicking lint off his sleeve. So she had no doubt that, even though he might love Zoe in his own twisted way, he *would* carry through on the threat. So this time when he'd told her to go, she'd gone. Thankfully she had enough tenure and foresight to ask for a leave of absence from work.

Eddy turned to face her. "Go kill Sullivan. You have one week."

She opened her mouth then closed it. He'd not given her permission to speak yet.

A slight smile tilted one edge of his mouth. "Very good, pet." He gave an approving nod. "You may respond."

"A week?"

He lifted his brows. "I've given you six weeks already, two of which you squandered by being stubborn. I hardly think you need more than another week."

She clamped her lips together and gave an abrupt nod. Arguing with him would accomplish nothing except to have him shorten the deadline even further.

He sighed and shoved his hands into the pockets of his trousers. "I'm not such a bad guy, Livvie." He shrugged. "I just know what I want, and I'm willing to do whatever it takes to get it—and that includes killing everyone who gets in my way. Some women find that kind of confidence appealing. Attractive, even."

What kind of women? The ones with a death wish?

She licked her lips. "May I ask what it is you want? Why is it so important that Rory Sullivan be killed? What did he do to you?"

Olivia thought for a moment he wasn't going to answer her, feared that she may have gone too far when his face darkened. But it was remembered rage that colored his features, not anger directed toward her.

"Let's just say there's a man I want to destroy, and I'm beginning by removing everyone who's important to him. Starting with his friends." His lips parted in a grin. "I hear he's fallen in love, so very soon I'll be ready to take that away from him, too. Although"—he tapped his chin—"if she's fetching enough, I may have to use her before I kill her."

"*You'll* kill her?" The words left her mouth before she could stop them. She bit her lip, preparing to be smacked because of the incredulity in her tone.

The smile faded from his face, and his eyes narrowed, though he didn't lift his hand to her. "Yes. The male friends are peripheral, not enough for me to bother with personally. But a wife?" The grin returned, this time so full of malicious glee it wrapped ice around her gut. "To watch his face, the agony in his eyes as I fuck her and then kill her, with him powerless to stop me?" He nodded. "That is something I must do myself."

Well, if he was going to use Olivia to do some of the dirty work, she damn well deserved to know why. "Who is this man? Why do you hate him so much?"

Eddy turned away from her. "Merr . . ." He broke off and shook his head. "He had everything—a loving family, wealth, power, and the poor sod couldn't stand that he wasn't normal." With his heightened emotions, Eddy's New York accent slipped a bit and took on a British flavor. He shook his head again. "It should have all been mine. If his father had just done what I'd asked—*begged!*—things might have been different."

He trailed off, seeming to be lost in his thoughts. After a moment he shrugged. "Never mind. It's not something you need to know." He glanced over his shoulder at her, eyes hard. "All you need to know is that for your daughter to remain safe you have a job to do."

Eyeing the distance between them, Olivia wondered if she could catch him off guard long enough to kill him. She could morph her fingers into claws now, just like he did. She might be able to do it.

It would only take one quick slash across the throat.

But then what about Zoe? There was at least one body-guard standing outside her door, his bulk casting a shadow onto the floor of the hallway.

Olivia briefly closed her eyes. She'd never be able to do it. She couldn't kill Eddy and go for the bodyguard before he could get to Zoe.

She had no other choice. She must finish the job she'd been given.

Thinking back over the last few days, she remembered her first impression of Rory Sullivan. Tall, dark, and dangerous.

An earnest protector.

Sexy as hell. But . . .

He had to die.

He's a sneak peek at Jill Shalvis's
INSTANT TEMPTATION,
coming next month!

"I didn't invite you in, T.J."

He just smiled.

He was built as solid as the mountains that had shaped his life, and frankly had the attitude to go with it, the one that said he could take on whoever and whatever, and you could kiss his perfect ass while he did so. She'd seen him do it too, back in his hell-raising, misspent youth.

Not that she was going there, to the time when he could have given her a single look and she'd have melted into a puddle at his feet.

Had melted into a puddle at his feet. Not going there . . .

Unfortunately for Harley's senses, he smelled like the wild Sierras; pine and fresh air, and something even better, something so innately male that her nose twitched for more, seeking out the heat and raw male energy that surrounded him and always had. Since it made her want to lean into him, she shoved in another bite of ice cream instead.

He smiled. "I saw on Oprah once that women use ice cream as a substitute for sex."

She choked again, and he resumed gliding his big, warm hand up and down her back. "You watch Oprah?"

"No. Annie was, and I overheard her yelling at the TV that women should have plenty of both sex *and* ice cream."

That sounded exactly like his Aunt Annie. "Well, I don't need the substitute."

"No?" he murmured, looking amused at her again.

"No!"

He hadn't taken his hands off her, she couldn't help but notice. He still had one rubbing up and down her back, the other low on her belly, holding her upright, which was ridiculous, so she smacked it away, doing her best to ignore the fluttering he'd caused and the odd need she had to grab him by the shirt, haul him close, and have her merry way with him.

This was what happened to a woman whose last orgasm had come from a battery-operated device instead of a man, a fact she'd admit, oh *never*. "I was expecting your brother."

"Stone's working on Emma's 'honey do' list at the new medical clinic, so he sent me instead. Said to give you these." He pulled some maps from his back pocket, maps she needed for a field expedition for her research. When she took them out of his hands, he hooked his thumbs in the front pockets of his Levi's. He wore a T-shirt layered with an opened button-down that said *Wilder Adventures* on the pec. His jeans were faded nearly white in the stress spots, of which there were many, nicely encasing his long, powerful legs and lovingly cupping a rather impressive package that was emphasized by the way his fingers dangled on his thighs.

Not that she was looking.

Okay, she was looking, but she couldn't help it. The man oozed sexuality. Apparently some men were issued a handbook at birth on how to make a woman stupid with lust. And he'd had a lot of practice over the years.

She'd watched him do it.

Each of the three Wilder brothers had barely survived their youth, thanks in part to no mom and a mean, son-of-a-bitch father. But by some miracle, the three of them had come out of it alive and now channeled their energy into Wilder Adventures, where they guided clients on just about any outdoor adventure that could be imagined; heli-skiing, extreme mountain biking, kayaking, climbing, *anything.*

Though T.J. had matured and found success, he still gave off a don't-mess-with-me vibe. Even now, at four in the afternoon, he looked big and bad and tousled enough that he might have just gotten out of bed and wouldn't be averse to going back.

It irritated her. It confused her. And it turned her on, a fact that drove her bat-shit crazy because she was no longer interested in T.J. Wilder.

Nope.

It'd be suicide to still be interested. No one could sustain a crush for fifteen years.

No one.

Except, apparently, her. Because deep down, the unsettling truth was that if he so much as directed one of his sleepy, sexy looks her way, her clothes would fall right off.

Again.

And wasn't that just her problem, the fact that once upon a time, a very long time ago, at the tail end of T.J.'s out-of-control youth, the two of them had spent a single night together being just about as intimate as a man and woman could get. Her first night with a guy. Definitely not his first. Neither of them had been exactly legal at the time, and only she'd been sober.

Which meant only she remembered.